THE
HEART
of the
BUDDHA

a novel

ELSIE SZE

EMERALD
BOOK CO.

Published by Emerald Book Company
Austin, TX
www.emeraldbookcompany.com

Distributed by Emerald Book Company
For ordering information or special discounts for bulk purchases, please contact
Emerald Book Company at PO Box 91869, Austin, TX 78709, 512.891.6100.

Cover design by Greenleaf Book Group LLC

Publisher's Cataloging-in-Publication Data
(Prepared by The Donohue Group, Inc.)

Sze, Elsie, 1946-
   The Heart of the Buddha : a novel / by Elsie Sze. -- 1st ed.

   p. : ill., maps ; cm.

   ISBN: 978-1-934572-30-6

1. Sisters--Fiction. 2. Monks--Bhutan--Fiction. 3. Twins--Fiction. 4. Bhutan--Fiction.
5. Adventure fiction. I. Title.

PR9199.4.S995 H43 2009
813/.6   2009930901

Part of the Tree Neutral™ program, which offsets the number of trees consumed in the production and printing of this book by taking proactive steps, such as planting trees in direct proportion to the number of trees used: www.treeneutral.com

TreeNeutral™

Printed in the United States of America on acid-free paper

09 10 11 12 13 14   10 9 8 7 6 5 4 3 2 1

First Edition

To my father and mother,
Hon-Ngi and Elizabeth Chin,
with love

Acknowledgments

My profound gratitude to Kesang Tshering, who showed me Bhutan and has remained a most helpful mentor on matters relating to Bhutan throughout the writing and revising of this novel. My sincere thanks to Sonam Jatso, who patiently and thoroughly answered my numerous questions on Bhutan during the earlier stages of this novel's formation.

I am very thankful to Howard Solverson, whose account of Father William Mackey's life in Bhutan in his book *The Jesuit and the Dragon* was a great inspiration during the writing of this novel. Mr. Solverson's book is mentioned on several occasions in this novel as a book read and appreciated by its protagonists.

My deep appreciation to my writers' group in Toronto, Leanne Lieberman, Elizabeth MacLeod, Roz Spafford, Dianne Scott, Ania Szado, and Anne Warrick, for their unfailing moral support, encouragement, and constructive comments for the novel. To Ania Szado, I am very grateful for her careful and insightful editing of the final drafts.

I am immeasurably indebted to Sam Sze for his time, commitment, and expertise in planning and formatting the entire layout of the book, and to Tim Sze for his staunch and competent online technical support. Their involvement in this cherished work has meant more to me, their mother, than words can ever express.

Finally, *The Heart of the Buddha* would still be just a dream without the unconditional backing and understanding of my husband, Michael, who not only catered to my whim to return to Bhutan for my research, but also went that extra length trekking the Himalayan foothills with me. My love forever.

ASIA

with Bhutan and neighboring countries

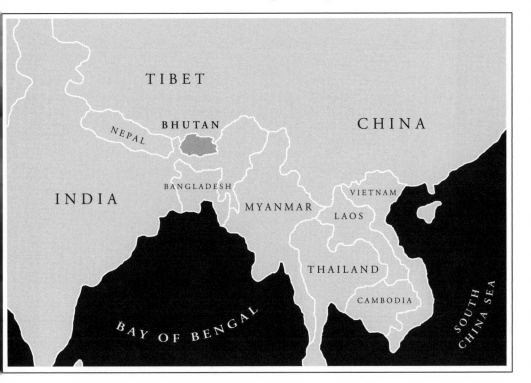

BHUTAN

locations of places cited in the novel

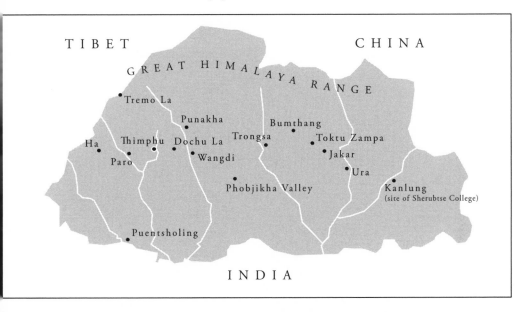

THIMPHU

sketch map of places cited in the novel

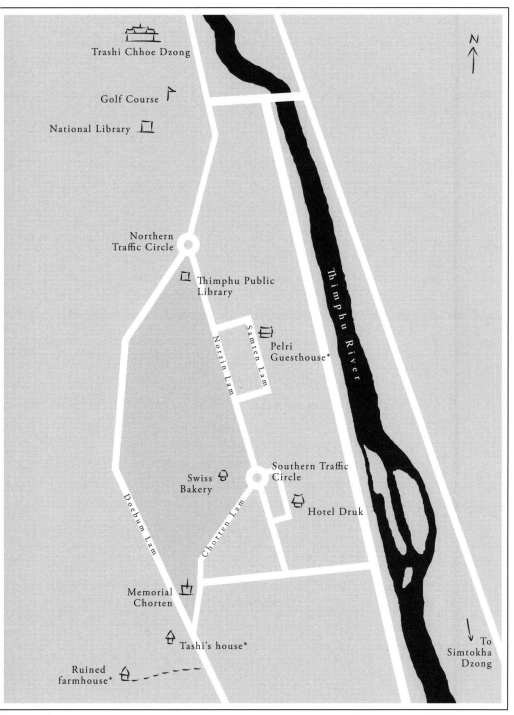

Trashi Chhoe Dzong

Golf Course

National Library

N

Northern
Traffic Circle

Thimphu Public
Library

Samten Lam

Norzin Lam

Pelri
Guesthouse*

Thimphu River

Swiss
Bakery

Southern Traffic
Circle

Doebum Lam

Chorten Lam

Hotel Druk

Memorial
Chorten

Tashi's house*

Ruined
farmhouse*

To
Simtokha
Dzong

*Fictitious Places

Author's Note:

At the end of this volume, readers will find a glossary of terms used throughout the book to convey the Bhutan experience. Some words in the glossary may be familiar to readers as terms associated with Buddhism, while others are common Bhutanese words.

1

THIMPHU, BHUTAN, FEBRUARY 10, 1999.
Approaching the traffic circle at the north end of town, I saw a woman in a light-colored long garment a distance ahead, of Marian's height and build, walking with Marian's gait, and wearing her hair up the way Marian sometimes did. I could only see her back, but what I saw sent my pulse racing. Immediately I stepped into the circle, barely missing a sleeping dog on the pavement and running almost into the path of an oncoming car. When I looked in front again, she had vanished. Frantically, I scanned nearby shops and side streets in the gathering dusk. There was no trace of the woman who could be my twin sister. In tears, I headed back in the direction of the Hotel Druk.

Darkness enshrouded the capital as I made my way south on Norzin Lam. Stores were boarded up for the night. Only a few shabby restaurants and bars where locals hung out were still open, dimly illuminated with small flashing neon signs. Few pedestrians were on the streets. Only the dogs were plentiful. They seemed to come alive with nightfall, roaming the streets in packs. I picked up my steps as I turned into Wogzin Lam and the square with the clock tower, thankful that the well-lit glass entrance to the Hotel Druk was in view.

As I crossed the square, I noticed a dark human form, somewhat bulky, standing below the clock tower. I had a creepy sensation that the person was watching me. I shuddered, my overworked imagination playing a trick on me. I quickened my step and soon entered the warm, bright ambience of the Hotel Druk.

2

I WAS IN BHUTAN LOOKING FOR MY SISTER. I had not heard from her in over two months. As far as I was concerned, she was missing.

Marian had gone in May 1998 to work as a librarian in Bhutan's capital city, Thimphu. Her contract was for six months, "not long in the span of a lifetime," as Marian said. When no dissuasion worked on her stubborn mind, I gave her my reluctant blessing and saw her off to Bangkok, en route to the remote, little-known Himalayan kingdom. After all, she was twenty-six.

The country had no Internet service, and so, other than an occasional quick and costly phone call, we resorted to good old-fashioned letter-writing. "Snail mail" was more a literal than metaphorical attribute of the postal service in Bhutan. Marian's first letter, sent about the same time as the phone call she made to our home in Toronto upon her arrival in Thimphu, reached me some three weeks later.

Her early letters told about the riveting sights and magical scenery of the country, her work at the public library, the occasional weekend trips out of Thimphu, and the interesting locals she had met. Nothing too personal, nothing Dad or even Esther, whom Dad married five years after Mama died, couldn't read. At first, she included some photos with her letters, but she soon stopped doing so, for the quality of the prints was not great and she would bring her film home to develop. Then, about four months into her contract, I received a disturbing letter from her, confiding that she was at a crossroad where one direction could raise her to the pedestal with saints and another take her down the path to perdition. Yet she did not elaborate. It was better that I read about it in the memoir she was writing, she said, for a clearer understanding of the situation. An inconsiderate teaser she was. That very evening I called her at her guesthouse.

"Don't overreact, Ruthie. Nothing bad's happening. Just a decision I have to make. Trust me."

"Tell me."

"Not over the phone. Look, I'm okay and more excited about my life than I've been in a long time, so stop worrying. The stuff I've been writing—I'll mail it to you. That'll explain everything."

Nothing more was mentioned about the road taken or not taken in the few letters that followed. Then, about mid-November, I received a registered packet from Bhutan. Inside were a letter and a small loose-leaf binder containing pages and pages covered with Marian's handwriting.

> Pelri Guesthouse
> 7 Samten Lam
> Thimphu, Bhutan
>
> October 21, 1998

Dearest Ruthie,

I am near the end of my contract. You should be proud, for I can honestly say the library is in better shape than before I came.

I am sending you what I've written so far about my life here. Call it a memoir. I write whenever I have the urge to, and when there are events, impressions or feelings to document. This is a work in progress, as I am still living my story, and the outcome is yet unknown. Nonetheless, what I have written so far will prepare you for my homecoming, and whatever surprises I may bring.

About my plans for the next while, I will stay in Bhutan for another two weeks after my contract ends at the end of October, till my visa expires in mid-November. Then I will travel a bit in Southeast Asia before heading home. Why not make the most of the luxury of unemployment before tying myself down to another job?

If all goes according to plan, I will be home for Christmas. Tell Dad I love him. Hi to Esther too.

xoxo,

Marian

I wasted no time reading the pages Marian sent and finished it in a sitting. I would have loved it, if it were only fiction in an exotic setting, if Marian weren't writing about herself. As it was, I came away more anxious about her than ever before. I understood what she meant about being at a crossroad. I was fearful she was tottering on the threshold of a realm of danger from which I could not save her. Only she could decide her future. I dreaded the outcome.

Then, about a week later, on November 22nd, I received a bizarre phone call from a stranger, who said he was calling from Bhutan, someone who identified himself by the name of Tenpa Norbu. Surprisingly, he spoke Mandarin, which I had mastered at an early age. While Marian and I had inherited some of our father's Portuguese features, our full-blooded Chinese mother made sure that we learned Mandarin growing up in Hong Kong, for she believed Mandarin, rather than our native dialect, Cantonese, would be spoken there in future. Tenpa Norbu asked for Marian Souza. I said she was traveling abroad, that I had no notion where exactly she was at the moment. He knew Marian had worked at the public library in Thimphu. He said he was a friend.

"Do you have a message for her?"

"I fear Marian might have been involved in an act of fraud," he said,

4

throwing me into a state of alarm. "If she is still in Bhutan, I can help get her out, if I know where to find her."

"Fraud? My sister would never do anything like that. You have the wrong person!"

"Whether she is guilty or not, I can help her," he continued. "I'll call back in two weeks. Find out where she is if she phones. Remember not to mention my call, for she may misread my good intentions and hide from me if she knows I am looking for her."

In none of Marian's letters had she mentioned Tenpa Norbu. Neither had the name appeared in her memoir. In the days following his call, my heart beat faster every time the phone rang. I was becoming a nervous wreck, praying for Marian to phone and dreading Tenpa Norbu's call.

Three days later, she called collect. Her voice sounded distant and muffled from the poor connection. She said she was still in Bhutan.

"But your visa's expired! I thought you were traveling in Southeast Asia. When are you coming home?"

"I'll leave here as soon as I can."

"Marian, are you in trouble?"

"Not really. Don't worry. I'll be okay."

I told her about Tenpa Norbu. Immediately, she sounded frantic.

"He called? What did you tell him?"

"I told him you were out of the country. Nothing more. Who is he?"

"Someone I—never mind, I'll explain later. But if he calls again, don't tell him I'm still here. He means no good. Tell him I left Bhutan. Tell him I'm coming home soon."

"When? When are you coming home?"

"As soon as I can, but not right away. It's hard to talk over the phone. All this static. Will take me half a day to explain." She paused. "Have you read what I sent you?"

"Yes. I am worried, Marian. How could you—how are things developing?"

5

"Not as I had wanted, but I'll be okay. Things have happened since what you've read so far. I can't leave right now. That's why I'm phoning, so you won't worry. I'll write to explain everything. Real soon."

"Why can't you leave Bhutan now? You can't or you won't? You can't live in a dream that will never become reality. Marian? You hear me? Besides, I don't know who this Tenpa Norbu is, but if he's up to no good as you say, you have all the more reason to leave that country immediately. I want you out of there!" My voice bordered on hysteria. Then, more calmly, I added, "You said you'd be home for Christmas."

"I'm sorry. I don't know about Christmas at this point. I'll leave as soon as I can."

"Where are you staying now? How can I get in touch with you?"

"There is no phone where I am. Snail mail is sporadic and may get lost. I'll write you. I miss you, Ruthie. Tell Dad I miss him. Bye for now. Love you!"

The phone clicked.

On December 5th, Tenpa Norbu phoned again. I said Marian had not called but that I had received a postcard from her in Bangkok, and she was coming home soon. Whether I sounded credible to him, I could not tell. He thanked me politely and hung up.

In the next few weeks, I waited for the letter that Marian had promised to write, which would explain everything. Even if she were to write and mail it soon after her call on November 25th, it would still take weeks to arrive. As expected, Christmas came and went without Marian. Dad was disappointed. I gave a vague explanation that Marian was still helping out in Bhutan and couldn't leave just then.

By early January, when still no letter had arrived, and with no further phone call from Marian, I was losing sleep. Why hadn't she come home? A total blackout of news of my sister. Was she afraid to tell me of her whereabouts, that I might seek her out? Was she afraid that I might betray her to Tenpa Norbu? Who was this man to her? What if he really wanted

6

to help her? And then there was Pema. How I wished she and Pema had never met.

3

MARIAN HAD TURNED IN HER RESIGNATION after three years at the reference desk of Toronto's municipal library. Government documents were too dry and uninteresting for her. She wanted change, a new environment, new challenges. She had dropped by the university's Department of Information Science to see what might be advertised on the hiring board. A very unusual posting caught her attention. *A trained librarian needed to reorganize English language collections in the public library in Thimphu, Bhutan. Term of service: six months. Attractive salary. Travel expenses and medical insurance covered. Apply to: Mrs. Virginia Campbell, c/o Canadian Institute for Aid to Developing Nations.*

Until then, I'd had no idea where the country was. The day she told me about the potential job opportunity there, she opened the atlas to Asia and tapped her index finger on a small but visible patch to the northeast of India, about the size of Switzerland. There, cradled in the folds of the Himalayas, was the Kingdom of Bhutan, with India to the west, south, and east, and Tibet to the north.

"But why, Marian?"

"Ruthie, I'm between jobs, unattached, and not going anywhere with my life. I'm not about to vegetate here, waiting for something to happen."

"You think going to Bhutan will make a difference in your life?"

"I don't know. But if nothing else, at least I'll have an experience few will ever have." She paused and continued as if to herself, "I just want to find myself."

That was Marian, baffling at times, her feet hardly touching the ground, a total dreamer. Still, her reasons for going away for a while would have made sense, if it was to anywhere recognizable on the face of the globe. But Bhutan? I was not happy at the prospect of losing my only sister and best friend to a place so remotely situated and so little known. Whether or not the fact that I saw the light of the world five minutes before Marian made me more authoritative, I had never been able to shed the older-sister syndrome of giving unsolicited, often unsympathetic, advice.

"That country doesn't even have a constitution," I said, quoting my findings from the Internet while making supper. "No political parties, no freedom of assembly, of the press or religion." I emptied spaghetti into a strainer.

"I can instill some of my own values there." Marian grinned impishly. She tasted the mushroom sauce with a spoon and smacked her lips.

"They'll lock you up."

"No, they won't."

"At least kick you out."

"I'm not going there to stir up a storm, or upset their apple cart, that is, if they grow apples. I'm only going to fix up their *li-bra-ry*, Ruthie. It's a job," she paused, half-smiling to herself while stirring the sauce, "*and* an adventure."

"No electricity in most parts of the country, no TV broadcasting, not to mention the Internet. A total blackout."

"The more exciting it will be. You just wonder what they do after dark, eh?" She gave a wicked chuckle.

"I've read of travelers getting really sick in that part of the world. Bacteria in the water. Parasites in the meat. And little medicine, except the indigenous kind."

"I'll take all the recommended shots before I go. I'll drink only bottled water and be really cautious with everything I eat, okay? As for the meat, have you forgotten I'm vegetarian?"

So much for scare tactics.

"There'll be no church to attend, only Buddhist temples," I said meekly, losing her, and turning to the Ultimate for help.

Marian tapped her forehead. "I don't need to get physically inside a church to do my bit of worshipping, under adverse conditions, Ruthie."

As usual, she got the better of me. I was always the one to talk sense, but Marian with all her philosophical sensitivity often won the debate and left me tongue-tied. And with the reluctant admission that she was probably right. Mama used to say of our temperaments that Marian and I were like the two halves of a yin-yang circle, different as the black of one half and the white of the other. And then perhaps, like the yin-yang circle, we complemented each other, and our differences made us whole.

"Well?" I pumped Marian when she came home from her interview with Mrs. Campbell.

I was hoping she had failed, or that she was so discouraged by what she had learned from Mrs. Campbell about the living conditions in Bhutan and the state of the public library in its capital that she would not take the job even if it was offered.

"The place is simply a paradise. It's not of this world, from the pictures she showed me."

"What about the job?"

"That's the problem. She was quite frank with me. The library's in a horrid state of neglect. She has seen it herself."

"That's not very encouraging." I was ecstatic.

"On the other hand, it will be a challenge I don't mind taking on if I'm hired. I'd be helping an underprivileged country, and at the same time doing what I do best where it counts most."

So long as she had not heard from Mrs. Campbell or the Canadian Institute, there was a chance that Marian had not gotten the job. In a time of downsizing in the Canadian job market, there must have been a lot of other librarians out of work, ready to take on the most pitiful of libraries, even if it meant going to the ends of the earth, or, in the case of Bhutan, the top of the world.

My hope was dashed when Marian received a phone call from Mrs. Campbell, telling her she had been hired. It turned out that the funding of the library project was coming from Virginia Campbell herself, who, according to a librarian friend of Marian's, was a former editor for a Canadian publisher and the widow of a wealthy, prominent Toronto lawyer.

The next couple of weeks saw Marian more excited and enthusiastic than she had been in a long while, as she prepared for her incredible journey.

"I want to write about my time there, something creative and true," Marian said during one of our last suppers at home before she left. Holding a spoon of soup suspended between her bowl and her lips, she looked into the distance with a hunger in her eyes that no food could satiate.

"*My Sojourn in the Dragon Kingdom?*" I volunteered.

"Or *How I Lost My Heart in Bhutan, and Found My Soul*," she said.

"That's so platonic. Hope Bhutan lives up to your expectations." I heard sarcasm in my voice, and added with redeeming sincerity, "Will I get to read it?"

"Absolutely," she said between slurps of soup. "You may be the only one to read it. I have no intention to publish right now."

4

DAD, ESTHER, AND I RANG IN THE NEW YEAR WITHOUT MARIAN. As soon as offices reopened after the holidays, I called the Canadian Institute. I was told, to my consternation, that Virginia Campbell had passed away in December, and the institute had not heard from Marian.

"Can you contact somebody in Bhutan about my sister?" I asked the institute director.

"I'm afraid it's not going to be easy. You see, this library project wasn't one of ours. Its funding didn't come through us but came directly from Virginia Campbell. She wanted her money to be spent specifically on the public library in Thimphu. We had agreed to be her agent in making the initial contact. Mrs. Campbell then took over the selection of a librarian. She told us about her chosen candidate, and we notified the Bhutanese government to arrange a visa for her. I'm afraid our part in the project ended there."

"But aren't you responsible for the welfare of people who have gone out through the institute?"

"People on our own projects, yes. But, as I explained, this was not one of ours. I wish we could help you, Miss Souza, but we've not heard from the Bhutanese government regarding this library project since your sister went to Bhutan. You may not be aware of it, but both your sister and Virginia Campbell had signed a waiver releasing us of all responsibilities for the project and for Marian's well-being during her term of work there. I'm sorry about your sister. She may just turn up at your doorstep any time."

I then called the public library in Thimphu. I was told by a woman whose distant voice was hard to hear that Marian had not been back to the library since the last day of her employment there, October 31st. It was assumed she had left Bhutan. I phoned the Pelri Guesthouse in Thimphu where she had stayed. I was told she had checked out at the end of October, although she had left some of her belongings in storage there, to be picked up later. She had not returned.

Once I had made up my mind to go look for Marian, I booked my trip on the Internet with a tour company, Bhutan Best Tours, which would also arrange for my visa. I was able to take three weeks off in February from Precious Blood Hospital, where I worked as an office administrator. I would have a licensed guide for the twenty-one days there, since no self-guided tourists were permitted in the country. The daily charge of two hundred American dollars would require my diving deep into my credit resources, but I would go to any lengths to get Marian home.

When I told Dad of my decision to go to Bhutan to look for Marian, he gave me his full moral support. And when he extracted from me the information about the cost of the trip, he asked me to stop by his café one day and quietly but firmly pressed a check into my hand, saying, "Come back with her safe, Ruth. That's all I care."

Indeed, Dad had always believed in my good sense. He also seemed to think I had the telepathic intuition to know where Marian would be, from my past record…

Marian did not come home for a few days when she discovered Dad was serious with Esther Jackson.

When Mama died of liver cancer in 1990, seven years after we immigrated from Hong Kong to Canada, it seemed our home had lost its heart. Marian and I started university a year later. We decided to live at home and commute to the university in downtown Toronto, for Dad's sake.

After Mama's death, Dad's business became his life. He spent long hours in the coffee shop he had managed and later taken over in Toronto's East End. He experimentally installed a couple of Internet stations inside the café. Business boomed. He added a few more computers. Then gradually, he succumbed to middle-age loneliness, when a rather comely fifty-year-old widow gave him the eye. And then more.

Marian did not like Esther from the start. In her words, she did not like Esther's overpowering perfume, her loud chuckle, her babbling manner of speech, her bragging about her lawyer son, her affected ways with Dad.

"You're not reacting rationally," I said. "I don't see any incriminating evidence from your far from generous observations that prove her unsuitable for Dad. We are all adults, so behave like one. It's been five years since Mama died, and Dad needs someone."

"Rational or not, I don't fancy her taking the place of Mama in Dad's life, and in his home, our home."

That sentiment of Marian's reached a climax when Marian and I came home one morning after an overnight stay at a friend's cottage to find Esther puttering barefooted in our kitchen, wearing a dressing gown, making breakfast as she hummed an off-tune rendition of *Love Me Do*. She smiled complacently at us. Marian immediately walked out of the house, drove away in the secondhand Honda she and I shared, and did not come home that night or the next.

Dad was worried. Esther was upset. I called Marian's friends, but no one knew her whereabouts. She was not working at the time, having just graduated from library school.

On the morning of the third day of her disappearing act, as if jolted by a current that only twin siblings know and share, I made my way to Highland Cemetery, where Mama's ashes were kept. After waiting two hours in the columbarium, I saw Marian entering and walking up to Mama's niche. I accosted her. I cajoled, argued, cried. After much painful convincing, I took her home.

14

A few months later, Dad married Esther. Marian and I moved out of our family's split-level home in Scarborough and rented a two-bedroom apartment in a modest low-rise complex in mid-town Toronto. Esther kept a jovial front with us, and she avoided stepping on Marian's toes.

This time, however, it wasn't going to be so easy. Looking for Marian in Bhutan was like looking for one special pebble on an unfamiliar beach.

5

I LEFT TORONTO ON FEBRUARY 7, 1999, FOR BANGKOK. Funny, with all my misgivings about Marian's going to Bhutan, I had remained reasonably calm while preparing for my own journey. I would survive the trip and return home safe. My mission was to get Marian safely home too. There lay the anxiety, challenge, and uncertainties.

In Bangkok, I stayed one night at the Siam Hotel by the airport, waiting for my morning flight to Paro, the only airport town in Bhutan. The air conditioning in the hotel afforded a most welcome reprieve from the steaming, humid air of the city.

Near the Druk Air counter at Bangkok's airport, I sat next to a Buddhist monk of short, stout stature. Although it wasn't easy to tell his age with his shorn head, his unblemished face suggested he could not be more than mid-thirtyish. He looked friendly, his slight overbite giving the illusion of a constant smile.

"Going to Bhutan?" he asked in a somewhat high-pitched voice.

"Yes." I forced a smile. I had never talked to a Buddhist monk before.

"Tourist?"

"Yes." Then curiosity took over. "Are you from Bhutan?"

"My family live in Thimphu." He spoke good English. "Now I live near Dharamsala, India. You know Dharamsala? The Dalai Lama lives there." The last bit of information he volunteered with a measure of pride.

"Have you seen the Dalai Lama?"

"All the time."

He then told me he had just been to Myanmar to visit the temples there and was on his way to Punakha, about seventy kilometers east of

Thimphu. Before long, he was telling me he first studied to be a monk in Thimpu. I was surprised at how open he was to a stranger.

"I go home one month every year to see my family, and this time also to attend Punakha dromche." I looked blank. He chuckled and explained that dromche was the name of a festival, and took place once a year in Punakha. He said it was the first of the big festivals of the year in Bhutan. "You should go," he said, broadening his smile. "All festivals take place in dzongs—you know, those big buildings with temples, monasteries, offices—big place, usually not open to visitors. You have chance to see inside Punakha Dzong if you go to dromche, February twenty to twenty-four this year."

I nodded, making a mental note of his recommendation. We soon boarded. That was the last I saw of him, for a while.

"Good morning, Your Majesties. Good morning, ladies and gentlemen. Welcome on board Druk Air Flight 28 to Paro," a woman's melodious voice sounded over the PA system.

A well-groomed young female attendant with tasteful makeup, hair combed smoothly back into a bun, and wearing a blue Bhutanese national dress came by. She offered candies from a basket.

"Is there royalty on the flight?" I asked her, nodding toward the curtained front section.

"It's the Queen Mother and two princesses, back from holiday in Bangkok," she answered. True, with air traffic between Bhutan and the rest of the world confined to two Druk Air planes, how else could anyone, royalty or commoner, fly in and out of the kingdom?

The plane made a quick stop at the airport at Kolkata, formerly Calcutta, to pick up a few more passengers as well as cargo. I found myself sitting next to a hill of jute sacks for the remainder of the flight. The arid landscape beyond Kolkata gradually gave way to layers of mountains looming grey and purple in the distance and becoming luxuriant and vibrant shades of green as the plane glided over them. Mountains and valleys interlocked into one another like fingers of hands clasped in prayer. My fervent prayer was to find Marian within the layers of that terrain.

I had taken with me the only source of information I possessed that ought to be helpful in finding Marian. Her memoir about her time in Bhutan was my only key to the mystery of her disappearance. All the way to Bhutan, I reread the pages of the memoir, wherein lay Marian's secret.

6

📖

From the Memoir of Marian Souza

PARO/THIMPHU, MAY 1, 1998—*ARRIVAL*
I can hardly believe that I, Marian Souza, have arrived in the Himalayan Kingdom of Bhutan. I am scared yet excited, as my sister Ruthie would say, "feeling the itch, dreading the pain." Nevertheless, I am ready to take this mysterious land in full stride.

I had hoped to catch a glimpse of the snow-covered peaks of the Himalayas as I flew into Bhutan, but none was in sight. The lush green mountains and valleys among the foothills were nevertheless breath-taking. Someone sitting near me said the plane coming in from Nepal flew over Everest. When I go home, I should arrange to fly by way of Nepal to see the real Himalayas.

I was met by a clean-shaven stubby fellow in his late thirties, with a pronounced round face, rather dark complexion, a fresh short haircut, and wearing dark-rimmed glasses. He had on what looked like a long bathrobe, pulled up to the knees and secured at the waist with a belt—the national costume for men, I was told, called *gho*. It was made of some thick, cottony, orange-checkered material. Grey knee-highs covered most of the exposed parts of his legs, and he wore black leather shoes.

"Souza? Welcome to Bhutan. Sonam Wangdi from Thimphu Public Library," he said, breaking into a broad smile and holding out a pudgy hand. He spoke reasonably good English.

"Very happy to meet you, Sonam. Call me Marian," I said. "I'm so excited to be here, and looking forward to working with you."

He gave me a disarming smile, exposing teeth stained alarmingly blood-red, which I had read was the result of betel-nut chewing, a Bhutanese addiction. He walked me through Immigration, retrieved my bags, and led me out of the tiny one-level airport building to a rather shabby Toyota Land Cruiser parked nearby.

The road from Paro to Thimphu was a paved road alongside a river, the Paro Chhu, with terraced rice fields extending across the valley on both sides. All along, on the edges of the road and fields were two- or three-story whitewashed houses, with windows framed in decorative painted wood panels, and the upper floors protruding somewhat over the ground floor. Roofs had shingles held in place only by stones. Long and narrow flimsy flags in white, red, green, yellow, and blue flapped on poles planted further up on hillsides.

"Prayer flags," said Sonam, pointing to them. "Mantras on them. When the wind blows, the prayers are heard."

At some point, we came to a confluence of two rivers, the Paro Chhu and the Thimphu Chhu. We stopped to stretch. He pointed out three chortens where the road forked into two. These were white cement structures, about two stories high, not accessible from outside. One was round at the base, shaped like a bell with a pointed top. The one in the middle had a square base rising up to a circular top, ending in a gold spire. The third was a square structure topped with a smaller square structure like a two-tiered wedding cake.

"They contain Buddhist relics. You gain merit if you walk around chorten, but remember always in direction of a clock," Sonam said.

"Merit?"

"For better next life, when you are reborn."

"I've always thought one gains merit from doing good deeds."

"That too. There are many ways to gain merit. Also donating to temples, planting prayer flags, turning prayer wheels. Many many ways." He flashed his betel-nut smile.

A big red barrel painted with colorful symbols on the surface hung from the ceiling of a pavilion nearby.

"Prayer wheel," Sonam indicated. "Many mantras inside."

He grabbed the wheel's wooden handle, and walked with it clockwise, turning the wheel as he did so. More merit gained.

We passed a farmhouse with a painting on its front white wall of what looked to me like a big fat red sausage, with a happy face, rolled-up eyeballs, a funny mustache curled up at the ends, and apparently wearing a rain hat. At its base were two round circles. A sausage on wheels dancing in the rain.

I asked Sonam if that was an auspicious symbol. He grinned.

"That's a phallus."

"A what?"

"A phallus. To drive away evil. You see many wood ones hanging from roofs."

I began to notice those objects hanging from roofs everywhere, each pierced with a wooden sword. Sonam said the sword stood for power. If the phalluses in Bhutan could ward off evil, they must be pretty powerful, and presumably quite virile. And I thought I had come from a liberated society to one where inhabitants were in all likelihood sexually conservative.

At intervals, our car passed locals walking by the edge of the road, men in ghos driving their cattle, women in the national dress, ankle-length, carrying big baskets on their backs, of twigs or pine cones. Children waved to us, their rough wind-burned faces bright and beaming.

Situated in a broad valley protected by mountains, Thimphu fell short of my concept of a nation's capital. It struck me more as a settlement of low houses concentrated in the center of the town, with some farmhouses scattered beside terraced rice fields a short distance from the main hub.

We saw more cars as we neared town. We drove around a traffic circle, where a white-gloved policeman in a blue uniform was directing traffic. We continued down Norzin Lam, described by Sonam as the main street of Thimphu, a two-lane street lined with two-, three-, or four-story white-washed buildings, mostly businesses on the ground level. External walls and wooden window frames were painted with colorful pictures of lotus blossoms, wheels, and symmetrical border patterns. As we neared the center of town, there were more pedestrians, men in ghos, and women in what Sonam called *kiras*.

"The women look so graceful in their national dress," I remarked to Sonam, "but it looks pretty complicated to put on."

"Doesn't take my wife long every morning." Sonam then described to me the process of putting on a kira, involving the wrapping of a piece of ankle-length fabric around the body and over the shoulders, secured in front by a hook at each shoulder, and tied at the waist with a woven belt.

"I'd love to try one on some time, but I'll probably need your wife to help me."

The Pelri Guesthouse, where I will be staying for the next six months, is a large two-floor wood-based building in the traditional design, north of the main section of the town, on Samten Lam. All the guest rooms are on the upper level. Below is a restaurant. The place caters especially to foreigners on extended periods of stay. My room is simply furnished with a foam mattress bed, a nightstand, a dresser with a mirror, an armchair in upholstery of a multicolored woven fabric, and a wooden desk and chair and looks quite Spartan, except for the beautifully stenciled designs of lotus flowers and wheels along the upper edges of the walls. I have an attached bathroom that has a shower and a seat toilet. It is better than what I expected, for the daily rate of six hundred ngultrums, about sixteen Canadian dollars. And what's more, there is a small exercise room with the bare minimum of an exercise bike, a rowing machine, a bench, and some free weights. For sure, I will be making good use of the "gym".

As for the other most basic of human needs, my first two meals consist-ed of vegetarian curry with Bhutanese red rice and dahl, which I liked. I tried emadatsi, another item on the Bhutanese daily menu, and my throat burned for a long time afterwards. No more chilies for me. Sonam told me about the Swiss Bakery downtown, which should satisfy my sweet palate and craving for caffeine.

The public library, situated on Norzin Lam, near what Sonam referred to as the northern traffic circle, was closed for a holiday today, my first day in Bhutan. I have only seen it from the outside, a street-level broad storefront decorated with elaborately painted designs of flowers, wheels, and swirls on window frames, just like ones on most other buildings of the capital.

The next six months promise to be an amazing eye-opener, a genuine breath of fresh air, as I set out to embrace a new culture, meet interesting people, and most likely learn more from them than what I can probably impart to them, in the time allotted to me to lend my so-called expertise to a developing nation.

7

$$\text{📖}$$

From the Memoir of Marian Souza

THIMPHU, MAY 2, 1998 — *THE LIBRARY*

A mid-fiftyish Bhutanese woman with rather ungroomed streaking grey hair walked into the library soon after I arrived this morning, my first day of work. She wore a white long-sleeved blouse under her black kira. Most women wear short jackets over their kiras, but she was not wearing one.

"You the new staff?" she asked curtly, throwing her tote bag on the desk.

"I'm Marian Souza, the librarian from Canada. You must be Jigme," I said, going over to where she was standing, and extending my hand. Sonam had told me there was another person on the staff, Jigme Chomo. While Sonam was the caretaker, Jigme looked after the circulation and organized acquisitions consisting mostly of book donations and a small quantity of materials bought with the dwindling annual membership fees and overdue fines.

Jigme took my hand hesitantly, without a smile, then dropped it almost immediately. Her hand felt cold and rough.

"I manage the library, keep everything in order," she said with a sweep of her hand. "Make sure books come back. For ten years I look after the library." She gave me an I'm-the-boss look.

To establish my position from the start, I said in as pleasant a voice as I could muster, "I've been authorized by the Bhutanese government to manage this library for the next six months. I understand much reorganization is needed. Let's start immediately. I will need your help, and Sonam's, to make this project a success. We will hold a staff meeting this afternoon."

Jigme was taken aback, stared at me, and was sour but reasonably co-operative the rest of the day.

The library consists of three street-level rooms, the two larger ones in front for public use, and the smaller end room for the staff. The public areas are furnished with badly scratched oblong wooden tables and low-backed wooden chairs. A metal magazine rack is at one end of the front room, displaying some embarrassingly dated copies of the *Readers' Digest*, *Time*, *National Geographic*, and a few Indian and South Asian periodicals. Several copies of the *Kuensel*, Bhutan's national weekly newspaper, lie on the tables. A small desk by the street entrance serves as the circulation desk, apparently Jigme's sentry post.

The middle room is the main reading room. A musty smell of old un-used books pervades. The stacks consist of dreary grey metal shelving. Some black labels on the shelves are peeling off. *New label maker*, I wrote on my notepad of things to get and do. Where the shelves are not full, books have fallen on top of one another. *Bookends*.

The card catalog, an archaic contraption not seen for a long time in libraries back home, sits in a corner of the main reading room. Rods for holding the cards upright are missing from some drawers, so that many cards are lying flat inside. A spot-check indicates the catalog is far from accurate. Its condition is something Jigme cannot justify even if she tries. I am not out here to find fault with local library attendants who have never taken Librarianship 101, but I will fix up that catalog yet. It may not be as big a headache as it seems, for I have a good mind to discard a big portion of the existing collection.

And the collection, to call it pitiful is an understatement. The 1979 edition of *Black's Medical Dictionary*, *The World Book Encyclopedia* 1985, *Britannica* 1984. And what is a copy of the 1980 edition of *Who's Who in America* doing in a Bhutanese public library? *Weeding*, I wrote in my to-do list. The most current and useful items are a few sets of recently published children's encyclopedias, gifts from the Queen Mother of Bhutan.

The fiction shelves are jammed with mass market paperback editions of old bestsellers, with covers torn, pages dog-eared. Nothing is discarded, nothing replaced. And where are *Wuthering Heights* and *David Copperfield*? And what is a poetry collection without T. S. Eliot, Tennyson, or Wordsworth? *Acquisitions*.

As I took note of the problems in the library on this my first day here, I realized the mountain of work ahead of me. I am excited by the challenge. With six months and a decent budget, I can make a difference. Ruthie will be relieved that I will have no time to get myself into any kind of trouble.

8

From the Memoir of Marian Souza

THE SWISS BAKERY, MAY 13, 1998 — *TASHI*

This afternoon, a tall young woman in an orange kira and matching jacket walked into the library. I was in the main reading room when she came hesitantly over.

"Miss Souza?" she asked, looking a little shy.

"Yes, Marian Souza," I answered, surprised. "And you are?"

She bit her lower lip. "Tashi Campbell. My grandmother told me about you. Said I could find you here."

"You must be Mrs. Campbell's granddaughter! I'm so pleased to meet you." I offered my hand, and she gave it a gentle shake.

The day I signed the contract with Virginia Campbell, she told me she had a granddaughter living in Thimphu. Her son had married a Bhutanese while he was on volunteer service as an English teacher in Bhutan years ago, and he lived in Bhutan until his tragic death from a rabid dog's bite.

Tashi Campbell was a beautiful girl, with keen brown eyes, mildly high cheekbones, and an almond-shaped face. Her complexion was lighter than that of most Bhutanese. Her dark brown hair was relatively short, covering her ears, pageboy-fashion. She must have inherited her height from her Canadian father, for she was about five foot five, taller than most Bhutanese women. The kira complimented her tall and slim figure.

"Happy to meet you too. I was just running some errands for my mother, and thought I would come in to say hello."

"Do you live close by?"

"At the other end of town. But in Thimphu, everywhere is within walking distance." Her English was as good as any I had heard in North America, minus the common slang back home.

"Look, I'm finishing in twenty minutes. If you can stay, perhaps we can walk down Norzin Lam and stop for coffee at the Swiss Bakery. I've heard good things about it."

She nodded, looking pleased. She picked up a copy of the *Kuensel* and sat down at one of the tables.

We left the library together, with Jigme, who was locking up, staring after us. At the Swiss Bakery, a neat little circular café, I ordered a vegetarian sandwich, coffee, and a rum ball, the only sweet I could see. Tashi had a bottle of the local apple juice and a bag of homemade chips. She had to be home for supper, she said.

Tashi told me she had been to Canada twice, with her father to visit her grandmother, but had not been there since his death nine years ago.

"I heard about the—accident. Your grandmother told me. I'm very sorry," I said, not sure what else to say.

She stared at her cup. Then, looking up at me gravely, she said, "I was nine. I was there. He was defending a dog that was being attacked by a pack of dogs. The other dogs left. Then he went up to the dog he saved and patted it on the head. It bit him."

"Nothing could be done for him?"

Tashi shook her head. "No one knew the dog was infected until it was too late to fly my father out to Bangkok for the injections. We didn't have the serum here."

I shook my head. Such a senseless loss would never have happened back home.

"Mama and I were not allowed to see him near the end."

I shuddered at the thought of someone dying from rabies, the virus attacking the nerves and the brain, until the victim was as mad as the dog that bit him.

"Did they get the dog?"

"They identified the dog, and kept it in a cage until it died." Seeing my disturbed look, she continued, "You must know in Bhutan the killing of any sentient being is strongly discouraged."

"Even when its suffering becomes unbearable?"

"Merit is gained in suffering."

"Even for a dog?"

"Yes, because all sentient beings go through rebirth."

I was silent for a long moment. It wasn't easy to take in the whole tragedy, the sufferings borne by the man and the animal.

"Your father's death must have been very hard on you and your mother," I said.

"Mama and I missed Papa very much, but Mama said we shouldn't be sad. My father died defending a sentient being. His merit was great, and he has probably reincarnated to a higher state of existence, closer to nirvana."

"Was he Buddhist?"

"He was a Christian until he converted to Buddhism. My grandmother was not pleased about that, just as she didn't like Papa marrying a Bhutanese. She wanted Papa to take us back to Canada, but my mother didn't want to leave Bhutan, so we stayed on. My grandmother came for my father's funeral." Tashi sipped her juice, and continued, "She visited again four years ago. Mama was not too happy about her visit. She was afraid my grandmother might talk me into going to school in Canada, and then perhaps I wouldn't come back. Mama was right; my grandmother did ask me if I wanted to go to Canada with her."

"And you didn't want to?"

"I had to stay. I was only fourteen. Mama would never let me go. Besides, I would be sad leaving my mother then."

"Would you like to go to Canada, now that you're older?"

"My immediate goal is to get into Sherubtse College after I graduate from high school next year. But yes, I do want to go to Canada some day. I want to leave Bhutan and see the world."

I like Tashi Campbell. When we left the Swiss Bakery, I knew I had found a new friend in her. And the rum ball was luscious, simply sinful, almost worth a trip to Bhutan.

9

From the Memoir of Marian Souza

DOCHU LA, JUNE 7, 1998 — *THE NAKED FELLOW*
    May came and went. I soon settled into a routine, the idea of which I normally baulk at. But with my life in Thimphu revolving only around the library and the guesthouse and the short distance in between, there had been little room for the extraordinary, and not much to write about. Until last Sunday.

That was the day Sonam took me to Dochu La as he had promised. Dochu La, a mountain pass, over three thousand meters high, about twenty-some kilometers from Thimphu, was a forty-minute drive along the Punakha Trail, on a bumpy paved road. Sonam said that, on a clear day, from Dochu La one could see Gangkhar Puensum, the third highest mountain in the Himalayan range, and the highest within Bhutan.

Bright and early that morning, Sonam packed me, his wife, Dolma, their six-year-old son and four-year-old daughter, and a picnic lunch into his old Land Cruiser, and we set off. We cut through a botanist's paradise of hemlock, chir pine, and blue pine. White magnolias and red and white rhododendrons bloomed wild among the evergreens. Sonam parked his Cruiser on a flat space at the top of the pass, not far from a small chorten and a forest of prayer flags making flapping noises in the wind. He had warned me that June was not a good time to see the Himalayas from the pass, but we lucked out that day, for the mist cleared just as we reached the top, and we saw the snow-clad peaks in the far horizon. Through a high-powered telescope in the cafeteria, which was a bungalow selling local woven fabrics and serving tea and cookies, Gangkhar Puensum, with its snow-covered folds and slopes, was magnificent and intimidating. A chart on the wall showed its elevation as seven thousand five hundred meters, and still unclimbed, because the Bhutanese government had forbidden climbing, for fear of inciting the anger of the mountain gods.

We lunched on the pass, not far from the chorten and the prayer flags. After gorging myself on curried vegetables and fragrant steamed rice kept hot in thermal canisters, I left Sonam, Dolma, and the kids watching a family erect a new prayer flag on the pass, and wandered downhill into the surrounding wood. A call of nature sent me further into the brush. I crouched low, hidden in the tall grass. Quickly I performed my duty, afraid that some lurking snake might get curious, even suspicious. It was then that I heard a voice, a robust baritone, singing a melodious and peppy song, probably in native Dzongkha, for I could not understand a word. Frantically, I pulled up my panties and jeans, adjusted my T-shirt, and looked around. No one was in sight. The singing came from round a bend on the gentle slope.

I made my way to the bend, and scanned a little clearing by a mountain brook. About ten meters from where I was, a man, stripped to the skin, his back to me, was heating rocks over a fire. He had an athletic form, with broad shoulders, brawny arms, a well-proportioned torso: an Apollo in action. As he bent his back, I could see the knots on his spine from the nape down. My eyes lingered on the crouched figure, the stretching of taut tanned skin over sinewy muscles, the tantalizing movement of firm, trim buttocks. Flushed at my own curious indulgence, I diverted my eyes. Nearby was a rectangular hole in the ground, about four by eight feet, and seemingly lined with wood. Water from the brook had apparently been channeled into the hole along a dug trench. As he piped out cheerful high-low notes, the naked fellow rolled the hot rocks into one end of the hole with a large piece of bark, creating a lot of steam when the rocks hit the water. So it was an outdoor steam bath, a hot tub, Bhutanese-style. I wanted to make a quiet exit, but before I could move, the naked fellow stood up, and walked around to the other end of the bath. His front was in full view for a few good seconds before he jumped into the water, and in those seconds I saw him in all his naked glory.

Embarrassed and frantic, I started going back in the direction I had come. But my movement must have caught his attention. He saw me. Surely astounded, he called out something from his pool.

"I'm sorry, so sorry," I yelled back, half turning, my face probably red as a beet, for I felt the heat. "I didn't know you were here." I was rooted to the ground.

He surprised me by answering in English. "Water is very good. Good hot bath," he said. He didn't sound embarrassed or upset at all, which relaxed me a bit.

"It must be very nice," I called back, facing in his direction but not focusing on him. "Enjoy your bath. Bye!"

As I was about to make my way back into the brush, my eyes fell on fabrics hanging from the branches of a tree close by, maroon color, his garments. They were the long flowing skirt and shawl of a Buddhist monk.

He called out something after me, probably some pleasantry. I did not look back. As soon as I had rounded the bend and was out of his sight, I breathed more easily.

I did not mention my experience with the outdoor bather to Sonam or Dolma. All the way home, I was quiet, unable to get the incident out of my head. Not that I was excited by a vision of the male anatomy, although the subject did seem to possess rather fine physical endowments. Perhaps it was his relaxed disposition as he prepared the bath in the woodland setting, the losing of self in nature's domain. Or the baritone voice warbling pleasing notes. Perhaps it was the sight of a monk's robe hanging from a tree—I could never imagine any priest bathing nude under the gaping eyes of Mother Nature.

10

From the Memoir of Marian Souza

THE CHORTEN, JUNE 13, 1998 — *THE MONK*
Tashi Campbell stopped by the library yesterday. She looked upset, saying she wanted to talk. She couldn't talk in the library, especially in the presence of Jigme, who was all but hostile to her.

I walked with Tashi down Norzin Lam when I finished at five, in the direction of the Memorial Chorten at the southern end of town, near where she lives with her mother.

"I'm really angry," Tashi began. "I took *Brave New World* out from the public library recently and read it. It gave me an idea for my independent topic essay. I discussed the dangers of unquestioning conformity in society."

"Great topic."

"I used homogeneity in our country as an illustration, like the compulsory national dress, the sole practice of Buddhism, and the intolerance of other religions here, and I said blind conformity could be detrimental to the survival of the human spirit."

"Good for you."

"Today I was called to the principal's office. The headmaster said I was too critical of my society and government, and I might get into trouble if I continued to write like that." Tashi was in tears. "My essay was disqualified for my own good, he said, to make me more mindful of what I would write in future. I'm given a chance to write another essay, because of my good record."

"This is outrageous! They can't do that to you. It's an infringement on the freedom of expression!"

"I need a good mark for that essay, for Sherubtse."

"I'd like to read your essay, the one they threw out."

"The headmaster destroyed the copy I handed in, but I'll give you the one I have at home." She paused. "I wish I could apply to colleges elsewhere."

"Your grandmother could help you there."

"But my mother would not let me leave." She gave a little sigh. "Maybe in a few years' time."

"I agree you should finish Sherubtse first."

We had turned into Chorten Lam. The Memorial Chorten came into view. It is one of the most prominent landmarks near the southern outskirts of Thimphu, taller than any of the chortens I have seen. An impressive monument it is, in the style of Tibetan stupas, with a high white square base, an inverted torch-shaped top, and a golden spear-like spire. Unlike most chortens, the Memorial Chorten can be entered. Tashi and I paused at the gateway to its juniper-lined entrance path.

"I'm just a little way up from here," Tashi said, pointing to the slope on the far side of Doebum Lam.

"I'd like to meet your mother some time."

"I'll arrange something. Hey, thanks for listening."

"Remember, don't lose sight of your dream."

Tashi smiled and nodded. I watched her as she continued up the dirt path. She turned to wave and soon disappeared from view.

Since I was at the entrance of the chorten, and my evening, as usual, was free, I thought I might as well go in for a look. I walked down the pathway to the wooden door. My pulse quickening a little, I entered its dark recess.

Several altars formed a big circle around the center of the interior, each dominated by statues of Buddhist deities. A stuffy smell of incense permeated the gloomy atmosphere, illuminated mainly by altar lamps and daylight through the doorway. I left my shoes with a few other pairs on the floor just inside the threshold. I saw no one from where I stood by the door. I started to walk around the center core, a little afraid of the wrathful looking statues, which seemed to outnumber the peaceful ones. One appeared to be a demon god entwined with a female, naked to the waist, in a sexual embrace. I was pondering over its possible religious implication when I heard someone clearing his throat behind me. I turned to look into the eyes of a monk. My first reaction was fear of transgression. But there was no sign of reprimand on the monk's face. He was actually nodding at me with a faint smile, as though he knew me. Suddenly I was thrown into deep distress as I realized he was the naked monk! Except that he looked quite different fully clothed in his long red robe. And this time he caught me looking at some statues seemingly in the act of copulation. What smutty pursuits he must think I had.

"You're—" I stammered.

"Dochu La, the *dotsho*, last Sunday." He smiled again, this time more broadly, and when I looked questioningly at him, he added, "The hot rock bath."

"Oh yes, I remember," I said, and wished I hadn't said that. "This is my first time here. Just wondering at these statues. I'm not Buddhist." I gave a nervous laugh, shrugging at the coupling figures.

"This is one of our bodhisattvas with his consort," he explained, his eyes on the figures. "In Tantric Buddhism, we believe sexual energy can be a positive energy to help in the transformation of the normal self to the enlightened state." He studied my face, perhaps waiting for my reaction.

I nodded, trying to look impressed though not comprehending what he said. "Are the bodhisattvas like saints?" I asked, digressing from the topic of the usage of sexual energy.

"Yes, they are saints, compassionate toward all sentient beings. They regard the sufferings of others as their own. They can enter the state of enlightenment, except they are delaying entering that state, and instead choose to be reincarnated in order to help others who are suffering in the cyclic movement of rebirth, that they may reach enlightenment as well."

"Very noble of them," I said, and instinctively added, "and Christian, loving others as themselves."

"Are you Christian?"

"Yes, I'm a Catholic. I'm afraid all this is new to me."

He glanced at his watch. "If you like, I can show you around since I have some time today." I hesitated for a second, then nodded. He continued, "By the way, you were walking in the wrong direction. You always circumambulate a holy place clockwise."

How could I forget? With that, he put out his hand to point me in the right direction.

I was, surprisingly, no longer uncomfortable with the remembrance of our first encounter. I was even glad I had a guide to explain the objects inside the chorten. As he led the way, he explained the tormas prominently displayed on the altars, describing them as ritual cakes made from flour and butter. The tormas were dyed in soft colors and carved into ornate floral patterns. Bowls of water were placed at the altars as offerings. The altar lamps were butter lamps, he said, burning wicks steeped in cups of pure yak butter. The heat from one lamp was turning a small prayer wheel placed above its flame. It reminded me of the revolving lanterns in Hong Kong during the Mid-Autumnal Festival. My monk guide stopped in front of a framed photograph of the late King Jigme Dorji Wangchuk, father of the present king of Bhutan.

"He was a very popular king, the father of modern Bhutan," he said.

"And the present king?"

"Like his father. A benevolent king. He's well-loved."

"But he's an absolute monarch. You have no constitution." I thought of Tashi's essay.

"We have a National Assembly and a Council of Ministers to help the king make decisions for the welfare of the people. We are a very happy and peaceful nation." He spoke with sincerity in his tone, while looking at me with a glint in his eyes, as if amused by my brusque statement about his country's political system.

We walked up to the second floor, where more statues of saints and deities resided, then made our ascent to the third and top level of the chorten. A huge statue of the Buddha sat in a lotus pose facing a big window, his back to the interior.

"Few people come up to this floor. I find it very peaceful here, especially in the company of Sakyamuni," he said, gesturing to the statue of the Buddha.

"I've read about him as Siddhartha Gautama. He gave up a life of luxury as a prince in search of enlightenment and attained it in his lifetime."

My monk guide nodded, giving me an appreciative look. Perhaps he didn't think me such a complete idiot after that.

Back on the first level, he pointed to an arrangement in a vase, of white feathery seeds with solid white centers, displayed like a peacock feather fan, on an altar.

"They are seeds from the Indian bean. The center of the seed looks like a heart." We walked up to a foot-long, canoe-shaped dried seed pod leaning against a corner on a table. My monk guide scooped out a few of the seeds still clinging inside the pod, and offered them to me. "The heart of the Buddha," he said, looking at me. I took the seeds in the palm of my hand, studied them a bit, took my little notebook out of my purse, and put the seeds between its pages.

Outside the chorten, while I put my shoes back on, the monk told me he was from Trashi Chhoe Dzong. Sonam had shown me the dzong from the outside, a very grand yet intimidating structure with gold-topped towers and high fortress walls. It contains the offices of the king and is the summer residence of the Central Monastic Body. I told the monk about my assignment at the public library.

"Have you been to our National Library?"

"No. I understand it houses mostly Buddhist religious books."

"True. It has volumes and volumes of Buddhist teachings and philosophy, as well as a big collection of sutras. You'll be impressed."

"Any English books?"

"A few, on Buddhism, Bhutan, some Himalayan history. I enjoyed reading *Seven Years in Tibet*." He smiled. This time I noticed his good white teeth. He was obviously not a betel nut addict. "But most of the books are in our native Dzongkha, and Choekey, which is classical Tibetan, the language of our holy books."

We walked down Chorten Lam together. He was visiting a monk at a goemba—a monastery—in town that evening and would not be returning to the dzong, he said.

"You know, even though English is the first language taught in schools here, I've found that most Bhutanese are not very fluent in it. But your English is so good. Where did you learn it?" Indeed, he was fluent, exceptionally well-spoken. What betrayed the fact that English was not his mother tongue were his rather formal manner of speech and the extra care he took in pronouncing every word correctly.

"I started learning English when I entered monastery school. Later, I was sent to a monastic school in India when I was twenty and had more chance to study and speak English there. I love to read English books. They are probably my best teacher."

"What type of English books?"

"I read books on Buddhism in English. But I also like books about places, especially exotic places."

"Like Bhutan?" I couldn't resist being facetious.

He shrugged his shoulders, like a schoolboy being teased, and continued, "To me most places outside Bhutan are exotic. I once read *Chariots of the Gods*. The unexplained phenomena fascinated me. Stonehenge, Easter Island, the Egyptian Pyramids. I travel through books."

"Most people do. What else have you read?"

"I enjoyed *A Tale of Two Cities*."

"Wow, I didn't think Buddhist monks read fiction. I'm surprised and impressed. Have you read other works of Charles Dickens?"

"*A Christmas Carol*. I like that too, even though I am not a Christian."

"You don't have to be a Christian to appreciate the spirit of compassion in the story."

"I agree," he nodded.

We exchanged a brief look, perhaps an intimation of camaraderie. We had reached the southern traffic circle where a policeman was guiding traffic on a raised kiosk.

"Well, this is where we part," he said. "It was a pleasure seeing you again."

I blushed at his reminding me, no doubt unintentionally, of the first time he saw me, or, rather, I saw him. I did not offer to shake his hand, not being sure if handshaking with a monk was acceptable social grace. We nodded to each other and said "Good-bye," and while he went off down a smaller street, I turned onto Norzin Lam, in the direction of my guest-house. I did not get his name. I did not know if it was proper to ask.

Today Tashi came to the library to work on another essay. She showed me the essay her school had rejected. By any standard, it deserved an A. But there was nothing I could do about it.

On the other hand, I may befriend the monk if he ever shows up again. My association with him should be harmless. After all, he is protected by the sanctity of his monkhood, and so am I.

11

From the Memoir of Marian Souza

THE LIBRARY, JULY 20, 1998 — *THE BOOK*

Another month has passed uneventfully. Ruthie wrote that she was going to Cancun in late June. A week on the beaches of Moon Palace, or lounging by the hotel pool, rubbing sunscreen lotion on her limbs, sipping a tequila sunrise. How absolutely heavenly. How enviable. How decadent.

Here, on the opposite side of the globe, I tread my daily route between the guesthouse and the library, along Samten Lam and Norzin Lam, umbrella in hand on rainy days, avoiding puddles and sleeping dogs on pavements, and greeting red-toothed locals who have come to regard me as a familiarity, me in my T-shirt and blue jeans. I can now identify them by the stores they keep, and I pass each man or woman with a smile, a nod, or a wave of the hand. "*Tashi Delek*," I say, and receive the same greeting in return. Children call out hello, some walking me all the way home from the library in the late afternoon, as though I were the Pied Piper with his happy followers.

July has brought the monsoon season and with it an abundance of rain, overcast skies, and mostly grey and gloomy surroundings. There is, however, a somber and austere beauty in the rain, the low heavy clouds covering the mountains, the fields laden with ripening crops, and the forests lush with a rich dark green. All is not lost, depending on one's mood.

The first shipment of books I ordered from a jobber in Bangkok arrived the first week of July, and that kept me busy for a while. The new label maker I ordered out of a catalog also arrived. I had fun playing with it, making new labels of different sizes for just about anything worth labeling in the library, and having Jigme replace old dilapidated ones.

Jigme has remained cold and distant toward me since the first day. We have no conversation outside of work-related matters. To my relief, she complies quietly with all my requests for work to be done and has not challenged the way I run the library. After all, she must realize I am the authority on the subject. Her disagreeable manner toward me stems from the fact that I am undermining her former position as boss of the library, and I have noticed her still ordering Sonam around. As for Sonam, he is the sweetest person to have for a coworker, cheerful, obliging, dependable, and concerned about my well-being. His presence in the library has brightened the work atmosphere, especially on days when Jigme's face seems darker than the rain clouds.

There is not much to do outside of work. One of the things I miss most is my tennis. To keep in shape, every day I wake up at sunrise to Bhutanese music on my alarm clock and get on the exercise bike for a good 45 minutes before I start the work day. The evening hours are hard to fill. The government banned all private television reception several years ago, although I have seen private homes with satellite dishes. The video rentals in town carry mostly Hindi movies with no English subtitles. Besides, I am not keen on watching a video on a nineteen-inch television screen with six other people in the compact parlor of the guesthouse. The only cinema in town also shows Hindi movies, again minus English subtitles, and I have heard the place is poorly ventilated with only a few inefficient ceiling fans. So I usually read in my room after supper until bedtime. Few people go out at night, not because of the crime rate, which is next to nonexistent, but because the numerous dogs, tame as they may look in the day, gather in packs when night falls, barking and howling at every street corner of Thimphu.

Just as I was thinking there seemed little to look forward to in terms of excitement in my life here, I got a pleasant surprise.

It had rained all the morning. Sonam had the day off and Jigme had called in sick. I would be alone in the library except for the users coming in, mostly students after school. I was shelving some new books in the deserted middle room around noon, my back to the entrance, when I heard whistling coming from the outer room. I recognized the tune to be *You Are My Sunshine*. Then it stopped. I knew the whistler had entered the room where I was squatting, legs apart, putting some books onto a bottom shelf, certainly not a vision of grace. Without changing my posture, I turned my head, and saw first a pair of well-worn canvas shoes, then the lower hem of a dark red robe. I raised my head and gazed into the eyes of my monk guide, beaming down at me.

Quickly I straightened myself, smoothing my hair with one hand as I did so.

"I've brought you a book," he began cheerily before I could utter hello.

From under his arm, he produced a paperback, its cover showing a painted depiction of a collared priest in a black cassock looking out to a field, and beyond the field a dzong.

"A book?"

"*The Jesuit*"—he pronounced it "Jesoo-it"—"*and the Dragon*, the biography of a Canadian priest who was invited by the late King Jigme Dorji Wangchuk to set up the education system in Bhutan. I took it out of the National Library for you, because you are Catholic and you are Canadian."

"Then that must be the book for me!" And immediately I regretted sounding facetious. I took the book and thanked him profusely.

I hadn't been too observant of his attire the last time we met in the Memorial Chorten, but this time, I noticed he had on a deep red vest with yellow trim and a long rust-red skirt. A large shawl of the same red as his skirt draped over his left shoulder, leaving the biceps on his right arm exposed. The incongruous items were his footwear, the running shoes worn without socks.

"I haven't been in this library in a long time," he said, looking around the room. He browsed the new books on the cart. He picked up a copy of George Orwell's *Animal Farm* and read its covers with interest.

"Two legs good, four legs better," he read and chuckled.

"It's not a Buddhist treatise on the sanctity of animals," I said, catching his mood.

"I know. It says here it's a political satire."

"You really impress me with your command of English. You told me you started learning the language when you entered the monastery. How old were you then?"

"I was six."

"You were six? Get out of here!"

"What?" he asked, looking stunned.

"Sorry, it's just to mean I don't believe you." He looked relieved and at ease again. "But you were six? So it must not have been your own choice to become a monk." How deprived he must have been of a normal childhood.

"It's an honor in every family to have a son become a monk. I could not have hoped for a better vocation."

"And have you found your vocation as a monk? I mean, are you happy?"

"Yes, I am very happy. I would not have chosen otherwise."

"You remind me of someone my sister Ruthie and I met on Lantau Island long ago, when we were growing up in Hong Kong. I mean, your background and hers. Her parents put her in a Buddhist nunnery at the age of eight or nine. She was content with the life designed for her—looking forward to it. I've sometimes wondered where she is now." I could feel his eyes on me as I returned to my shelving. His gaze made me self-conscious. I wanted to keep on talking. Purposely I looked over to *The Jesuit and the*

Dragon I had set on the table nearby and asked if he had read it.

"Yes, I read it. I'm glad I did. It taught me something about Christianity."

"You are liberal, you know, and widely read. Are most monks like you?"

"No two monks are alike."

We giggled.

"You know what I mean." I feigned exasperation.

"I know what you mean, and what I mean is every person is an individual," he said, still carrying a spark in his eyes.

"But not everyone dares to be different."

He looked down, perhaps embarrassed by my intended compliment, and smiled thoughtfully to himself. Then, looking at his watch, he said, "I'd better go now. Enjoy the book."

"Would you like me to return it to the National Library when I'm done?"

He looked hesitant. "I took it out in my name. Foreigners are permitted to use the materials only inside that library. It doesn't seem right if you return it." He paused, then continued decisively, "I go to the Memorial Chorten on the eighth, fifteenth, and thirtieth day of every month, our auspicious days in the Bhutanese calendar. You can find me there between four and four-thirty in the afternoon. Perhaps you can bring the book there when you finish."

"I'll do that," I said, happy to have a chance to see him again. "I'm really glad you came by. What a pleasant surprise, especially on a miserable day like today." He looked pleased. I continued, "By the way, how should I address you?" How could I not know someone's name after three encounters?

"People call me Lopen Pema. Pema is my first name, and lopen is a form of address for a teacher monk."

"I'm Marian Souza. Marian is my first name, Souza my family name."

"Marian," he echoed and nodded. "It has a good sound." He stopped, as though he was hearing my name again, before heading toward the outer room. "Well, I really have to run. Duty calls." Waving his hand, and turning his head to look quickly in my direction, he walked out of the middle room.

It was still raining outside. I returned to my work, humming *You Are My Sunshine* quietly to myself. For the rest of the day, my mind kept wandering back to Lopen Pema, the stubby hairstyle, the red robe and shawl, the over-worn canvas shoes. I placed Lopen Pema in his early thirties, about five-ten in height, tall for a Bhutanese. His high cheekbones reminded me of a northern Chinese. His somewhat narrow but keen, intelligent eyes, together with his rather thoughtful expression, seemed to hint dangerously that he could read one's mind. There was a humble yet confident manner about him, suggesting that he was mindful of his station as a monk, yet assertive as an individual.

I was still thinking about Lopen Pema and his surprise visit when Tashi came in after school. She said she got a decent mark for her makeup essay on the safe topic of conservation awareness in Bhutan. Then she saw *The Jesuit and the Dragon* on the desk and picked it up with interest.

"Someone took it out of the National Library for me," I explained, not anxious to disclose the identity of that someone, for it would entail my giving away the embarrassing story of how I met Lopen Pema the first time.

"It was the priest in the book, Father William Mackey, who started Sherubtse Public School, and that became a high school, and then later Sherubtse College," Tashi said. "Most Bhutanese people have heard of Father Mackey."

"I'm sure I'll enjoy the book."

And I know I will finish it in no time, so that I can return it to Lopen Pema.

12

I PAUSED IN MY READING OF MARIAN'S MEMOIR, while I deplaned in Hong Kong for a four-hour layover on the way to Bangkok. Hong Kong, my birthplace, and Marian's, where we spent the first eleven years of our lives. I remember well the novice nun we met on Lantau Island when we were kids, the one Marian mentioned to Lopen Pema.

The day after our arrival at Lantau, just a half-hour ferry ride from Hong Kong Island, Marian and I woke, before Dad and Mama, to a reddening sky and sweet birdsong. We slipped quietly out of the little rented cottage up on Po Lin Hill. The dewy morning air smelled refreshingly sweet with midsummer fragrance, and the purple morning glories on the cottage fence were just beginning to open after a night's sleep. A little footpath, sheltered by poplars and bamboos on both sides, wound downhill to the Po Lin Temple and Monastery, and uphill to higher unknown grounds.

As we were plucking a few new shoots off the bamboo stalks not far from our cottage, I heard rustling in the undergrowth and spied a brown and white dwarf rabbit skipping just a few steps from where I stood. Fascinated, I dropped my handful of bamboo shoots and went after it, with Marian at my heels. It led us uphill, until it stopped near a thicket, and Marian and I crouched down on the dirt to watch it nibble at an apple core. Suddenly, I heard shuffling nearby and, looking up, found myself staring at a girl. She had cropped hair and wore a Chinese jacket and pants of stern dark grey. On her feet were black Buddhist cloth sandals. Marian and I stood up to the same height as the girl, but there was the look of an older person in her expression. At the moment, she seemed uneasy.

Marian stood close to me, scrutinizing the girl with curiosity bordering on rudeness.

I smiled. "Where did you come from?" I asked in Cantonese.

Without a word, she pointed up the slope.

"My sister and I are here on holiday from Hong Kong," Marian chimed in. "Are you also on holiday?"

"I live here, in the Buddhist nunnery," the girl answered quietly.

"I thought only nuns live in a nunnery," I said.

"I'm preparing to be a nun when I grow up," the girl replied in a louder voice, her chin tilted up a little.

"Why?" Marian asked for both of us.

The girl did not answer. She cast one last look at Marian and me and turned to walk uphill, leaving us puzzled. Later that day, we saw her again, carrying a heavy sack and following an old Buddhist nun in the village market. Marian went up and touched her on the shoulder. She turned and nodded faintly in recognition but did not say a word. She seemed afraid of the nun, as though communicating with outsiders would bring on reprimand. She soon went on her way, following the nun, but not without looking back at us.

When we next met again the following morning, apparently by chance, at the same spot where Marian and I had watched the rabbit, we exchanged smiles and names. Her name was Wong Yee Ying, Wong being her family name, and Yee Ying, her given name.

"So why have you decided to be a Buddhist nun?" Marian asked again.

This time, Yee Ying answered hesitantly, "It was not for me to decide. My pa and ma brought me here."

"Why did your parents do that?" My sister was certainly not a mistress of tact.

"My pa and ma sent me to the nunnery to honor the Lord Buddha." She paused, and continued, "Pa is a fisherman, and Ma had all five of us—I have four younger sisters—to take care of. Now that I'm at the nunnery, I

48

have enough to eat, and Pa has one fewer mouth to feed. This is better for everyone."

We met with Yee Ying every morning of our week on Lantau, before she began her day of prayer and work.

"What do you do at the nunnery?" I asked during a mid-week rendezvous.

"I learn to chant, and I work for the nuns. I go with them to funeral wakes to chant for the dead. The elder nun says I will be spending my life in prayer and good deeds, cut off from worldly desires and worldly cares, and I will gain a lot of merit for the next life."

She sounded more grown-up than she actually was. I was not sure what worldly desires were, or worldly cares. Neither did I understand her notion of merit. I felt sorry for her. Her life seemed dreary and dull compared to mine and Marian's.

As the week progressed, Yee Ying became more relaxed. She laughed and joked and was fun to be with. Marian and I were enjoying her company. Once, when we were late getting to our meeting spot, her face lit up as soon as she saw us.

Yee Ying taught us a ditty about a little cloud that had traveled the world over only to find that it was happy when it returned to its village by the sea.

> *I've wandered across the heavens,*
> *Riding on the wind;*
> *I've touched the wings of birds,*
> *And seen the ends of the earth;*
> *But I was not happy*
> *Until I returned to where I started out,*
> *My village by the sea,*
> *Yes, my village by the sea.*

ELSIE SZE

"Do you miss your folks, Yee Ying?" I asked on our last morning on Lantau.

"Sometimes. But I try not to think of them."

"I don't know if I'll recognize you if I see you again when they have shaved your head. To tell you the truth, I can't tell Buddhist monks from nuns because they all have shaved heads," I said.

"Our elder nun says it is good that monks and nuns look the same, because it is only when we look different that we have temptations of the flesh."

"What are temptations of the flesh?" asked Marian.

"The man and woman thing," explained Yee Ying, looking embarrassed.

"But the hair on the head is not the only thing that makes a man different from a woman, you know," I said. At that, Yee Ying covered her mouth, and we both tittered.

"Yee Ying, will you still remember us when you are a nun?" Marian asked after a while.

"You must understand I have to be free from all attachments in the world when I am a nun." She talked so much like an adult.

"Including friends?" I asked.

Yee Ying nodded slowly.

The three of us spent the last minutes of our short-lived friendship lying on our backs side by side under some poplars, looking up at the blushing morning sky through the chinks in the silvery rustling leaves. I remember being sad because we were leaving Lantau the next day which meant we wouldn't be seeing Yee Ying anymore. But perhaps, even then, I could sense that she would be wiping us out of her consciousness when she became a nun, and her mind would be free from the memories of people who had meant something to her.

I reboarded my plane for Bangkok, and returned to Marian's memoir.

13

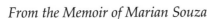

From the Memoir of Marian Souza

THE CHORTEN, JULY 31, 1998 — *THE THIRD FLOOR*
As I was reading *The Jesuit and the Dragon*, my mind kept wandering to Lopen Pema, wondering what was on his mind while he was reading the book, if it inspired him with its exposition of Christian values, Buddhist though he was.

Father William Mackey spent over thirty years of his life in the service of Bhutan, and all for what? Not for the purpose of proselytizing. He was no missionary in the conventional sense. He did not attempt to convert a single Bhutanese to Christianity during all his time in Bhutan. The truth was he had grown to love the Bhutanese people. Love. The closest word the Buddhists used was compassion. Did Lopen Pema see in Father Mackey's selfless love that essential Buddhist principle of compassion? From my limited understanding of Buddhist doctrines, it was compassion for others that motivated the bodhisattvas to remain in the cycle of rebirth, that they might help others and teach them the way to enlightenment.

Yesterday was the first auspicious day since I finished the book, the eighth day of the sixth month in the Bhutanese calendar. I went to the Memorial Chorten to return the book to Lopen Pema. I was eager to talk about Father Mackey with him. Since Sonam and Jigme were going to close up the library that day, I left work earlier than usual and was at the chorten at ten to four. I stepped over the threshold onto the cold hard floor of the dark interior. I slipped off my sandals by the door. I circumambulated the center core of altars. My heart was beating faster in expectation of seeing Lopen Pema any moment.

He was not in sight on the first level. I went up the spiral stairs to the second floor. He was not there. The third floor, which I scanned from the top of the stairs, was deserted. Feeling uncomfortable alone up there, only in the company of the statues and the sacred paintings and embroideries called thangkas, I was about to make my way down when I heard the swishing sound of cloth, followed by that of quick breathing, coming up the stairs. Quickly I stepped onto the third-level floor, and walked over to the east window, near the big statue of the Buddha. In a few moments, Lopen Pema's bristly head appeared. The pleasure I betrayed at seeing him was probably accentuated by my earlier disappointment in thinking that he might not show up. He appeared surprised and happy to see me.

"I finished the book and want to return it to you," I said immediately, not moving from my position.

"How did you like it?" he asked, still breathing fast.

"I liked it very much." There was a short uncomfortable pause. I glanced around me and asked, "Are you here on official business?"

"Not exactly. I come on auspicious days to pay respects to the Lord Buddha and the bodhisattvas." He inched a little closer toward me, then stopped, as if mindful that he should keep some distance between us.

"More merit?"

"Just a little something extra I do." He nodded slightly. "It's also to test my physical endurance. Our supper is at three-thirty. On auspicious days, I skip supper and come here. I have to walk fast, for the dzong is at the opposite end of town. I have to be back at five for a learning session." He looked awkwardly at his watch.

"What do you learn?"

"I practice dances for the tsechu. You must come to the Thimphu tsechu, the biggest festival of the year in Thimphu. It's at the end of September. That's the only time you can enter the dzong." As he spoke, he walked gradually toward a small altar opposite the banister.

"End of September. I should still be here." I approached him. I took the book out of my shoulder bag and held it out to him. He took it in a reverent manner, bowing his head slightly.

"Thank you for lending it to me. I thoroughly enjoyed it. What do you think of Father Mackey?"

"Father Mackey was a real Buddhist," he said in a jolly manner. Then more seriously he added, "He was a blessing to the Bhutanese people. He loved them, and they loved him."

"He was also a real Christian. He served others regardless of who they were, and what their religion was. I'm proud of him," I said.

We proceeded slowly along a wall of thangkas, like two visitors at an art gallery, discussing the paintings.

"I'm sorry we have no church here for you," he said, astonishing me.

"Thank you for thinking about me. But the place is not the most important thing. If Father Mackey could live in Bhutan for thirty-odd years and still be a Catholic, I think I can manage for six months."

"True, the place, and in fact all the rituals and paraphernalia connected with worship are not the essential things, even though they serve important purposes."

"I thought Buddhist monks, especially the Tantric orders, put a lot of emphasis on visual and physical manifestations of worship."

"That's true. But one must look beyond the superficial and focus on what is essential."

We stopped pacing and faced each other.

"Are you considered a rebel in your order?" I asked.

He suppressed a smile. "I don't want to give you a wrong impression of me. I believe in what my religion teaches, and I obey the monastic rules."

"In other words, you are a good monk," I teased. Was I taking too much liberty with him?

"There are no good or bad monks. Besides, it's not what we do that defines us. It's the motivation, the thought behind the act."

"Are you a monk for life?" I asked, undaunted by his gentle rebuttal.

"Yes, our commitment is for life. That does not mean a monk cannot leave the monkhood, but that is only under very unusual circumstances. Remember, monks are happy to be monks. We regard our station as an honor, and a privilege."

"I guess so," I pondered, shrugging my shoulders, "regardless of whether it's one's choice to begin with." We had resumed walking. "What else do you do at the dzong?"

"I chant and meditate. I am also a part of the dialectics group. One of my biggest enjoyments is debating with my fellow monks." Regarding me with interest, he asked, "So how long are you staying in Bhutan?"

"Six months. My contract is for six months. I'll be here until the end of October."

"You should see the country before you leave. The mountains are very beautiful. I recommend a trek."

"I'd like to go on one. I suppose you've been?"

"Several times with other monks from the dzong. We went on the Jhumolhari trek twice, to the base camp of the sacred mountain. I have also been on the Rodang La trek in Eastern Bhutan. My family live not far from Lhuentse, one of the big towns in the east."

"You have brothers and sisters?"

"Two sisters and a brother. They are all younger. My sisters are married, but my brother lives with my parents in a farmhouse my mother inherited. What about you? Your family?"

"I have a twin sister. Our father remarried some years after our mother died. He runs an Internet café in Toronto."

"And you live with?"

"My sister. We share an apartment in Toronto."

A guide and three foreign tourists came up to the third floor. They went around the room, the guide explaining various statues and thangkas to the tourists. We moved away from the path of the group.

Lopen Pema looked down at his watch.

"You have to go, I suppose."

"I may be able to stay a little longer today," he said. "I think I'll skip the debate session."

I refrained from asking if he would be in trouble for skipping. After all, he was a lopen. He should be allowed to make changes to his timetable occasionally. We walked slowly over to the big statue of Sakyamuni, and looked out of the window toward the eastern sky.

Rumbling came from his stomach.

"You must be hungry, skipping supper and walking here." He looked embarrassed, and I regretted my remark.

"Skipping a meal now and then is not only good for my karma, but also good for the body," he said cheerfully.

"And when you don't skip your meals, do you eat meat?"

"Yes, our monks can have meat except on auspicious days, but we don't usually get it. Rice and dahl make up our usual daily diet. We only have meat when donors bring us some."

"I don't understand why you're eating meat when you preach the non-killing of sentient beings."

"You ask difficult questions, don't you," he said with a playful frown. He thought for half a minute, and continued, "But you are right. It is very hard to justify killing. The essence of Buddha's teaching is compassion and not inflicting harm on other sentient beings. True, the best is to give up meat altogether—"

"Like I do. I'm vegetarian because it gives me pain to think that an animal is killed to satisfy my gluttonous impulses. There's also the good health factor. Sorry for interrupting. Please go on."

"Buddhists who eat meat, including monks," he pointed to himself, "are taught to be intensely aware of the pain and suffering of the slaughtered animal, to feel compassion for it, to pray fervently for its higher rebirth."

"Still it's hard for me to reconcile the action with the principle."

Unfrazzled, he continued, "We believe that connecting with the slaughtered animal through chanting mantras and praying can greatly benefit the animal in its rebirth. Still, we do accrue some negative karma when we eat meat, even though we don't kill the animal ourselves or order its killing."

"The best way is not to eat meat at all, so you don't encourage butchers by giving them business," I persisted. "I suppose it's difficult for anyone to be free from some bad karma, since people are interconnected and dependent on others one way or another for survival."

"Very insightful."

"Besides, we are all human." I looked down and fidgeted with my hands.

"Yes, we are human," he murmured. I could feel him looking at my hands.

The tourists and their guide had left the floor, and we were alone again. We kept our stance beside each other, half an arm's length apart, gazing out with Sakyamuni to the distant fields and hills. I was enjoying Lopen Pema's presence, his modest, unpretentious manners, the ease, freedom, and honesty with which we were able to converse. I liked being there with him, sharing his stolen moments from regimen and duty.

"This is such a peaceful refuge—no wonder you like to come here." I looked sideways at him. "I've learned a lot from you. I enjoy talking to you. Do you mind if I come sometimes when you are here?"

Without turning to me, he bowed his head, so that I could not see his face. After what seemed an eternity, during which I went through agony, afraid I had said something improper, he raised his head and looked at me.

"I don't think we should be running into each other again, Marian, because we walk very different paths." He spoke softly, as if trying to apologize as he rationalized.

"True," I said, almost inaudibly. If only I could dig a hole in the earth at that moment and bury myself in it. My consolation was that he remembered my name and had addressed me by it.

"I hope I didn't hurt your feelings. That's far from what I want."

"I understand."

"I have to go. Thank you for bringing back the book." His voice had lost its enthusiasm.

"I guess I should be going, too," I said sheepishly, the elation I had felt being with him transformed to inexplicable depression and shame.

We started toward the stairs.

"After you."

He waited for me to lead the way down the stairs. On the first level, I waited by the doorway while he circumambulated the altars. Back into the light of the late afternoon sun, he turned to me. We murmured a quick good-bye, and our eyes met for one brief poignant moment. Then he hurried down Doebum Lam in the direction of the dzong, *The Jesuit and the Dragon* tucked under his arm.

14

From the Memoir of Marian Souza

THE CHORTEN, AUGUST 8, 1998 — *THE FIFTEENTH DAY*

In the days following my return of the book to Lopen Pema at the Memorial Chorten, my sensible voice gained sure ground over the delinquent and irresponsible part of me. I put in more hours than I normally would at the library. I faxed compiled lists of book titles for purchase to jobbers in Bangkok and India and weeded a sizable section of the collection. I even sat with the Peace Corps couple from Wisconsin in the dingy living room of the guesthouse after dinner a couple of evenings. I was proud of my discipline. Every time images of Lopen Pema sneaked into my brain, I sent them back to oblivion.

Then, on the morning of the fifteenth day of the month, which was two days ago, I woke up feeling restless. I had not slept well the night before. And that morning, I felt I had lost the mental resistance I had been trying to build up. Suppressed thoughts of Lopen Pema crept back into my mind — his kind, intelligent eyes, appealing smile, the sincere and patient manner in which he talked to me. And I could not rid myself of the image of the tall brown athletic body under the trappings of a monk's robe. I was nervous all day. I looked at the clock many times. At three-thirty, after telling Sonam and Jigme I wasn't feeling well, I left the library and, as if driven by an irrepressible force, headed as quickly as my weakened legs could carry me south on Norzin Lam.

"Hello, Lopen Pema, I've had a long and trying day, and I've come to find some peace and quiet."

"I understand, but I'm afraid your intention might be misunderstood. You know what I mean, don't you, Marian?"

"Yes. I should go."

"You know I don't mean to hurt your feelings, Marian."

"I know, but it's best I leave."

Should I turn around before I make a complete fool of myself? That afternoon as I walked toward the Memorial Chorten, I could only go with my heart. My feet kept carrying me onward until I saw the golden spire of the chorten and soon the rest of the great structure.

Our eyes met as I emerged onto the third floor. We were engulfed in a wave of passion. He opened his arms, his robe like widespread wings ready to take me in. We met in the center of the hall. He wrapped me in his shawl. I felt his hardness, his arched body bent over mine, his lips smothering me with feverish kisses.

In my schoolgirl days, I would have gone to a priest for confession for what were termed impure thoughts.

I finally arrived at the chorten, my heart pumping so hard it hurt, my mind in excruciating turmoil. I entered. I did a quick scan of the first and second levels, then went up to the third, my chest heaving. No one was there. I waited, in the emptiness and silence.

He was late. It was almost twenty minutes after four when he finally came up to the third level. I stood at the far end of the room, my back to the stairs. As he emerged at the top of the stairs, I turned, as if wondering who it might be. At the sight of him, my defense system broke down. I dropped my pretense of innocence and waited humbly for his rebuke. Inevitably, our eyes met across the room. There was no sign of rejection in his expression, only quiet joy. Without a word, boldly we looked at each other, while the space of the entire floor kept us apart. I could feel our pulses racing toward each other, our thoughts meeting halfway, as though on a bridge over a raging rapid.

"How are you, Marian?" Pema finally broke the silence with his deep voice.

"I shouldn't be here," I said, my voice trembling and my heart palpitating in my ears. "I'm sorry."

"Don't be sorry. I am very happy to see you. It was I who told you I would be here." He sounded gentle.

We remained where we were standing, silent, he at the top of the stairs, his hand still on the banister, and I against the opposite wall, uncertain of what I should say or do. I had no idea what would have happened next, if we hadn't heard voices coming up the stairs. Pema quickly walked over to the window where the big statue of the Buddha sat with his back to us, while I turned to stare at some thangkas on the wall. Funny how guilt can make us self-conscious, even fearful. A guide came up with a couple of visitors. Pema and I glanced at each other. He headed slowly for the stairs, and I did the same after a few seconds. We did not stop until we reached the ground level. I followed him at a distance behind, as he paid his respects to the saints.

We exited the chorten. He would be late for his debate session. He turned to me with an intense look of hopelessness mingled with hope. We did not utter a word. Then he hurried down Doebum Lam in the direction of the dzong. He did not once turn his head.

Our meeting lasted only ten minutes. But in those ten minutes, I had abandoned all good judgment. I had chosen the direction I would take at the crossroad. There was no turning back.

15

From the Memoir of Marian Souza

TASHI'S HOUSE, AUGUST 21, 1998 — *THE KIRA*

Lopen Pema did not show up today, the thirtieth of the sixth month in the Bhutanese calendar. I left the Memorial Chorten disappointed and hurt after waiting for an hour.

He has made his choice, and I will abide by it. It is for the best. The hardest part is for me to get over him; but I will, in time.

Last week, a new guest arrived at the guesthouse, Marvin Coe from Washington, D.C. He is a volunteer with the United Nations, an engineer, and will be in Bhutan for a year. He is probably in his late fifties. What interests me is that he will be taking time off to do a trek in the fall. Trekking in Bhutan is something I have wanted to do, especially since Lopen Pema has recommended it. I may join Marvin Coe if the timing is right.

Tashi and her mother, Choedon, invited me to their house on the second weekend of August. They live just outside the southern end of town, not far from the Memorial Chorten. She had met Stewart Campbell while working at the reception desk of the Hotel Druk in Thimphu where he stayed during his term of teaching. They fell in love and, as Tashi put it, decided to commit themselves to each other. In Bhutan, making such a commitment is as good as any marriage ceremony. Being a rich man's son, Stewart had never been short of means. He rented a house for himself and Choedon in Motithang, a high-end residential area of Thimphu. Tashi was born a year later. They lived there until his death in 1990. Since then,

Choedon had moved back with Tashi to the farmhouse she inherited at her mother's death.

Following her stint of working at the Hotel Druk, and especially after her husband died, Choedon devoted her time to weaving at home. Tashi said her mother's woven kiras were of superior quality and highly coveted by the cottage industry stores in Thimphu.

I met Tashi outside the Memorial Chorten that early Saturday evening. She took me along a mule track off Doebum Lam, the north-south road that ran the length of the town, meeting Chorten Lam just south of the Memorial Chorten. Lopen Pema usually takes that road going from the dzong to the chorten. Thimphu must be one of the rare capitals of the world where dirt paths and rice fields are within a stone's throw of the main crossroads of the nation. We made our way up the path, past happy children with wind-burned rosy cheeks who called to me "Hello!" and "Bye!" as they rolled metal hoops down the slope in an improvised game. An old man passed us with his cow and exchanged some pleasantry with Tashi. He smiled at me, revealing broken red-stained teeth.

Choedon and Tashi's house was a typical two-story farmhouse with whitewashed external walls and a gabled roof of shingles secured with stones. The window frames were decorated with paintings of lotus blossoms, wheels, and swirls. A picture of the mythical bird, the garuda, was painted on the front wall above the doorway. And a wooden phallus hung from a corner of the roof, pierced with a wooden sword.

We cut through a small courtyard and stepped into the *okhang*, the ground level, used for keeping animals for the night and in the winter in the old days but converted into an entrance hall since. We climbed up a ladder carved out of a tree trunk to the second level, the living quarters. The interior of the house was dark, illuminated only by waning daylight through the windows. A lightbulb hung from the ceiling at the top of the stairs. Tashi quickly pulled the little chain to turn it on as she reached the top. Most farmhouses in the rural areas still had no electricity.

Choedon greeted me, shaking my hand warmly. She was a stout woman who looked fortyish, with a spread around her waist accentuated by the bulkiness of her kira. But behind her plumpness were refined features and a sweet countenance, which Tashi seemed to have inherited. She must have been an attractive woman before events in her life and her increasing years took their toll.

I watched Choedon prepare the meal above the *bukhari*, a kind of stove that Tashi explained was introduced by the Swiss to Bhutan in the sixties. A pipe ran from the stove to the exterior through a high opening in the wall, channeling smoke and exhaust fumes out of the house. Tashi offered me a chair, but I opted for the floor which had a nicely patterned woven mat on each side of the bukhari.

"We had nice sofa and furniture in Motithang when my husband was alive, but I wanted to move back here after he died. My home is here," Choedon said, as she chopped up potatoes and cauliflower for a curry. "I want Tashi to grow up a Bhutanese." She looked at her daughter, who was placing a cup of butter tea and a bowl of fried corn snack before me.

We had dinner sitting on the floor, near the bukhari. The food was good, especially the momos, which reminded me of Chinese dumplings, except that Choedon put cheese and squash inside, for Tashi had told her I was vegetarian. After dinner, I tried the ara, a home-distilled drink made from fermented wheat. The alcohol content was high, and after the second round I was a bit tipsy. Choedon suggested I spend the night in their house. By then it was completely dark, and I wasn't keen on walking back to the guesthouse with packs of wild dogs as my escorts. So I agreed to stay, which made Tashi very happy.

Tashi took me into the choesham, the altar room, which doubled as a guest room. Three statues, each about three feet in height, sat at the altar. The center statue was the Buddha, Sakyamuni. On his right was Guru Rimpoche, who brought Buddhism to Bhutan from Tibet in the eighth century. On his left was the Shabdrung Rimpoche, who united and ruled the country in the seventeenth century. Seven bowls of water were on the altar, as well as a single flickering butter lamp. All around, hanging on the walls, were thangkas of bodhisattvas and deities. A large one beside the altar was of Pema Lingpa, who, as Tashi explained, discovered many religious treasures for Bhutan in the sixteenth century. I asked about the image of a wrathful blue figure wearing a leopard skin, framed in a ring of fire. He had snakes on his body, fierce eyes, and teeth and a tongue that formed a horrid snarl. Tashi said that was Channa Dorji, the god of power and victory, a good deity. He held a metal instrument called a dorji, looking like a baby's rattle, onion-shaped at both ends, signifying the thunderbolt.

Tashi closed the window, sliding a wood panel across it. It was unnerving being alone in the darkened altar room, lit only with the lone butter lamp, and especially in the company of Channa Dorji and his thunderbolt. Lying on a mattress on the floor, I closed my eyes and prayed till I fell asleep.

In the morning, Tashi was churning butter tea as I walked into the kitchen.

"I like rice and chili for breakfast," Choedon said as she toasted slices of bread on the bukhari, "but Tashi likes eggs and toast, just like her father." She laid out before me boiled eggs, buttered toast, and apricot jam, and then settled down to her rice and chili.

"Tashi told me you're a fine weaver," I said as we were finishing breakfast.

Choedon looked pleased. "I learned the craft from my mother. She was one of the best."

She beckoned me into an adjoining room. There I saw her loom. It had two warp beams with a wooden frame set against the wall. The warp slanted against the wall, away from where the weaver would sit. Choedon demonstrated the weaving process, sitting on the floor and leaning back against a wide leather strap that kept the color threads stretched as she nimbly wove them into the background cloth. Then she laid out two finished kiras on the floor. I touched one admiringly. It had a light green background with a small peachy-pink geometric design.

"Yours, Marian," Choedon said, nodding at the fabric.

I was taken aback. I offered to pay her, but she would not hear of it.

"Tashi will take you to a store in town to get matching jacket and blouse. You also need a belt," Choedon said, following my outpouring of gratitude.

Later, Tashi took me to a shop on Norzin Lam where I picked out a matching pink jacket, a white blouse with a cloud pattern, a handwoven belt, and a matching pink and green *rachu*, a shoulder cloth for festive occasions. I also bought two silver ornamental hooks to keep the kira in place at the shoulders, although two big safety pins would have served the same purpose.

Tashi helped me put on the kira in my room at the guesthouse. It was a very complicated process, wrapping around and folding back and forth. I looked at myself in the mirror. I could pass for a full-blooded Bhutanese.

16

📖

From the Memoir of Marian Souza

THE DZONG, SEPTEMBER 30, 1998 — *TSECHU*
The library is closed for three days for the Thimphu tsechu, which runs this year from September 30th to October 2nd. It is the biggest annual religious and social event of the year in the capital. It is being held inside Trashi Chhoe Dzong. Sonam has been talking about it for weeks. Even Jigme loosens up whenever the tsechu is mentioned.

I had debated whether to go to the festival or not, solely because of Lopen Pema. I had been disciplined the last month, not even going close to the Memorial Chorten on auspicious days. However, it would be ridiculous of me to stay away from the tsechu because of my foolish crush on a monk. Besides, with the crowd, there should be little chance of us running into each other. With this reasoning and a clear conscience, I went with Sonam and Dolma and their children to the dzong today, the first day of the tsechu. I wore my kira, rachu and all, and felt very much at home among all the local women there.

It seemed most of Thimphu and many from other towns and villages were there. Mothers came with their babies tied to their backs in cloth carriers. Men, women, and children put on their best ghos and kiras. The colors of the kiras were vibrant, simply resplendent.

I took pictures of a few eight- or nine-year-old boys in their ghos and rubber shoes. They loved to be photographed. How I wished I could adopt one of them and take him home, not that any child in Bhutan was up for adoption. They might look grubby and snotty, but they all had families who provided for them, however frugally. They might never have watched television in their lives, but they looked a happy bunch, content with their lot, not missing much. No beggars in the capital, and no pick-pockets at the tsechu.

The sacred dances, accompanied by music of cymbals, drums, horns and bells, took place in the big courtyard of the dzong, surrounded by lhakhangs and buildings containing the monks' quarters. The dancers wore colorful costumes, some with masks of animals and demons, others without. Some masks were monstrous, others funny. The dances, known as cham, portrayed stories of Buddhist saints and deities in their victories over evil. Sonam said there was merit gained just from watching them. I said there couldn't be an easier way to nirvana.

Between sacred dances, girls in uniform kiras and high-heeled clogs performed folk dances and songs, tapping and swaying to the haunting rhythms of the *yangchen*, resembling a dulcimer, and the *dramyen*, some kind of a lute, as well as the flute and fiddle. Sonam explained that the dances and songs were in praise of their wise and benevolent king, to ask for blessings on him, the country, and the people, and to glorify the harmonious coexistence of man, all sentient beings, and nature.

I had a refreshingly good day. I did not see Lopen Pema. I had not expected to. Of course I wasn't consciously looking for him.

I will return tomorrow for the second day of the tsechu. The dances are supposed to be fantastic.

17

From the Memoir of Marian Souza

THE TSECHU, OCTOBER 5, 1998 — *BLACK HAT DANCE*

I walked alone to the dzong the morning of the second day of the tsechu, again dressed in my kira. The courtyard was already full of people, mostly locals, with a small minority of tourists. I saw a group of some ten foreign women, probably American, their local guide talking to them in fluent English.

The first ritual dance of the day was the Black Hat Dance. To get a better view, I climbed onto the circular cement ring enclosing a huge tree trunk, and stood there with other spectators. The dancers emerged, monks in flowing brocade robes of brilliant multicolors and ornate patterns. They wore pointed wide-brimmed black hats, adorned with feathery decorations. Colorful scarves hung from the brims, swirling as the dancers spun. They formed a wide circle as they twirled, raising their heads skyward like figure skaters entering a spin. They danced to the rhythm of drums and gongs, twenty-one of them, their hands in symbolic gestures, their felt boots stomping the ground, now converging in the center of the courtyard, now separating in a gyration of motion, the wide skirts of their robes flared like open umbrellas spinning in a dazzling array. My heart vibrated to the sound of the drums, so loud was their beating.

I zoomed in on a few of the dancers, my finger busily clicking away at the camera. Then slowly my eyes focused on him among the dancers. He was majestic in his robe of multicolored brocade, with a black apron in front displaying the image of some fierce-looking deity, and scarves swirling around his black hat, his every movement full of grace and virile energy, magnetic and commanding. He was the best dancer out there. I followed him with my eyes. Gradually, all the other dancers seemed to have faded into the background, and all I could see was Pema, spinning and whirling in regal splendor, his boots beating the earth to the sound of the drums. Pounding. Thundering. He was the conqueror of demons, the victor over evil. He was deity reincarnate with divine power to subdue, and a man in harmonious union with his spectators. Just before the dance ended, he tilted his head in my direction. In that moment, he must have seen me standing on the cement pedestal, for he broke into a conquering smile as our eyes met for one fleeting second. I smiled back, all the yearning that I had managed to suppress returning with full power, enveloping me, drowning me in a sea of emotion. And then, he was gone. The dance was over. The dancers had all left the courtyard.

The sight of Pema and the happiness it generated were too sudden, too unexpected, too soon ended. I stood my ground through the next couple of performances by masked dancers, anticipating Pema coming to me after getting out of his costume. Thirty minutes elapsed. No Pema. Forty-five minutes. No Pema. An hour. No Pema. Tears filled my eyes, as I made my way toward the entrance of the dzong, full of loneliness and self-pity. The disappointment was excruciating. Just outside the dzong, a young voice called "hello" from behind. I turned and saw one of the boys I had wanted to adopt the day before. He came up and handed me a piece of paper folded several times. I unfolded it. It was a blank piece of paper, but in the center was a seed from the Indian bean.

My mind was set. I burned with impatience for the next auspicious day, only three days after the tsechu. Today. I left work at three-thirty, feigning a headache, and hurried to the Memorial Chorten.

I waited on the deserted third floor, standing in the shadow of the far wall, beside one of the altars. He was late again. It is so hard to describe how I felt while I was waiting for Pema, the anguish of uncertainty, the hope that I really meant something to him, the fear of rejection. At a quarter after four, he arrived.

"Hello, Lopen," I said, trying hard to sound normal. As soon as he looked in my direction, I continued, "I've come to tell you how beautifully you danced the other day." With my opener, if I had misunderstood him, I had a way out of the situation.

He did not look surprised. His face only glowed.

"Thank you, Marian," he said. "And I want to tell you I saw the most beautiful girl in a kira the other day at the tsechu." He looked at me in a way as to make me blush.

We walked slowly toward each other until we were three quarters of an arm's length apart. He took my hand in both of his and held it to his quivering lips. His big brown hands felt warm and dry. Soothing. His fingers were long, like a pianist's, his nails close-cut and clean. Trembling, I touched his face with my other hand and felt the rough ends of emerging stubble. We inched closer, but his bulky garments were a barrier between us, soft but sure, keeping our bodies from touching. Instead, we studied each other's face, searching out each other's thoughts, indulging in the intensity of the moment that was consuming us both.

We heard voices from below, and quickly stood apart. The voices died down. No one was coming up. He led me to a bench. We sat down, inches apart, our hands unobtrusively touching between us.

"What are we going to do?" I asked in a low shaky voice.

"I have to think. I am too happy and too confused right now, Marian. I want very much to see you."

"I want to see you too," I echoed. "In fact, I've thought of you ever since I met you at Dochu La, in your birthday suit." We both laughed softly, and he looked more embarrassed than the day I saw him naked at his hot rock bath.

"I am spending the night at a goemba in town next Monday. Can you meet me here at four o'clock?"

"Nothing will keep me away."

He looked at his watch. He told me to remain upstairs until he had made his exit, so as not to arouse suspicion. Quickly he squeezed my hand, stood up, and with one last lingering look, he rushed down the stairs and was gone.

18

📖

From the Memoir of Marian Souza

THE RUINED FARMHOUSE, OCTOBER 16, 1998 — RENDEZVOUS
I went to the Memorial Chorten again last Monday, October 12th, when Pema would be spending the night in town. To avoid Jigme's suspicion, for she might wonder at my frequent indisposition, I told her and Sonam that I would be going in to the library last Sunday to unpack the new shipment of books that had just arrived, and I would be taking the Monday off instead.

Somewhere along Norzin Lam on my way to the chorten, I met Marvin Coe, the UNV staying at the Pelri Guesthouse. He asked where I was heading. I told him the Memorial Chorten, since I had no time to think of a fib. He then said he would like to go along to see the monument, if it was okay with me. I was frantic, but what could I say? So he walked alongside me to the chorten.

It was a quarter to four when we arrived at the chorten. I went around the first and second floors with Marvin. After a while, he was losing interest in the coupling statues. By the landing on the second level, we met Pema coming up. Quickly I looked away. Marvin was undecided about ascending to the third floor, and, seeing a monk, he immediately asked Pema what was up there that might be worth seeing. Pema told him there were more statues and more altars, and many tourists would end their visit on the second floor. Pema then continued his ascent to the third floor without looking in my direction. So then Marvin was ready to leave. What about me? I told him I was gathering material for an article on Tantric Buddhism, and therefore would stay behind a little longer.

As soon as I knew Marvin had left the chorten, I went up to the third floor. Pema was waiting at the top of the stairs. As usual, the room was empty except for us. He took my hands and pressed them to his lips while looking earnestly at me. He said he was not expected at the goemba till seven. We had almost three hours.

Three hours were more than all the time we had ever had, more than I could hope for. I asked where we could go. He told me to take Gongphel Lam just south of the chorten, till I came to a footpath on my right that led into the rice fields. Beyond the rice fields was a ruined double-story farmhouse with a black roof, in the middle of an uncultivated field. I should wait for him outside the farmhouse. It would be a fifteen-minute brisk walk for me. He would join me there shortly.

I found the farmhouse easily and waited anxiously for Pema in its shadow. The cool October air cut through my thin cotton blouse, and I wished I had a sweater with me. Before long, I saw the flowing red robe of a monk heading along the footpath leading into the fields. It was Pema. I stayed in the shadow of the farmhouse, out of view of any inquisitive soul who might be traveling on the road skirting the fields.

Pema soon arrived. Without a word, he took my hand and led me through a broken door into the okhang. Daylight seeped through the windows and the chinks of the upper floorboards. Telling me to wait inside, Pema went out again and soon came back with a long wooden board he pulled off a broken fence. He laid the board on the dirt floor, saying there would have been a lot of animal manure on the ground in the old days. Everything was long dried up. Still, he did not want me to sit on the bare earth.

Having completed his housekeeping chores, he stood up. He turned awkwardly toward me, put his hands on my shoulders and said in a hoarse voice, "Marian, I wish I could provide you with a better place."

"I don't want a better place, as long as I can be with you." I was trembling with the anticipation of having him to myself at last, away from the seeing eyes of gods and men, if only for a couple of short hours.

He must have sensed I was cold, for he took off his shawl and wrapped it around me. Then, still standing and looking nervous, he gently drew me to him. He buried his face in my hair, inhaling its shampoo fragrance. I felt his firm hands on my back, his strong, bare arms enveloping me. I opened up the shawl and wrapped it around us both. His vest was pressed against my blouse. I felt his body heat, the thumping of his heart. I could feel him, his virile energy. He kissed me, first lightly, touching his trembling lips to mine, then more and more urgently as I opened my lips to his.

"Pema, what will happen if we are found out?" The question had been on my mind for a while. By then, we had sat down on the board.

"A year ago, a monk at the dzong was discovered having a sexual liaison with a girl from a village." He tightened his arm around my shoulders. "I remember the day of his reckoning. The monks were assembled in the main chapel. He was stripped by the discipline masters so that he was completely naked before everyone's eyes. They tied him to a pillar. He was whipped nine times with a cat-o'-nine-tails, each time by a different lopen. I could see clearly the marks left by the tentacles of the whip. He was made to pay five thousand ngultrums to the Central Monastic Body and sent back into the laymen's world in shame for the rest of his life."

"Pema, I'm so frightened. I don't want this ever to happen to you. What shall we do?"

He smiled sadly at me, which worried me.

"I'll think of a way for us, Marian," he said.

"Didn't you say monks could leave the monkhood?"

"Yes, a monk can leave the monkhood and return to the world, with a penalty of five thousand ngultrums. I have saved up over the years from payments for ceremonial services, and I can borrow some from my family, so money is not the biggest problem." He looked hesitant.

"So what is?"

He let go of his hold on me and covered his face in his hands. I waited. When he finally looked up, he was serious.

"I just need time to think, to come to terms with my position, and my faith." He clasped his hands together, making a tight fist. His facial muscles were tense. Then he looked at me, and his face softened. "I want so much to be with you. Please be patient for me. I'll think of a way for us both, I promise."

"Whatever happens in the end, I want you to know this moment is the happiest for me."

Pema wrapped his shawl tightly around us while we sat on the plank. "I feel the same too. I've had beautiful experiences in my life, but I've not known such happiness as this."

"Before we met, what was your best moment?"

Slowly, dreamily, Pema looked away, his lips forming a faint half smile. "The first autumn I was in India studying under a Tibetan high lama living near Bodh Gaya, I made a pilgrimage to the Ajanta caves in Central India. Twenty-seven caves in all, carved out of granite, some dating back to the second century BC, India's oldest Buddhist shrines. A giant statue of the teaching Buddha sat in every cave, chiseled out of the rock. Some caves also had smaller Buddhist statues and friezes all around the interior. Some even showed mural paintings depicting the life and times of the Buddha." His eyes shone as he spoke, as though he had returned to the bowels of the earth and was inside the cave temples again. "Imagine the lifetimes of labour and sacrifice to accomplish this monumental work of devotion. That moment is still very clear to me, Marian. Standing there, in the darkness of one of the caves, lit only with light from the entrance, surrounded by images of the enlightened ones, I felt like I was entering their realm, or at least standing on the threshold of it, looking in. Perhaps the darkness inside the caves brought me closer to the saintly beings, by filtering out all distractions that light could bring. There were monks' cells in some of the caves. In that instant, I could not want more than to spend my life in one of those stripped cells. If I were to find one moment that I would call my best, it would be that moment, that day I visited the Ajanta caves," he turned to me again and added gently, "until I met you. I am in love with you, Marian."

We kissed in the waning daylight. Soon, it was total darkness in the ruined farmhouse, but we did not need to see. The closeness was all.

"I feel very special because you love me, Pema," I murmured. After a pause, I asked, "There are many beautiful girls in Bhutan. Have you ever been attracted to one?"

"Do I sense jealousy?" He laughed teasingly. "Don't forget I am a monk. I don't look at women as a rule, let alone get close to them." Then, more seriously, he said, "I had not wanted to fall in love with you, Marian. At first, I thought I was safe with you because you were not one of us. Surely, I could befriend a foreign visitor. But I became attracted to you. You are someone I feel comfortable with, someone I can talk to freely, even in the little time we have spent together. You understand me more than anyone else. You and I seem to share common views on many aspects of life, even though our backgrounds are so different. I fell in love with you, in spite of myself."

Pema did not make love to me that day. Whether his restraint was brought on by his station or his intrinsic values, I respected it. Enough to say that the little time we had in the farmhouse meant as much to us as what a lifetime of loving each other would. It seemed deep down we knew each other. It was as if we had been lovers in a previous existence. Perhaps our coming together was meant to be. I felt abundantly and immensely blessed that day. After all, of the three virtues—faith, hope and love— wasn't the greatest love?

19

WHAT HAPPENED IN THE RUINED FARMHOUSE on October 12, 1998 constituted the last entry Marian sent me. Like her love affair with Lopen Pema, her story was as yet unfinished. I wanted to know the ending, which no doubt would lead me to Marian. However, I had the intuition that, at the time of my journey to Bhutan to look for Marian, the ending was still to come, and it had not yet been written.

If only I could console myself with the conviction that her passion for the monk was nothing but an infatuation, an indulgence in the thrill of a passing moment that time would obliterate. But that little voice in me that told me where to find her when she went missing before also told me she loved Lopen Pema.

What did Lopen Pema mean when he told her he needed time to come to terms with his position and his faith? He said he would think of a way for both of them. Was he going to give up the monastic life for her? Five thousand ngultrums were all it would take to buy his passage back to the world. He still had a chance to choose, like Yee Ying on Lantau Island, the novice nun whom Marian and I befriended as children.

Seventeen years after my first visit to Lantau Island, I returned to the nunnery there in 1997, on a trip to Hong Kong, hoping to see Yee Ying again.

I stepped over the threshold into a small courtyard of the somewhat dilapidated nunnery and was led by an old woman into a prayer hall dimly lit by altar lamps. A Buddhist nun in a long grey habit and cloth sandals entered. The folds around her eyes and her puffy cheeks indicated her advanced years. Her face revealed no emotion of sorrow or joy, befitting one who had severed her ties with the world and was living a passionless life of detachment and inner peace.

"Namo Amitabha," she pronounced the Buddhist salutation in Cantonese, her clear melodious voice at last betraying her gender, which her appearance might have concealed. "May I ask what brought you to our humble abode, miss?"

"I've come to find an old friend who I believe has become a nun. Her name is Wong Yee Ying."

The old nun paused for a moment, appearing puzzled, and replied in a polite and quiet manner, "There is no one here by that name. Perhaps you are mistaken that she is in this nunnery."

"Have you not even heard of her name? She was a young novice here in 1980. She must have long become a nun. I am visiting from Canada and was hoping to see her," I persisted, filled with disappointment.

"I'm sorry, miss. I know no one by that name," the old nun repeated patiently.

The ringing of bells from across the courtyard prompted her to excuse herself. I assured her I could find my way out.

It would have been such a surprise for Yee Ying to see me, unless one would not experience surprise when one had left the ways of the world, or unless she had totally forgotten me and Marian. Alone in the prayer hall, I looked around me. My eyes had grown accustomed to the dim lighting, and I saw scroll paintings of Buddhist saints hanging on the walls. This was where Yee Ying would spend a great part of her day, her life, if she were living here. Perhaps she had taken up a new name, and the old nun did not know the name she used as a girl. Sister Bernadette at my old school was Countess Valentina Pagniello before she became a nun. Any moment Yee Ying might walk in. *Remember me? I am Ruth Souza. My sister Marian and I met you here on Lantau. It's been seventeen years. Remember the song you taught us, about a little cloud traveling to the ends of the earth, or something like that?* But then, Yee Ying might be residing in another nunnery. Catholic nuns I knew were relocated from one convent to another, sometimes from one country to another, depending on the mission of their order. There was also the possibility that Yee Ying was not a nun. Perhaps she had left the nunnery before her final commitment. Perhaps at some point while she was a novice, she chose to leave the life of detachment and emptiness, to re-enter the world.

Whether it was the notion that Yee Ying might be free from a life that was not initially her choice that I found comforting, or the strange quietude of my surroundings, I did not know. Feeling in no hurry to make my exit, I sat down on the wood floor, on a mat against the wall across from the altar. I leaned my head against the wall and closed my eyes to rest. Somehow, the solitude was pampering, the silence intoxicating, almost a luxury. I opened my eyes. I saw the Buddha sitting effortlessly in his lotus position. Slowly, I bent my knees, crossed my feet, turned my soles up until my ankles hurt. I could not do it. Perhaps with practice I could. I pulled myself up. It was time to leave.

20

I RETURNED MARIAN'S MEMOIR TO MY CARRY-ON BAG as my plane
approached Paro. The landing at Paro Airport was surprisingly smooth.
If the visibility was not good, we were told, the plane wouldn't be landing,
since the airport was not equipped with radar detection devices. "What
you see is what you get" was the order of the day.

"It always works! No chance of errors from those faulty radar systems,"
a man said from behind, as we stood in the aisle of the congested cabin
waiting for the attendant to open the plane door.

The airfield was in a valley surrounded by mountains. The sky was
clear as I emerged from the plane and stepped down to the tarmac. In
spite of the high altitude and time of year, there was no snow anywhere,
not on the hills all around, and not on the ground. The temperature felt
like early spring in Toronto. I crossed the field to what was probably the
smallest passenger terminal building in the world, a modest single-level
house with designs on door and window frames as Marian had described.
At last, I was walking the same land as Marian, breathing the same air,
under the same sky.

A man in a blue striped gho, his hands behind him, walked up to me as
soon as I stepped through the gate into the passengers' hall.

"Welcome to the Dragon Kingdom, Miss Souza. I'm your guide, Karma
Penjor, from Bhutan Best Tours," he greeted. I must have been easily
identifiable, with just a handful of foreign-looking passengers on the
flight and me being the only woman traveling alone. Karma gave me a
genuine smile and my hand a firm shake, a reassuring start for a taxing
journey, though he had no notion at the time of the true purpose of my

trip. I followed him as he went through the rigmarole of getting my visa and baggage in a most efficient manner.

I would place Karma anywhere between twenty-five and thirty-five, for he seemed to have one of those young faces on which age had trouble leaving its mark. A rich crop of black hair complemented his youthful look. With his medium height and rather athletic build, he could look smart in a soldier's uniform or a tennis player's outfit. As it was, in his gho, he looked like one who had come out of a Ming Dynasty novel, a hero of a bygone era, but for the fresh-looking Nikes he was wearing, over grey and yellow harlequin-patterned knee-highs. He spoke with a faint, rather pleasing accent.

My driver's name was Chimi, a young fellow with a constant grin and a minimal amount of English. He drove a rather new-looking yellow jeep, property of Bhutan Best Tours. Karma, Chimi, and I would be travel companions for the next twenty-one days.

We arrived at the Hotel Druk in Paro, where I would be spending the first night. Perched high on a hill not far from the airport, the hotel looked like an ancient palace. Tea was served in the deserted hotel dining room. Through a big picture window, Karma pointed to the Paro Dzong, a white fortress-like structure, perched on a hillside, the Paro Valley dotted with farmhouses in the fields, and, further on, the town of Paro, looking more like a settlement of low buildings.

Karma suggested a visit to the town before sunset. I complied, to be polite. I planned to tell him the true purpose of my trip that evening and have him change my travel itinerary accordingly. Chimi drove us downhill and parked at the foot of the Paro Dzong. We crossed a river through a covered bridge and walked along an unpaved road into town. I set my eyes for the first time on prayer flags that Marian had described, all flapping relentlessly in the breeze. I was thankful for my down jacket, for the air was nippy. We passed an archery field, where men in ghos were practicing for a tournament, according to Karma.

"You should see a real tournament," said Karma. "When an archer hits the bull's eye, his whole team sing and dance around him like children."

I nodded, feigning interest.

Paro was a town with one dusty main street lined with low houses with shabby storefronts, a very loose definition for a town. I saw a few cars here and there, but mostly people, children on their winter break from school, and adults going about their business as if they didn't have a care in the world.

I was glad for the walk. The fresh mountain air was therapeutic, the environment soothing. If only I were not on a mission to look for my missing sister, I could enjoy the place.

Up till then, Karma had no inkling of my real motive for coming to Bhutan. His company had faxed me a detailed itinerary for my twenty-one days, including a trek in Central Bhutan. I had approved it, intending to make changes to my travel plans upon arrival. After all, mine was a custom-designed tour, just for me. Having met Karma in person, I felt more comfortable confiding in him the purpose of my trip.

That evening, over dinner, I told Karma about Marian's disappearance, but only to the extent that Marian had not come home when I had expected her to, long after her work contract in Bhutan was over, and that she had not written or called. He looked at first bewildered, then gradually nodded attentively, as I told him that the last I had heard from her was her phone call from Bhutan two and a half months ago, on November 25th. I did not mention her memoir. Nor did I bring up the strange phone calls from Tenpa Norbu.

"So Karma, I need you to take me to places that may give me clues to my sister's whereabouts. You've got to help me," I almost pleaded.

"We should first check with Immigration to see if your sister has left the country."

"No, please, no Immigration. Her work visa has expired, and if she is still in the country, and I have good reason to think she is, she's staying illegally."

He nodded. "In that case, you don't want to call their attention to your sister."

My change of travel plans did not seem to upset Karma. After all, the assignment I laid out was a first for him, and he looked excited. Even though he had to report to his tour company the changes to my travel plans, the company did not have to know the real reason. I did raise my concern that the driver might wonder at my unusual itinerary.

"I'm not worried about Chimi," said Karma. "He's my loyal friend. His job is to drive anywhere I ask him."

"Tell me, Karma, is this a safe country? I mean—could something bad have happened to my sister?"

"Bhutan is the safest country in the world, Miss Souza. Very little crime. As for accident, people would have discovered by now if she was in any accident. Your sister must have other reasons to disappear."

21

"For every visitor to Bhutan, it is a sin not to see the Taktshang Monastery," said Karma, pointing to a big framed poster in the lobby of Paro's Hotel Druk the next morning. It was the picture of an isolated monastery perched on a bare and vertical cliff. "The monastery was built on a granite cliff nine hundred meters above the Paro Valley. It was heavily damaged by a fire last year. Still, it is awesome."

I smiled at his use of the attribute, which he must have picked up from his North American clients. "Why did they build it on such a high cliff?" I asked, to show polite interest, although my mind was far from the partially ruined structure on the rock.

"Guru Rimpoche flew here from Tibet in the eighth century, on the back of a flaming tigress, and landed where the monastery is today. He meditated in a cave there. He brought Buddhism to Bhutan," explained Karma, doing his guide's spiel. "The monastery was first built in 1684 on that sacred site. We call it the Tiger's Nest. Maybe we can see it when you come back to Paro, before you leave."

"Yes, maybe on my way back, if things work out favorably," I said, too preoccupied at the moment to be interested in a guru riding on a flying tigress to meditate in a cave.

At breakfast, I mapped out for Karma my initial plans. When we reached Thimphu, my first port of call would be the public library, in case Marian had left word with someone there about her plans before she left. Then the Pelri Guesthouse. Then there was Mrs. Campbell's grand-daughter, Tashi Campbell, whom I wanted to question. Karma assured me there would be no problem finding Tashi. Thimphu was no big city, and everybody knew everybody else.

"While we are in Thimphu, I'd also like to see the dzong," I said to Karma, with Lopen Pema in mind.

"Sure, it's called Trashi Chhoe Dzong. It's very grand. Now that the Central Monastic Body has moved to Punakha for the winter, I should be able to take you into the main courtyard, but I won't be able to take you inside the lhakhangs without special permission."

Perhaps Lopen Pema had also moved to Punakha for the winter. Then I would have to go to Punakha, which was on my original itinerary. He could probably answer a few important questions concerning Marian.

"Do all the monks from Thimphu go to Punakha for the winter? 'Cause when I was traveling in India once, I met a monk who said he was from the dzong in Thimphu," I fabricated my story, remembering Marian had written that Lopen Pema had been educated in India, "and I'm wondering if he's there now."

"Most monks go to Punakha, but a few stay behind to look after the lhakhangs inside Trashi Chhoe Dzong. We'll ask about your monk at the dzong."

That morning, we left Paro and headed for Thimphu in Chimi's jeep. I had arrived in the dead of winter, and the fields were bare except for scattered patches of golden mustard. I recognized the three chortens at the confluence of the Paro Chhu and the Thimphu Chhu, as Marian had described, but we did not stop. I was anxious to press on.

The Hotel Druk in Thimphu—the second one by that name that I had so far come across—overlooked the town square which was dominated by a clock tower in the center, no higher than the height of the three-story buildings all around. My room had all the basic amenities, plus a portable electric heater, since central heating was a sophistication yet lacking in

Bhutan. The first evening after I checked in, Karma told me to order anything I wanted from the hotel dining room menu for dinner, all included in my daily fee. Both he and Chimi lived on the outskirts of Thimphu. They went home for the night, he to a space he rented in a farmhouse, and Chimi to his wife and two children. I therefore dined alone.

After an early dinner of Chinese fried noodles, I took a walk down Wogzin Lam to Norzin Lam. *What if I ran into Marian?* There were just a few main streets in Thimphu, easily identifiable with the help of a map from my guidebook. I passed buildings that were two to four stories high, all in the traditional style with lots of painted decorations on walls, windows, and door frames. I soon came to one of the traffic circles that Marian wrote about. The streets, the circle, the shops, the dogs in her memoir all came alive. I thought of Marian walking down Norzin Lam not too long ago, on her way to meet Lopen Pema, her anxiety to see him, her fear of discovery, her hopeless obsession. Who was this man who had captured my sister's heart even as he conducted his daily affairs wearing a monk's garb and with a shaven head?

I made my way along Norzin Lam toward the north end of town, wishing Marian would materialize. I took a second look at every young woman I passed. Thimphu was not a big place, as Karma said. It was not unlikely that I would encounter Marian on the street, if she was still in the town. Before I knew where I was, I had walked a great length of Norzin Lam, and I came to a sign above a door that said Thimphu Public Library. I felt a sudden surge of adrenaline. The library was closed, the time being eight in the evening. So this was Marian's library. For six months, this was where she came to work, a place where she had left her footprints, as well as the legacy of a better library.

That first evening in Thimphu was when I caught a momentary glimpse, from a distance behind, of a woman in a light-colored kira that could be Marian, with her height, her gait, her build. The woman disappeared from view as quickly as I spotted her. Moments later, as I crossed the town square toward my hotel, I frightened myself with the sinister feeling that someone standing below the clock tower was watching me.

22

KARMA ARRIVED AT THE HOTEL DRUK about nine the next morning. After a breakfast of hot porridge and toast, we headed on foot for the library.

An older woman in a black kira was seated at a desk just inside the entrance, stamping a book for a borrower. A fresh-looking sign saying 'Information' hung from the ceiling above the desk. My guess was the woman was the Jigme in Marian's letters and memoir. I went up to her and introduced myself as Marian's sister.

"You looking for Marian?"

"Yes, I called from Canada a month ago. Did I talk to you?"

"I'm Jigme," she said, looking stone-faced. "I never saw her after she finished here. I think she went back to Canada."

"No, she hasn't gone home. I'm here to find her. Did she say anything that might give a clue as to where she might be going after she finished here?"

Jigme shrugged her shoulders. "Not to me. Maybe she working in another country."

"Had she been well? I mean, I haven't seen her since last May."

"She looked okay. Sometimes she said not feeling good, had to go home early." It was hard to tell from her expressionless face whether she had suspected any other reason for Marian's leaving work early on certain days.

"She mentioned Sonam in her letters. Is he here?" I could probably get more information and sympathy from him.

"No," she answered curtly.

"When will he be in?"

"Tomorrow, but he cannot help you." Then, looking at me with some curiosity, she asked, "How long you staying in Bhutan?"

"Three weeks. If you think of anything that may help me find her, please call me. Here's my number at the Hotel Druk. And please tell Sonam I'll be back tomorrow to talk to him."

Leaving Jigme looking a little perturbed, I entered the next room containing the open stacks, to browse the collection Marian had worked hard to rebuild. The shelves were marked with shiny black plastic labels with lettering showing subjects and their corresponding Dewy Decimal groupings. A crisp paperback copy of *Wuthering Heights* was in the fiction section, Marian's all-time favorite novel—she and her romantic obsession with unfulfilled love. And yes, Dickens had laid claim to a few slots. There was a brand-new collection of T. S. Eliot's *Poetical Works*. Tennyson too had found a place on the poetry shelf, as had Wordsworth, in an anthology of English Romantic poets. I opened it to my favourite poem, "Ulysses."

> Yet all experience is an arch wherethro'
> Gleams that untravell'd world, whose margin fades
> For ever and for ever when I move.

Was Bhutan the "untravell'd world" Marian had come to? A world where she found love and lost herself?

I returned to the small front periodical room. Magazines were neatly displayed in their designated spaces, marked with fresh labels on a metal rack. Karma was waiting patiently at a table, reading a copy of *Kuensel*. He stood up immediately, seeing I was ready to leave. I picked up the paper. "Chorten vandal sentenced to life," the headline read. Also on the same page, "Eight HIV cases detected in Bhutan." Little international news made it to the national paper. And nothing critical of government policies found its way to the paper's remotest corner. Surely there must be discontented souls unhappy with contentious issues even in the most fairytale paradise on earth?

"They are careful of what they print, aren't they?" I remarked to Karma, nodding at the paper.

He gave me a wondering look, and said, "Yes, it's a pretty good paper."

As we were getting ready to leave, Jigme emerged from the main reading room.

"You not only one looking for Marian. Someone else too."

"Who? When?"

"A monk. He spoke Dzongkha in funny way. Not from here. From Tibet. He came about three weeks after Marian left."

That meant about the third week of November.

"Did he give his name?"

Jigme shook her head and said, "He asked how many people working here. I told him me, Sonam, and Marian—but she left. He asked for picture of Marian. I got no picture. Marian took pictures with us on last day. Promised to send us when she got back to Canada. So I got no picture yet. He asked what she looked like. I said middle height, middle size, twenty-something, hair to shoulders. He asked where to find her. I didn't know, but told him to ask at Pelri Guesthouse."

23

WHAT JIGME SAID ABOUT THE TIBETAN MONK distressed me. How could Marian have any connection with a monk from Tibet? Why Tibet? My thoughts went to Tenpa Norbu who had phoned me from Bhutan. He said on the phone that he knew Marian had worked at the Thimphu library. Could Tenpa Norbu be the Tibetan monk? He never said he was a monk on the phone, nor did he say he was Tibetan. However, his knowledge of Mandarin supported the Tibetan connection. Since the Chinese takeover of Tibet, most Tibetans had become fluent in Mandarin.

As we exited the library, Karma must have noticed that I looked disturbed. Alone in a strange country, I had no one to turn to but my guide. Though I had known Karma for just a couple of days, I took my chance and told him about Tenpa Norbu as we walked back to the Hotel Druk for lunch, about his phone calls to Toronto, my suspicion that he might be the Tibetan monk who asked about Marian at the library, and my fear that he had found out more about Marian at the guesthouse, thanks to the lead Jigme had unwittingly volunteered.

"Don't worry about the monk," said Karma. "He's an unknown factor. Don't let him or this Tenpa Norbu, whether they are one person or not, disturb you and distract you from our original plan of finding your sister."

"You're right," I said, grateful for Karma's good sense. He had become a source of assurance in the short time I had known him. "By the way, when are we going to see the Thimphu dzong?" Back on track, I tried to hide my anxiety to locate Lopen Pema at the dzong with the feigned interest of a tourist.

"We'll go after four today if you wish. The administration offices will be closed at four, and we can enter the courtyard then."

"Do you suppose I could look up the monk I met in India while we are there?" I tried hard to sound casual.

"Oh yes, I'll inquire for you. There's a good chance he's gone to Punakha for the winter. What's his name?"

Slowly, self-consciously, I said, "Lopen Pema." Seeing Karma's puzzled look, I added quickly, "That was what he told me."

"Pema is a common name. And lopen is just a title for a teacher. Did he tell you his last name?"

I shook my head. Marian never mentioned a last name in her writing.

"It may not be as easy to find him then. Monks are everywhere in Bhutan. But at least you'll recognize him when you see him."

"I hope so. It's been a few years." I gave a nervous laugh.

"Let's go back to the hotel for lunch. We have several hours before four o'clock. Where would you like to go after lunch?" asked Karma.

"The Memorial Chorten," I said.

An impressive monument it was, the Memorial Chorten. We stepped over the threshold, slipped out of our shoes, and walked on the cold, hard floor. In the darkish, eerie interior, I followed Karma around the central altars, as he prostrated at some and explained to me the different statues of bodhisattvas, many in carnal poses with their consorts as Marian had described. To Karma, they were very much a part of the nation's religious psyche. To me, the sexual explicitness was embarrassingly out of place in a spiritual context.

We went up a narrow dark staircase to the second and then the third floor. Everything I touched, Marian might have touched. Scenes in her writing of her secret meetings with Lopen Pema on the third floor flooded back to me, as though I were witnessing the unfolding of their love, illicit by the rules of his monastic life, sacred in Marian's heart. There was the larger-than-life statue of the Buddha looking out of a big window. Could he be turning his back on the lovers in censure, or, by not looking at them, condoning what they felt for each other?

We descended the spiral staircase from the third to the second level, pausing on the second level landing to wait for some foreign tourists to come up from the ground floor to the second. It was then that I had a chilling sensation for the second time that I was being watched. I looked up and down the stairwell, and seemed to catch a fleeting glimpse of a shadow on the wall above me, cast by someone on the third level. I had not seen another soul when Karma and I were up there. My imagination could be deceptive, playing tricks on me again. I had to stop scaring myself. I, Ruth, the sane and sensible.

As we were leaving, my eyes fell on a long, brown dried-up half of a seed pod on the floor, leaning upright against a corner beside an altar. I went close to it to take a better look. A few of the white feathery seeds still clung to the inside.

"Indian bean," said Karma.

"I know. The heart of the Buddha." I forced a smile at Karma, who seemed surprised. He saw the tears that were welling up in my eyes.

24

AT FOUR IN THE AFTERNOON, Chimi drove us to Trashi Chhoe Dzong, situated north of the town, just past a golf club. From a distance, the dzong looked like a city within white fortified walls, extensively spread out. The four corners were marked by four towers above multi-leveled red roofing, all topped with golden pinnacles. And in the middle was the central tower, higher than the rest.

While Chimi waited by his jeep, Karma put on his kabney, a long white shawl of raw silk with tasseled ends, flipping it around his back, knotting it loosely at his side, and wearing it like a wide cross-shoulder sash. We passed stately stone steps leading to a majestic entrance framed by red and golden pillars and ornate wood trimmings painted with the familiar dragons, wheels, and swirls. Karma said that was the entrance for the king and the ministers. We entered the dzong through a humbler entrance, for ordinary folk but nonetheless decorated with similar elaborately painted designs. Two huge brass prayer wheels, each taller than a man, flanked the entrance. Karma gave each one a couple of turns, grabbing its wooden handle near the base as he walked clockwise. A bell tinkled from above every time a rod protruding from the top of the barrel hit it as the wheel turned.

We only got as far as the courtyard, which was paved with rectangular stone slabs and enclosed on four sides by two-story buildings with balconies all around. Karma said the buildings housed the chapels and monks' quarters. It was a spacious area, the scene of the Thimphu tsechu, as Marian had described, where she watched Lopen Pema at the Black Hat Dance, a dance that in all probability robbed her of her senses and triggered the events that led to her disappearance.

"The Thimphu tsechu takes place here every September." Karma's voice echoed my thoughts.

I nodded. "Is there someone I could ask about the monk I met in India?" I prompted.

"Oh, your friend Lopen Pema. I'll talk to the caretaker. Just wait here for me." Karma disappeared into one of the dark arched entrances off one end of the courtyard, leaving me alone, but not quite alone, for three young, barefooted novice monks, no more than nine or ten years of age, were happily chasing pigeons in the courtyard. Lopen Pema was once such a child. Perhaps years of monastic discipline and indoctrination had only suppressed but not stamped out the instinct my sister was able to reawaken.

The wait seemed forever. With luck, I could be talking to Lopen Pema any minute. I could not imagine how he would react when he found out who I was. Would he know where Marian was? What if he had bad news of Marian? Blood rushed to my brain, making my head throb. There was a nervous cramp in my stomach. I looked up. Long balconies surrounded the courtyard. Through the railings I could see doors opening into corridors at regular intervals. Beyond those doors were probably the dark recesses where monks spent most of their limited free time. The uncanny feeling I was being watched crept in again. I had to contain my paranoia, or I wouldn't last the three weeks.

After about fifteen endless minutes, Karma reappeared with a monk. They headed toward me. I noticed the monk was an old man, walking with a noticeable bent posture and an uncertain step. As he came near, I could see the wrinkles of time registered on his face.

"Miss Souza, this is Lopen Gap Thinley. He has been here a long time. You want to ask him about Lopen Pema?" Karma feigned a deliberate questioning look at me.

"Yes, Lopen Gap Thinley, I met Lopen Pema in India. We were traveling on the same train, and we got to talking, for it was a long train ride." I was certainly not a natural at concocting tales. "He mentioned he was from the dzong in Thimphu, and since I'm visiting your city, I asked Karma if there would be a chance I might find him here." Karma nodded as I looked in his direction.

The monk knitted his brows. "What is his name?" he asked in careful English, his weak voice shaky.

"Lopen Pema." There was a hollow tremor in my voice.

"Pema. Pema what?" Slowly he drawled out each syllable.

I shook my head. "I only know him as Lopen Pema."

"Is he old or young?"

"About thirty." Marian had described him as in his early thirties.

"Lopen Pema Khandu is in Punakha, but he is over fifty. Gelong Pema Phuentsho is also in Punakha, but he is fifteen," the old monk pondered aloud, taking his time. He shook his head, and my heart sank. Then lifting his eyes to me, he said with more gusto than before, "Unless you mean Lopen Pema Tshering, who is in Jicho Goemba in Bumthang. He is about thirty-two or three."

"Did he go there from here?" I tried to sound calm.

The old monk nodded. "About two months ago."

"December?"

He nodded again and did not volunteer more information. Tempted as I was to ask more, I refrained from doing so, for I might arouse his curiosity, even suspicion.

"Thank you, Lopen. I guess I won't be seeing Lopen Pema this time."

As we walked to the waiting Chimi and his jeep, I turned to Karma.

"Can we go to Bumthang?"

"I thought you would ask this question." Karma smiled. "Bumthang is a big district in Central Bhutan. It's great for trekking."

25

A FTER LEAVING TRASHI CHHOE DZONG, Karma and I decided we would have dinner at the restaurant of the Pelri Guesthouse where Marian had stayed, so that I could talk to the people there.

The restaurant was simply decorated and clean. Red-and-white checkered plastic tablecloths covered the tables. A small bar sat in a corner, where a few locals had converged as we walked in. Karma did all the ordering, and we ended up with curries, dahl, emadatsi, and a stew of dried yak meat.

A mid-fiftyish man walked in, and sat down at a table not far from us. He was Caucasian, with grey hair, matching sideburns, and a receding hairline. He sounded American when he spoke to the waiter.

"Karma," I said softly, "I have a feeling that man may be someone my sister had mentioned. I'm going to talk to him."

I finished a last morsel of food, wiped my lips, and walked over to the foreigner.

"Excuse me, are you by any chance Marvin Coe?"

"You've got him," he said, surprised. Then, looking at me, he added, "For a moment, I thought you were someone I knew! Whom do I have the pleasure of talking to?"

"Ruth Souza. You must be thinking I was Marian, my twin sister." I waited for my words to sink in, and then he broke into a smile.

"You're Marian's twin sister! Of course!" He stood up and shook my hand, inviting me to have a seat at his table.

It was strange how Marian and I had sometimes been mistaken for each other, in spite of the fact that the only thing identical with us was our height: we were both five four, although Marian described herself as a tad taller, as if a quarter of an inch on the doctor's scale could make a visible difference. While Marian inherited Mama's mild Cantonese features and darker skin coloring, I got our father's fairer complexion, a higher nose bridge and wavy brown hair.

"It's your eyes," Mama used to say with a measure of pride, "those large round eyes, and your smile, the way you pucker your lips and show your dimples." Dad called those our flashing moments of resemblance.

"So how's Marian?" Marvin Coe asked.

"I wish I knew," I said, feeling crushed. "I was hoping you could give me some information that would help me find my sister."

"Haven't you heard from her since she left here?" He stared at me with concern.

"She called from Bhutan, presumably Thimphu, on November 25th. Since then, I haven't heard from her. That's why I'm here looking for her."

Marvin pursed his lips and looked thoughtful. "Now, when she checked out of here late in October, or was it early November, she told me she was going on a trek with friends. She said she would be back to Thimphu before going home. I hadn't seen her since, and just assumed she had left the country."

"I didn't know anything about this trek she went on, and with whom."

"She had talked about joining me on a trek to the base camp of the Jhumolhari last fall. That's one of the sacred mountains here," he said.

"She did mention her interest in going with you."

"Then my plan fell through. I had a deadline and couldn't get away. I guess that was why she went with another group."

"Same route?"

"Yes, she said it was to the Jhumolhari. I remember her last day here. When she came to my room to say good-bye, she told me she was going with friends the next day. I was quite surprised, because she had not mentioned anything about it until that moment. And the strange thing was that she was rather evasive about which trekking company she had signed up with. There aren't a whole lot of them out there. I suppose you can call up each one to inquire about her and her companions on the trek."

By then, Karma had finished his dinner and come over to Marvin's table. He left Marvin his phone number at Bhutan Best Tours, so that Marvin could contact me should he have news of Marian.

I asked to see the guesthouse manager. We followed Marvin upstairs to the guest quarters. He soon found the manager, Kesang, a small gaunt middle-aged man with a thin mustache and a goatee. I explained the purpose of my visit.

"I understand my sister has left some of her belongings here. May I take a look at them?"

"Certainly. You look like Marian, so I know you are sister. You welcome to take them." He seemed more than ready to be rid of the luggage which had been in his storage for over three months. The thought that Marian might return to claim her belongings did not seem to have crossed his mind. He took Karma into a storage room, and they came back each carrying a big suitcase, which I immediately recognized as Marian's set of blue Samsonites that Dad had bought her as a going-away gift.

"Your sister very nice lady. I hope you find her soon," said Kesang.

"Did someone else come and ask about her?"

Kesang thought for a moment.

"Yes, few weeks after Marian leave. He ask where is Marian. I say I don't know, but because sooner or later she go home, I give him address and telephone number in Canada. He is a monk. From way he talk Dzongkha, he is not Bhutanese. He must come from Tibet."

I shuddered. The Tibetan monk was hot on Marian's heels. He came to the Pelri Guesthouse because Jigme told him about it. And he got our Toronto phone number from Kesang. I received Tenpa Norbu's first call on November 22nd. The timing was right.

"By the way, I have strange telephone call few days after monk came,"

Kesang said. "Woman voice, but she not saying her name. She only call my name, and when I ask what I can do for her, she hang up. Strange thing is way she say my name, *Kaysang*." He paused, looked at me intently, and continued, "That's how Marian say my name."

"About November 25th?" My voice was shaking.

Kesang thought for a moment. "I think so," he said.

That was also the last time Marian called me from Bhutan. Why did she hang up on Kesang? Why hadn't she returned to the Pelri Guesthouse to reclaim her belongings?

26

"KARMA, I'M CONVINCED the Tibetan monk asking about Marian at the library and at the guesthouse was Tenpa Norbu," I said as he walked me back to the Hotel Druk, each of us dragging one of Marian's suitcases along on its casters. Chimi had gone home earlier that day, so we had no car.

"Very likely. But we won't know why he's looking for Marian until we find her and then maybe she can explain. Or unless we can ask him face-to-face."

I cringed at the idea of confronting Tenpa Norbu.

"My biggest worry is that something might have happened to Marian, a woman alone in a strange country," I said. That fear had been gnawing at me ever since her silence began to raise concern.

"As I said before, I don't think anyone has harmed her, no, not in Bhutan. Tomorrow, I'll call the trekking companies to ask about your sister, find out which trek she took. She couldn't have gone on a trek without a guide. Don't worry. If she's in Bhutan, we'll find her, Miss Souza."

"Karma, thank you. I know this is not in line with your usual guiding duties."

"My pleasure, Miss Souza," he said quietly.

"By the way, I'm not used to being called Miss Souza. Why don't you call me Ruth?"

"I would rather address you as Miss Souza, if you don't mind. Miss Souza is easier to say. No tongue between the teeth." And we both laughed.

On reaching the Hotel Druk, Karma took Marian's two suitcases up to my room on the third floor. Elevators, like traffic lights, were nonexistent in the country. But who needed them when the tallest structures in the kingdom were the utses in the dzongs? Before Karma left for the evening, he assured me he would make arrangements for us to drive to Bumthang as soon as possible.

"And tomorrow I meet Tashi Campbell. I have a feeling she may know more about Marian than all the others I have met."

Back in my room, I had no intention of sleeping for a while. With my small Swiss army knife, I picked the lock of the larger of Marian's two suitcases.

Inside the suitcase were her summer clothes, a pair of black dress shoes, a pair of sandals, her Reeboks—she must have just worn her hiking boots on the trek—and her kira, a beautiful piece of woven fabric with the accessories as she described in her memoir. Her camera was there, along with a cloth pouch filled with rolls of undeveloped film. Sandwiched between layers of T-shirts was a red lacquer picture frame. The five-by-seven-inch photo was of our family, Dad and Mama with the two of us about the age of ten, on an outing to Shatin, in the then British-governed New Territories of Hong Kong. I was putting on my trademark smiley face for the camera, my lips curved tight into an upturned half moon, but Marian was frowning, either from the sun or something on her mind. On the not-too-distant hill in the background was the Amah's Rock, a compilation of three rocks giving the impression of the head and torso of a woman with a baby on her back. Legend had it that she was looking out to sea, day in, day out, waiting for her husband's return. The heavens took pity on her and changed her into a rock, a monument to woman's constancy.

I picked the lock of the second suitcase. Inside, the first thing that caught my eye was Marian's passport. So she did not have her passport with her! No wonder she could not come home. Why hadn't she reclaimed her luggage when such an essential item was there? Something must be keeping her from going back to the guesthouse. My worst fear, that she was dead and therefore had no use for the passport, surged to the forefront of my mind.

Her smaller suitcase was packed mostly with books. Among them were *The Oxford Dictionary of Current English, Buddhism for the Twenty-first Century*, a Bible, and her personal copy of *Wuthering Heights*. A jewelry box held mostly her favorite bangles, bracelets, and charms, nothing of great value, except for a pair of diamond studs Mama left her.

I fanned through every book for notes and scraps. A white bulging letter-sized envelope was lodged inside the Bible. It was sealed and addressed to me in Toronto, with Marian's return address as the Pelri Guesthouse but no stamp. My hand shook as I held the invaluable find. I was about to close the Bible when the pages it was opened to caught my attention—from 1 Corinthians 13. Three of the verses were marked with a yellow highlighter.

> . . . *if I have a faith that can move mountains but have not love, I am nothing.*

> *Now we see but a poor reflection as in a mirror; then we shall see face to face. Now I know in part; then I shall know fully, even as I am fully known.*

And the frequently quoted verse,

> *And now these three remain: faith, hope and love. But the greatest of these is love.*

Didn't Marian cite from the last verse in her memoir? They were in the closing lines of the last entry she sent me. I closed the Bible and returned it to the suitcase. With nervous fingers and a palpitating heart, I ripped open the envelope.

Pelri Guesthouse
7 Samten Lam
Thimphu, Bhutan

October 29, 1998

Dearest Ruthie,

By the time you receive this letter and the enclosed install-ment of my story, you will have read all the earlier segments I sent about a week ago. Please pray for Pema, as he is about to embark on a very difficult journey.

I finish at the library in two days, but I will stay in Bhutan till my visa expires on November 15th. If all goes well with Pema, I may be coming home with him soon after.

Love you,
Marian

27

From the Memoir of Marian Souza

THIMPHU, OCTOBER 28, 1998 — *THE SUTRA*

Pema and I met in the Memorial Chorten again yesterday. I got to the chorten at a quarter to four. Pema arrived soon after. As usual, we were alone on the third floor. We embraced behind an altar, as though we were living all our hours apart for those stolen minutes together.

"Marian, I have decided," Pema began after a while, as we walked along a wall, pretending to be looking at some thangkas.

I held my breath and prayed.

"Every time I thought of the future, you were there. I want nothing more than to be with you." He took a deep breath. "I have decided to ask for permission to leave the monastery."

I was full of joy. My prayer had been answered. We could fly to Bangkok from Paro, spend a few days visiting the glitzy golden temples there, so different from the humble, somewhat decrepit lhakhangs here, then fly home to Toronto. I would introduce Pema to Ruthie and Dad, Esther too, and all my friends. I would take him to the Tibetan Buddhist Temple in Toronto, so that he could blend into the Buddhist community there. I would never interfere with his religious practice. I would make sure he felt at home on Canadian soil. And I would love him forever with every breath and fiber in me. We would be married using Buddhist and Catholic rites. For a few moments, I was the happiest person on earth.

Then I noticed something seemed to be bothering him.

"But there is something I need to do first, Marian."

"I'll wait, Pema, as long as you will leave with me."

He nodded and smiled at me. "To explain what I need to do, let me go back several hundred years of our history."

I bit my lower lip and braced myself for what he was going to tell me.

"A fifteenth-century Bhutanese high lama, a rimpoche, had written an inspired sutra, thirty volumes of enlightened teachings and saintly wisdom, a treasure for Bhutan and for Buddhism. The sacred sutra was kept in a monastery in the Paro Valley until the seventeenth century, when the Tibetans launched several attacks on Bhutan from Phari on the Tibetan side, crossing Tremo La, a high mountain pass, and advancing into the Paro Valley. Even though the Tibetans were defeated each time by our great Shabdrung Rimpoche, this valuable text was secretly taken to Tibet and kept in a monastery, Thumpsing Goemba, a hundred kilometers from Phari." Pema paused, to give me time to absorb what he had said. "When its current abbot, Yeshey Tulku Rimpoche, and several monks from his goemba fled Tibet in 1959 during the Chinese invasion, they took the sutra with them, except for three volumes. Those three volumes were on loan to another goemba at the time. They have since been returned to Thumpsing Goemba. They are of vital significance to the teachings of the sutra, and consequently of paramount value to our faith. They are the heart of the sutra, according to Yeshey Tulku Rimpoche. A Bhutanese monk went secretly to Tibet in 1977 hoping to get the missing volumes back, but he was caught by the Chinese before he got to Thumpsing Goemba. He was not heard of again. Yeshey Tulku Rimpoche now resides inside Trashi Chhoe Dzong. He's in his nineties. His dream is to have the missing volumes of the sutra reunited with the rest of the set in Bhutan, before he dies." Pema paused. "Marian, I have volunteered to bring the three volumes back."

I was silent. Then the reality sank in. "But Pema, I understand the Bhutanese government forbids anyone to cross over to Tibet. And the mountains. It must be dangerous. And what about the Chinese side?"

"The border is guarded by our soldiers at a couple of places on the way to Tremo La. I'll do my best to avoid the checkpoints. Very few have crossed Tremo La to Tibet in recent years. Yeshey Tulku Rimpoche has a map of the region, which he got from traders in 1959 when he and some monks crossed Tremo La into the Paro Valley. This map will guide me. I'll be very careful to avoid Chinese border guards once I cross to Tibet. I should be back in ten days. I should go while the pass is still open, before the snow comes."

"I'll go with you."

"No, it's too dangerous for you, Marian. I can't let you go. Stay in Thimphu, and wait for my return."

I knew I would only be hampering him if I were to go along, especially with me being a woman and him a monk. "I will be dying every day you are gone. What if something happens to you? I won't even know. Do the monks at your dzong know you are going to Tibet?"

"Only Yeshey Tulku Rimpoche and my immediate superior. The Rimpoche has given me a letter with his official seal, requesting the monks at Thumpsing Goemba to give me the three volumes of the sutra. No Bhutanese is supposed to cross the border to Tibet, but my superior is willing to let me take some time off, closing his eyes to what I am going to do. But about you and me, no one knows, or about my intent to leave the monastic life after I'm back."

"No one must know about us," I emphasized, recalling the terrible punishment he described that befell a monk who was caught loving a woman. "Will the monks at this monastery in Tibet be willing to part with the sacred books?"

"I have Yeshey Tulku Rimpoche's letter with his official seal. He is still their abbot, even though he left Tibet years ago. I should have no trouble getting the books. It is good that I speak Tibetan. I became quite fluent in the language when I was studying in India, practicing with Tibetan monks who escaped to India when the Chinese invaded Tibet."

"Looks like you are all prepared," I said, my heart heavy as a big anchor. "When are you planning to go?"

"In three days. I have to complete the journey before winter comes."

"No, not so soon, Pema!"

I must have looked utterly frantic, for he said quickly, "Marian, when I come back, I'll notify my superiors of my intention to leave. Just think, only ten days and I'll be back."

"Is it for merit, Pema?" I was crying. "For your next life?"

"It will be good karma, but mainly I want to do one last thing, something important, for the Monastic Body, and for Bhutan, before I leave. I will leave without regret then. I have thought carefully about this, since our last meeting, before making up my mind. For my sake, let me go, Marian."

"I won't stand in your way, whatever you want to do. I'll wait for you. I love you."

Alone on the third floor, he held me as we stood beneath a statue of Chenrizig, the bodhisattva of compassion. Just ten days, and he would be back. He would meet me at the Memorial Chorten on November 10th, at four in the afternoon, even though that would not be an auspicious day. We would plan our future together then.

We said good-bye. I turned my back to the stairs, for I could not bear to see him go.

28

"**I** CHECKED ALL THE TREKKING COMPANIES," Karma said as soon as we met at the hotel the next morning. "Marian didn't sign up with any of them."

The last segment of Marian's memoir, the one she never mailed, had added immensely to my anxiety. The link with Tibet was beginning to make sense. But why didn't Marian stay in Thimphu to wait for Lopen Pema's return from Tibet? Why did she tell Marvin Coe she was going on a trek? If indeed she went on a trek, why did she not reclaim her luggage at the guesthouse upon her return? Did Lopen Pema return with the sacred books? Riddles piled upon riddles. Yet I could not voice my new concerns to Karma without betraying Marian and Pema, and that I would not do. One thing I was relieved about was that Kesang apparently did not mention Marian's belongings left at the guesthouse to the Tibetan monk. Consequences would be unthinkable if the monk had laid his hands on Marian's last entry embedded in her Bible.

Karma had arranged for me to meet Tashi Campbell at the Swiss Bakery at noon. Since it was a short distance from the hotel, he walked me over to the modest round structure that was the café. We had waited for a few minutes when a pretty young woman in a pink kira walked in. She answered to Marian's description of Tashi Campbell. Karma said he would return later to pick me up, and left.

I expressed my sympathy to Tashi for her grandmother's passing. She said it was a heart attack, very sudden.

We ordered sandwiches, apple juice, and rum balls.

"Marian hasn't come home. She phoned on November 25th from

Bhutan. Since then, I haven't had news from her. I'm quite worried. When was the last time you heard from her?"

"I haven't heard from her since she..." Tashi hesitated and continued, "since she left, but, all this time, I thought she had either returned home, or at least her family would know her whereabouts."

"Did she tell you where she was going?"

Tashi was silent for a moment. She looked directly at me, as though she was assessing me, perhaps trying to decide if she could tell me what she knew.

"She went on a trek," she finally said.

"That was what someone at the guesthouse said. Any idea when she left, and with whom?"

"She left the first of November, the day after she finished her job at the library." That was two days after Lopen Pema left for Tibet on October 30th. Then in a lowered voice, even though there were only a father and his young son sitting two tables from us, Tashi continued, "She went with a friend of mine. He guided her."

"Who?"

"His name is Dechen Jatso."

"Where did he take my sister?"

"To Tibet." Before I could raise my alarm, Tashi continued, "Let me tell you how this came about. On her last day of work, I stopped at the public library to see her. I walked in as her two coworkers were having a little farewell party for her. I waited, and we left the library together. She looked unusually agitated that day, as though her mind was somewhere else. She asked if I would have dinner with her. But I had promised to have dinner with my friend, Dechen, and I said she would be welcome to join us. I had told her about Dechen before. His father is a horse contractor in this region. He rents horses out to trekking groups. Dechen had gone secretly over to Tibet a couple of times with his father to buy horses and bring them back over Tremo La. It was illegal and dangerous, but his father knew the way,

110

for he used to cross the pass with his own father, who was a trader in the old days, before the Chinese invaded Tibet. Marian immediately agreed to join us for dinner. In fact, she seemed anxious to meet Dechen.

"Over dinner that evening, Marian asked Dechen about the trek across Tremo La to Phari, how difficult it was, and how dangerous. Dechen told her it was a very difficult trek. He said in addition to the rough terrain, high altitude, and the Bhutanese army posts on the way to the pass, there were Chinese soldiers at the border on the Tibetan side. He said the Phari border was heavily guarded by Chinese soldiers, mainly to prevent Tibetans from leaving Tibet.

"'What about Bhutanese going in?' Marian immediately asked.

"Dechen said that, other than his father and himself, he knew of no Bhutanese who had crossed Tremo La to Tibet. His father knew the pass very well, from the time he was a young man. The superior quality of horses at good prices had drawn him back to Tibet twice in the last few years. Both times he took Dechen with him to bring back horses. And each time they managed to avoid army guards on either side of the border."

"What would happen if they were caught?" I asked.

"That was what Marian asked. Dechen said if they were caught by their own soldiers, they would be sent to jail for three months, and whatever they brought across the border would be seized. On the other hand, if caught by the Chinese, there was no knowing what they would do. He said it would be advantageous if the person going in could speak Chinese and say he was on business if stopped by the Chinese." Tashi took a sip of juice, and continued, "It would be worse for monks to be caught crossing the border, for the Chinese were very strict on their activities and movements. If he were a monk crossing the border, Dechen said, he would dress as an ordinary man.

"The color faded on Marian's cheeks at the mention of monks. Then came the shocking proposition. She asked Dechen to guide her to Tibet, across Tremo La. She offered him a hundred American dollars a day.

Dechen thought about it, then agreed, but not without warning her of all the dangers. He had no job at the time. It was very good money. But he was not a licensed guide, and the arrangement was done under the table, so to speak. I tried to dissuade her, but she was determined. He asked when she wanted to go. She said the next day. Dechen and I were both taken aback. Before dinner was over, they had planned to set out the next morning for Paro."

The information Tashi gave was too much to swallow. What unimaginable dangers Marian submitted herself to, going after Lopen Pema into Tibet! The comforting thought was that Marian had survived the journey into Tibet, for she did call me from Bhutan on November 25th.

Tashi took a bite of her sandwich.

"Did Dechen show her a route?"

Tashi nodded, swallowed her food, and continued, "Yes. From Paro they would follow the Jhumolhari trail for a day before heading toward Tremo La. We finished dinner quickly, and they went together to get supplies for the trek before shops closed for the night."

"Did they make it there? Did he come back with her?"

"Yes and no to your two questions." Tashi laid a hand on mine before I had time to react, and continued, "You see, Marian told me and Dechen that she wanted to catch up with a friend who had left on the trek the day before. I saw Dechen after he came back from the trek. He told me they caught up with..." Tashi paused, and resumed softly, "with Marian's friend, just before they crossed Tremo La. Dechen guided them across the border. Marian's friend then went on his mission, whatever it was, while Marian and Dechen went into Phari. But the next morning, Marian told Dechen to return to Bhutan on his own while she would go after her friend. Dechen said he didn't want to leave her, but she was stubborn about going on her own after her friend. So he came back by himself."

"Did Dechen tell you who her friend was? Tashi, you can tell me. My sister and I have no secrets."

"Her friend was a monk," Tashi said quietly. She hesitated and, looking at me intently, continued, "Ruth, I knew about them. About ten days before her job at the library ended, I saw Marian meeting a monk at an old farmhouse not too far from my house. First I saw her walking fast to the farmhouse. That roused my curiosity. Then I saw a monk heading there. I couldn't see the monk's face from afar. They went inside the farmhouse and were in there for at least two hours. I never told Marian I saw them, so she didn't even know I knew. Her secret is safe with me." She lowered her eyes and was silent.

"I know about that meeting. She wrote to me."

"I had a feeling she might not come back this way after she caught up with him. I thought they would just leave from Tibet and never return to Bhutan. And that was probably why she dismissed Dechen and went after the monk on her own. But since she called you from Bhutan late in November, she must have come back. I don't know if the monk came back with her, but he probably did. The morning she left on the trek, I went to Dechen's house to say goodbye, for she didn't want to be picked up at the guesthouse and said she would meet Dechen at his house. You should see what she did to her hair. She had cut her beautiful shoulder-length hair very short since I saw her the evening before. She said it was for convenience on the trek. That was the last time I saw her."

"Tashi, you've been a great help."

"Marian had been a good friend to me. Sometimes I have ideas different from people here, which upsets them, but Marian listened to me, and she understood me. I miss her. I hope you hear from her soon."

"Where can I find Dechen?"

Tashi bit her lips. "That's a problem. Dechen got a job at the hydro plant near Phuentsholing after he came back from the trek. It's a long way south of here, at the border with India."

When Karma came to the Swiss Bakery to pick me up, I told him I wanted to go to Phuentsholing. I had asked Tashi for directions to locate Dechen Jatso there.

"Phuentsholing!" exclaimed Karma, startled at my sudden change of plans. "I thought we're going to Bumthang! Phuentsholing is in the south, on the Indian border."

"I know. How about going to Bumthang with a detour to Phuentsholing first?"

He looked flustered but soon regained his good-natured composure. "We can do that, Miss Souza. We have time. I'll tell Chimi we are heading south tomorrow." Then he added with renewed enthusiasm, "We can do some shopping on the Indian side. They have great merchandise there, and good bargains."

"Thank you for putting up with me, Karma, and for being so easy about it." He looked away, seeming embarrassed. "You and Chimi may need time to get ready for the trip. I'll walk to the library by myself. I want to talk to Sonam there."

I found the stout, bespectacled library worker alone at the circulation desk.

"Jigme told me you coming back today. I wish I have more information about Marian. I thought she went home. Now I worry about her."

"I'm hoping you can give me some clue, from things she might have said, her actions, or unusual occurrences."

The kindly man was thoughtful, and after a few seconds said, "She was very nice lady. When she first came, she told us about you and father in Canada. I took her on family trips. She enjoyed very much."

If Sonam hadn't taken Marian to Dochu La that fateful day when she saw Lopen Pema bathing in the open, things would have turned out differently, and I would have my sister home.

"Something wrong?" Sonam asked, noticing my silence.

"Just trying to picture Marian here," I said, blinking hard.

"She became very quiet later, not like in the beginning, and I often saw her moody at work, like she had worries."

I thanked Sonam, even though he had nothing new to add that was helpful. As I passed the stacks, my eyes fell upon a book I had missed the day before, *The Jesuit and the Dragon –The Life of Father William Mackey in the Himalayan Kingdom of Bhutan*, by Howard Solverson. The soft-cover book's white spine with large black lettering caught my attention.

"Sonam, where did this come from?"

"Marian ordered it from company called Society of Jesus in Bangkok. It arrived in brown envelope, not with big orders from Bangkok. Marian very happy to receive it on her last day. She cataloged right away. This was last book Marian gave me to put on shelf."

"May I borrow it? I promise I'll return it before I leave Bhutan."

"No problem," said Sonam, with a big smile.

29

THE NEXT MORNING, FEBRUARY 13, 1999, I was surprised to see Tashi waiting for me in the lobby of the Hotel Druk, a backpack on the floor beside her. I invited her to join me for breakfast in the dining room. Karma and Chimi would be coming by shortly after nine to pick me up for our drive to Phuentsholing.

"Ruth, I'm wondering if I could come with you to Phuentsholing," Tashi said rather awkwardly after we had ordered tea. "I'm free from now until the new term starts at Sherubtse, and I have little to do right now."

Tashi had graduated from high school that winter, and had gained the much coveted admission to Sherubtse College in the new term, which would not begin until March. Her request took me by surprise, but it suited me well. There was plenty of room in Chimi's jeep, and even though I was enjoying Karma's company, I was beginning to miss the tête-à-tête with a friendly female. Besides, having her with me would make it easier to question Dechen about Marian, since I had never met the man.

Karma was late. It was twenty after nine before he walked through the main entrance of the Hotel Druk, to find me and Tashi sitting in the main lobby.

"Sorry. Some trouble with Chimi's jeep. It's okay now," he said, joining us on a sofa.

Immediately I told him about Tashi's request to go with us. He had no problem with having her as an extra passenger, especially since I offered to share my room with her. Tashi said she would pay for the extra expenses, mainly food, that her coming with us would incur, but I assured Karma that I would take care of them.

"My tour company may not like me taking an extra passenger on my own, but some rules are made to be broken," said the enlightened Karma. Then, looking at my suitcase and overnight bag, and Tashi's backpack, he said, "Why don't you two ladies get into Chimi's jeep. It's waiting outside the front entrance. I'll take care of your bags."

As soon as Tashi and I were seated inside the jeep, to my surprise Chimi started to drive away without waiting for Karma and our bags.

"No worry, Miss Souza. Karma coming." He drove round a couple of blocks before returning to the hotel, stopping at the back door, where Karma was waiting with our luggage.

"Why all the secrecy, Karma? Are you trying to smuggle something out of the hotel?"

"Yes, in a sense," he replied, giving me a mysterious smile.

It was a rough six-hour ride to Phuentsholing. The forested road was bumpy, the traffic hampered by repair and construction. The lanes were too narrow for the caravans of lorries carrying Indian goods and produce to Thimphu. It was miraculous that two vehicles could pass each other alongside a deep gorge on a ledge apparently wide enough for the smaller of the two. Chimi honked noisily every time a lorry in front was moving too slowly for him, before he passed it at the first opportunity. At first I was uneasy about his apparent bad highway manners until I noticed the big words painted across the back of every lorry: BLOW HORN!

As we journeyed south, pines and hemlocks gave way to banana trees and betel palms, and the rich abundance of wild-grown rhododendrons and magnolias soon made room for the dazzling flame of the forest. We were entering the tropical zone.

Tashi asked for Dechen at the workers' quarters of the hydro plant just before we reached Phuentsholing. Dechen was at work. She left word for him to meet her for dinner at the Phuentsholing Inn in town at eight that evening. She added that she was not alone but had some friends with her.

"I don't want to give him the wrong idea that I've come alone to see him," Tashi said, with a wicked smile.

"Will he come?" I asked, considering the impromptu nature of her message.

"Oh yes, he'll be there," Tashi replied with confidence. "You see, Ruth, Dechen really likes me."

The Hotel Druk in Phuentsholing, the third one of the same name in the kingdom, was different in setting and décor from the ones in Thimphu and Paro. Situated in a garden of towering betel palms and bright red and purple bougainvilleas, the three-story pink structure resembled a tropical resort hotel. There was a dense fragrance in the air, and the breeze that touched my skin was comfortably warm and gentle, with a hint of humidity. Tashi and I had a room facing out to the main street of town, which was lined with rather decrepit low buildings with street-level shops. The archway to Jaigaon, the town on the Indian side, was in view just a short distance away.

A late lunch of the usual fare of curries and rice at the hotel dining room refreshed us. Afterwards, Tashi and I explored the town with its few congested streets, while Karma and Chimi did their bargain shopping across the border. The ethnic components of Phuentsholing seemed to be divided between Bhutanese and Indian. The law for Bhutanese to wear their national dress was not enforced in this border town, and so Karma and Chimi had changed into T-shirts and blue jeans. They looked different, not only because of their attire, but also because they seemed more relaxed and in a holiday mood as they left the hotel to walk over to the Indian side.

There was a continuous flow of human traffic between the two sides. The Indian influence could be seen and felt everywhere in Phuentsholing, which looked more like an Indian town than Bhutanese, with its rows of open storefronts, many run by Indian proprietors, selling items from clothing to carpets, Buddhist and Hindu artifacts to groceries and sundry goods.

Somewhere near the archway Tashi and I met three Catholic nuns in religious habit. They were ethnic Indians. I approached them.

"Hello, sisters, are you from around here?"

"We're from Jaigaon. We've come over for the afternoon," replied the oldest-looking of the three.

"Do you know if there's a Catholic church nearby?" I asked.

Immediately the three nuns gave me a look of kinship.

"You won't find any church in Bhutan. Not permitted, you know," one spoke up, "but there's one not far from here in Jaigaon." They gave me directions to the church.

"Are you going there?" Tashi asked as soon as we had said good-bye to the nuns.

"I guess not. I don't like walking in a strange town in a strange country on my own."

"I'll go with you, if you wish," said Tashi.

I was touched. A Buddhist from Bhutan accompanying me to a church. I had no reason to refuse her offer, and no excuse not to go.

We passed through the archway to Jaigaon, and followed the nuns' directions to the church, walking through streets full of grime and garbage, with young beggars at our heels, touching my sleeves, some carrying babies just a few years younger than they. Somewhere on a concrete island in the middle of a street was a dead cow, with swarms of insects buzzing over it. People carried on their usual business and cars went around it. A dead cow on a busy street was apparently not an extraordinary sight.

We found the church, a modest, whitewashed, low building marked by a big wooden cross above its gabled roof. A sign read *Our Lady of Perpetual Help Catholic Church.* I walked up the few front steps, and Tashi followed. The door was not locked. We entered. It was a one-room church with a central altar and a small side altar to its left and one to its right.

I knelt in front of the left altar presided over by an icon of the Virgin Mary holding the infant Jesus. I lit a votive candle for Marian. *Hail Mary, full of grace, the Lord is with thee.* I started reciting in my mind... *Pray for us sinners now and at the hour of our death.* For the first time since arriving in Bhutan, I felt I belonged. I had been deprived the last ten days of a house of God and the freedom to worship.

As I prayed, my eyes rested on the two painted side panels, each of a waist-length angel, flanking the center icon of the Madonna and Child above the left altar. Images from long ago floated back, of Marian and me, on the Feast of Christ the King. We were angels...

We were angels in white robes, wearing shimmering gauzy wings and tiaras crowned with a glittering star. We were angels walking in front of the Blessed Sacrament displayed in a bejeweled monstrance held reverently by the bishop under a canopy. We paved the way, sprinkling rose petals from the ribboned baskets we held. We were two of twenty angels handpicked by the nuns at Sacred Heart School to take part in the procession on the Feast of Christ the King. Big fanfare. To have been chosen as angels was an honor to us, to our parents. We were eight then.

Marian and I had been full of anticipation all week leading up to the Feast of Christ the King, attending briefings and rehearsals at school and trying on the garments. Mom took us to get new white sandals befitting angels. We were on our best behavior, like angels.

Sunday, the Feast of Christ the King. The slow beating of the drums resonated in my heart, vibrating and solemn. The altar boys followed the drummers, followed by church officials. We, the angels, came next, closest to the Blessed Sacrament. People lined the route of the procession. The crowd knelt as we neared, not to us, but to the Blessed Sacrament we heralded, although at the time I had a false sense of importance. We walked two by two. Naturally, Marian and I were a pair.

The procession started from the Catholic cathedral, continued along some mid-level streets of Hong Kong to the Botanic Gardens, returning to the cathedral for the celebration of the Eucharist, the Holy Mass, which was the highlight of the afternoon. A reception would follow in the church hall after the Mass.

The streets were blocked off, where the procession cut through. We turned onto Holly Street, where the crowd was thinner. Through a gap in the line of onlookers I saw a beggar in tattered rags sitting on the pavement against a wall. In his arms was a sickly little boy, whose drawn, deep-set eyes took up most of his face and whose limbs were no more than skin over bones. If only I could give them my week's allowance, which was jingling in my pocket beneath the angel's gown, but I could not step out to them. I had my duty as an angel to perform.

We soon turned another corner to a main street leading to the Botanic Gardens. By four in the afternoon, we had returned to the cathedral for the Mass. We angels took our places by the choir, to join in the singing. I looked for Marian but did not see her. She could have gone to the little girls' room and afterwards was too shy to take her place with us once the service had begun.

After the service, we filed into the church hall for refreshments. Women from the parishes kept replenishing the supply of sandwiches, cakes, and tarts on the tables. Angels, wings removed, mingled with family as well as other participants of the procession. Still, Marian was nowhere to be seen.

Mom and Dad came by for us soon after. They were alarmed that Marian was not at the Mass, nor was she at the reception. The organizers of the event were alerted to the fact that Marian had disappeared following the procession. A team of volunteers was formed to look for her in and around the cathedral. I was beset with guilt for letting her out of my sight, even though Dad and Mom did not lay a word of blame on me.

As the sun began to set on the Feast of Christ the King, I, led by an intuitive understanding of my sister, took Dad and Mom to Holly Street, to the spot where I had seen the beggar and the boy. There, we found Marian in her angel's gown, sitting on an old wooden crate, her wings folded neatly on the pavement beside her, watching the man feed bits of chicken from a sandwich into the sick boy's mouth. On the ground, by the man's side, was a ribboned basket of sandwiches, cakes, and tarts.

A week later, we passed by the spot where we found Marian. We saw the man begging for alms, but we did not see the boy. Perhaps he died. If he did, he did so knowing the angel of compassion had smiled on him.

My eyes became watery. *Dear Mary, please help me find my sister, Marian, your namesake, as I did before. Let her see the folly of falling in love with a monk. Dear Jesus, guide and guard her wherever she is, and bring her back safe to me.*

I sobbed until I felt a hand on my shoulder. I turned. Tashi was standing behind me.

"I'm just unloading here," I said, trying to smile through my tears. "It's comforting to be in a church again."

"I understand."

Outside, I thanked Tashi for walking with me to the church.

"Oh, that was nothing, Ruth. Marian would have done the same for me if I were looking for a Buddhist temple in a strange Christian country."

30

DECHEN JATSO ARRIVED AT EIGHT that evening at the Phuentsholing Inn, a young man in his mid-twenties, of medium height and build, with a wholesome smile and eager-to-please look. He wore a Hawaiian-style shirt and khaki pants, and brown leather sandals. Tashi, changed out of her kira into a fuchsia cotton blouse and blue jeans, had transformed from a Bhutanese beauty into a fresh-looking sporty teen. It was obvious Dechen was full of admiration for her and was anxious to be in her good books. Tashi, on the other hand, though happy at seeing him, seemed to be wary about any suggestive nuance from him. Because of the secretive nature of our subject, I had asked Karma and Chimi to have dinner on their own. Karma graciously complied, no questions asked. He and Chimi would have a great time painting the town red.

"Marian gone home to Canada?" Dechen asked as soon as Tashi had introduced me as Marian's sister.

"No. That's why I'm here to look for her. I believe she's still in Bhutan."

"Dechen, Ruth knows about the trek to Tibet. She would like to hear about it. Every bit of information you can give her may help her find Marian," Tashi said.

We ordered the inn's specialties, tandoori chicken, and charcoal beef ribs, and Indian beer. While we waited for the food, Dechen began his story in his manner of English.

"Marian in big hurry to catch up with friend who start on trek to Tibet two days ago. We ride in private car to Paro morning on November first. We reach Drukgyel Dzong—you know dzong which burn down many years ago—not far from Paro. From Drukgyel Dzong, we start on Jhumolhari trek. The trek not very difficult first day, not very steep climb through forest, but very muddy from heavy rain in October. I want to camp near Sharna Zampa, small village, first night. But before that is army checkpoint. Everybody pass that way must register at checkpoint. We have to avoid it, because I am not license guide. We cross river over log bridge about two kilometers south of checkpoint and walk on muddy trail on south bank. Soon trail end, then we cut through forest going up hill. We pass checkpoint without any problem, only few cuts to the skin. Your sister very tough lady." Dechen nodded at me, sipped his beer, and seemed to enjoy telling his story.

"We camp near Sharna Zampa first night, at about twenty-nine hundred meters. I have dome tent for your sister. I sleep under stars."

"What did you do for food?" I asked.

"Tins, bean, vegetable, bread, biscuit. She eat no meat. Also water, camping things, clothes and my sleeping bag all in my backpack. Her backpack not so heavy. She carry her sleeping bag, and clothes. She ask me for trek clothes for her to take to her friend. Lucky our sleeping bags can press into small bundles. Everything necessary, except gho."

"Why would she bring a gho to Tibet?"

"I don't know. I wear trek clothes every day. She say I will need gho when we get to Tibet." Dechen shrugged his shoulders. "My backpack too full, so she put inside her backpack."

"So that was the first day," Tashi prompted, steering Dechen back to the narration.

"Yes. Next morning, we start early. We take trail of Jhumolhari trek again, along Paro Chhu. We walk through forest, cross small streams for about seven kilometers. We come to trail left of Jhumolhari trail. Way to Tremo La.

"It is pave trail, easier to walk than mud, for about ten kilometers. Then trail end. Then we begin to go up pass. There is Bhutanese army camp guarding pass. I have map my father give me few years ago, grandfather's map, to follow to avoid army camp." Dechen looked from me to Tashi, pausing as if to build up the tension in his narration. "To cross Tremo La, first you cut through forest—hemlock, spruce, fir—then up rocky slope to forty-seven hundred meters. The pass not very wide, but altitude gain eighteen hundred meters from first night camp near Sharna Zampa. No mark trail. I plan three days to cross pass, first night going up, camp in forest, second night in rock cave below high point, and third day, cross pass to Tibet."

"Did Marian make it okay?"

"Yeah, she okay. She surprise me. Super woman, you know?" Dechen laughed. "We start out very early. Had to trek slow because of high altitude. She got breathing problem and headache second day, but after some rest, she okay. Climb six hundred meters a day difficult even for trek guides. And other trekkers have mark trail, but not us. Lucky I go that way twice before. So I find way up without guessing a lot. In November, we take chance with weather. Lucky weather good. Sunny all the way. There is some ice from last year, but not yet new snow. Usually new snow come after middle of November. But there are half-frozen mountain streams. Difficult to go up icy slope." Dechen finished his beer, and I signaled to a waiter to refill his glass. "Slowly, very carefully, we go up icy slope, me in front, and I tell Marian where to put her feet every step. First night after Sharna Zampa, we camp in forest. She sleep in tent, me in open, by fire I build. Next night, we sleep in cave. Very cold, over four thousand meters. I build fire in cave. We wear jackets and cover up in sleeping bags by fire. Fire is dead in the morning."

"I understand she caught up with her friend." That was the part I most wanted to hear. Dechen was taking his time and enjoying it.

"All the way, Marian look for friend. She want us to go faster, but I say no, normal person cannot go anymore faster in high altitude. I say we already gain one day because we make no stop in Paro. Can't go anymore faster. Then morning after we sleep in cave, before top of pass, we see something moving far up in front on bare rocky slope. At first I think it is a yak. No, it's a person! Marian very excited. She call out loud and wave."

"What did she call out?"

"Pema! Pema! Person must hear her for it stop moving. Then we go up rocks, very careful of loose rocks. Then I see more clearly it is man wearing wool hat, winter coat over—over red skirt." Here, Dechen paused, then said almost in a whisper, "He is a monk."

"Was he shocked when he saw you and Marian?" I asked.

"Yes, very shock. But also very happy. Marian and monk say little, only happy. Marian tell him I am guide for her."

"And you went on with them after Marian caught up with the monk."

"Yes. But first, Marian ask monk to take off monk's robe and wear my trek clothes she bring for him. I tell them to leave monk's clothes behind, but monk say no. He stuff monk's clothes in his backpack. If we are caught by Chinese soldiers and they search bags, we are all dead. We reach top of Tremo La about forty-seven hundred meters in afternoon. Then we go down about two hundred meters over rocks other side of pass. Another four hundred meters down is Chinese army post. Must avoid. So I take them north, over rocky mountainside to waterfall. We go down side of waterfall, very icy, very slippery. We slide down a lot. Get bruise and cuts. Then more rocky slope until we get to elevation about forty-two hundred meters. Some trees growing there. After that we come out to high plain. Phari only three kilometers south from us, but about two hundred meters higher. Not hard to walk there on open field. Almost dark by that time. Good to enter Phari at night.

"Monk say to me to take Marian to Phari that night. He has important job to do in other place, he say. He will meet us same place we say good-bye that night, near pile of rocks with prayer flags, in two days. So I go to Phari with Marian that night. She got room at hotel for her and room for me. But early next morning, she say she change her mind and she will catch ride to where monk is. At first I say no, stay and wait for monk in Phari. She say no, she must go after monk. Then I say I go with her, but she say no, she will go by herself. She has very strong mind. She pay me for my whole journey and tell me to return to Bhutan. She tell me to be very careful to avoid Chinese soldiers. And she make me swear not to tell anyone about her and monk friend. So I swear."

"You told Tashi, which is fine, but have you told anyone else?"

"No, never I tell anyone else. Tashi is friend of Marian. She know about me taking Marian to Tibet, so I tell her. But nobody else."

"So she went after the monk, and you came back to Bhutan?"

"Yes. First I make sure she get ride with good people. Lucky she got ride in bus taking children on school trip to Gyantse, west of Phari. She say where monk is going is not far from Gyantse. After I see her on bus, I buy food in Phari and start back to Bhutan same way I come."

And Dechen had apparently forgotten his gho that was in Marian's backpack.

31

DECHEN SUGGESTED TO TASHI AND ME after dinner that he be our guide around town, maybe even stopping at a disco, apparently a trendy pastime with the younger set of Phuentsholing. I declined his offer but encouraged Tashi to go with him. I left Tashi with Dechen, who cast me a grateful glance as we said good-bye. I returned to the hotel to seek out Karma.

I found Karma at the bar in the dining room, seemingly at ease in his shirt and jeans, enjoying a beer and chatting with the bartender and a few others. I called him to a table, while the fellows at the bar followed us with their eyes and made some remark in Dzongkha, to which Karma smiled and lent a deaf ear.

"How was dinner?" he asked as soon as we sat down.

"Good. Dechen was very helpful." I owed Karma an explanation for my sudden decision to come to Phuentsholing to talk to Dechen, especially when he had been so gracious about my change of plans, without so much as asking why. I braced myself for his reaction to what I was about to tell him. "Dechen was Marian's trek guide. He took her across Tremo La into Tibet."

"Tremo La! I didn't know if anyone had crossed Tremo La since the Chinese occupied Tibet! Why did she want to do that? It's a very difficult trek, and the Bhutanese government forbids anyone to cross to Tibet. Why didn't she join a trekking group to the Jhumolhari?" Karma looked utterly dismayed, and shook his head in disbelief.

"They made it safe over the pass," I said. I could not tell him the reason why Marian had gone to Tibet by way of Tremo La. But I added, "Dechen came back by himself, because Marian wanted to stay in Tibet for a little while."

"Alone? So she could still be in Tibet." Karma looked at me in bewilderment.

"But she was back in Bhutan the last time I heard from her, when she phoned me in Toronto in late November," I reminded Karma.

"Oh yeah. But how could she get back by herself? I'm afraid I don't understand, Miss Souza. This is beyond me," said Karma, throwing up his hands and looking more perplexed than ever. It was time to explain myself a little further.

"Karma, you might have guessed I wanted to go to Bumthang because the old monk at the Thimphu dzong said this Lopen Pema Tshering had gone to a goemba there." I paused, giving him time to acknowledge with a nod. "You also know I wouldn't sidetrack from my search for my sister to hunt down a monk who was a casual acquaintance I met on a train." Karma nodded again. "Has it crossed your mind then that there is a connection between Marian and—" I stopped, then continued in one breath, "and my wanting to find the monk I met in India?"

"I have wondered," he said, studying my face.

"It is important that you don't breathe a word about any of this to anyone, not even Chimi. Just say we are going to Bumthang to trek."

"You can trust me completely."

"Thank you, Karma," I said, my voice conveying my gratitude. I had come to rely on Karma as someone who could keep a secret and who had the open-mindedness and flexibility to bend rules as his better judgment dictated. I got up from the table. "Karma," I turned to him, just as he was picking up his beer to rejoin his buddies at the bar, "I want you to know I am very lucky to have you for my guide."

"Thank you, Miss Souza. It's my pleasure to be of service to you," Karma murmured, bowing his head in acknowledgment. He smiled at me with a thoughtful look, then quickly looked away, still wearing his smile.

Tashi came back to the hotel room we shared not long after I was in bed. I did not talk to her but stayed silently awake for a long time. I pictured Marian following Lopen Pema to the monastery in Tibet, where he was to recover the missing volumes of the sutra for Bhutan. When sleep finally overtook me, I dreamed of Marian with a shaved head and wearing the garment of a Buddhist nun, begging for alms from door to door in Thimphu.

We returned to Thimphu the next day, to drop off Tashi. I would spend another night at the Hotel Druk in the capital, before Karma, Chimi, and I set out for Bumthang. Tashi expressed a desire to talk that evening, so I suggested dinner in the town.

"Would your mother like to join us?" I asked.

"Maybe another time," Tashi said, looking reluctant.

We picked the Plum Café, a cozy little upstairs restaurant serving Indian food. We sat by the window, overlooking the southern traffic circle.

"This country is protected from change," I observed, watching the white-gloved policeman directing the thin traffic from his kiosk.

"That's one of the reasons I want to leave," Tashi said.

"You are a rebel, Tashi," I said, playfully frowning at her. I recalled what Marian had written about her, about her trouble with her school over an essay she wrote. "I thought the Bhutanese are contented to be here, and if they have to leave for a time for any reason, they always come back."

"You are correct about the Bhutanese sentiment, but I'm not all Bhutanese. I have my father's blood too. I want to see the world. And what's more, I'm tired of being one among six hundred thousand others, dressing alike, thinking alike, behaving alike."

Her barrage of words, fair or unfair, stunned me. "Yet, this is the happiest and most peaceful place on earth. You'll know what I mean, Tashi, once you've been outside." Tashi looked at me dubiously. "What about Sherubtse?" I asked.

"That's a stepping stone to something more exciting, I hope. When I was young, my mother was careful that my Grandmother Campbell did not have too much of an influence on me. Now I'm older, but my grandmother's gone." Looking at me earnestly, she continued, "Ruth, when you go back to Canada, can you look out for opportunities for me? I mean, if there's a job I can do, a school I can attend, anything, after Sherubtse."

"I can inquire."

"I got a letter from my grandmother's lawyer in Canada last week. She has left me some money, placed in a trust until I turn twenty-one, which will be two and a half years from now. I'll be financially independent and able to do things my own way."

"The money will certainly open up a lot of avenues for you." I was happy at the prospect of a turn of fortune for Tashi. "But what will your mother think about your leaving?"

Tashi heaved an audible sigh.

"She'll be heartbroken to see me go, but I've got to live my life the way I want it. She's the typical Bhutanese who will never leave. This is her life— her loom, her farmhouse, the prayer flags, the chortens and temples, the mountains. That's all fine, as long as she's contented. One should have the freedom to choose how to live one's life and find one's happiness. She's only forty-one, you know, and she can take care of herself. I'll miss her. But I'll make sure she is comfortable and not in need."

Looking at Tashi, I saw some of Marian's impulsiveness but perhaps not my sister's sentimentality, which had marked her a vulnerable victim of her own heart.

"Well, when you graduate from Sherubtse and you are in possession of your inheritance, if you are still of the same mind as you are now, I'll see what I can do."

We filled our glasses with beer and drank to each other's future—and to Marian's, wherever she was.

32

KARMA AND CHIMI CAME TO THE HOTEL DRUK early the next morning to pick me up for our trip to Bumthang. At the reception desk, the clerk asked where we were going.

"It's a secret," Karma answered quickly, and covered his abruptness with an impish smile. He asked me to get into Chimi's jeep, while he took my luggage to the back door of the hotel, as he did when we set out for Phuentsholing.

"Why all the hush-hush?" I asked after Chimi had picked him and my luggage up at the back door.

"My job is to guide and protect you, Miss Souza, and that's what I'm doing."

"Am I being followed?" My mind went back to the uncomfortable feeling I had of being watched the first couple of days I was in Thimphu.

"It may not be you someone is after, but your sister."

"Tenpa Norbu? The Tibetan monk?" I asked, not sure if I was referring to one person or two.

"Possible," Karma nodded. "But don't worry. You are in good hands. Chimi and I are your guides and bodyguards. Let's enjoy the ride to Bumthang. You have to see our country."

Chimi half-turned his head, nodded at Karma's words, and grinned his betel-nut grin. It was the fifteenth day of February, and the seventh day of my journey in Bhutan. We would spend the night in Jakar, the main town of Bumthang, and set out the next morning for Jicho Goemba, where Lopen Pema Tshering was supposed to be.

Our first stop was the village Wangdi, where Chimi filled up on gasoline and bought some food and water for the journey.

"We'll stop at Trongsa for lunch. There is a valley halfway between here and Trongsa, called Phobjikha Valley. Every November to March, the black-necked cranes from Tibet come to the valley to roost. If you like, we can detour into the valley to see them," suggested Karma.

Since we would not be heading for Jicho Goemba until the next day, there was nothing to lose by seeing a bit of the country on the way. So, at the next fork, Chimi turned his jeep down the road to Phobjikha Valley. As we drove downhill, we saw that the hillside was strewn with yaks, those massive black ox-like woolly creatures, slow in movement, but indispensable as beasts of burden and suppliers of milk, cheese, and even meat.

We were soon at the bottom of the valley. We parked at a fence by a field where some black-necked cranes were roosting. I was thankful for the binoculars I had brought along, for we could not get too close to the cranes. According to Karma, they chose their partners for life. They strutted in pairs, some in parties of three, the third being an offspring that had not yet found a mate. Such constancy in some of God's creatures, coming back to the valley every winter, attached to one mate for life.

Several grubby village children approached, with chapped rosy cheeks and wearing ghos and kiras that seemed a few sizes too big for them. They were attracted to my binoculars. I gave them each a turn to look through them. The price for the favor? A photo with me. The children posed eagerly for the camera, giving their sunniest smile, some with front teeth missing.

Before we left the valley, Karma took me to Gangte Goemba. Outside the temple, Karma, Chimi, and I removed our shoes. As soon as we entered the assembly hall, a young monk poured water into our cupped palms from a brass flask. Karma and Chimi quickly slurped it up, but Karma told me to wipe the water on my hair, since he knew I would not drink any water in Bhutan, except of the bottled spring variety. I watched as Karma touched his joined hands to his forehead, lips, and heart and prostrated himself at the altar. Three times he repeated his act of veneration. He then placed some ngultrums on a dish by a butter lamp. Chimi went through the same motions at the altar.

The interior walls of the goemba were covered with freshly painted depictions of saints and bodhisattvas, and of ancient Bhutanese daily life. The center statue at the altar was that of the Buddha, with one of Guru Rimpoche on his right and, on his left, Pema Lingpa, the sixteenth-century saint who discovered treasures mostly in the form of sacred texts of Buddhism for Bhutan. In front of the statue of the Buddha was a tall vase with a fanned display of white seeds from the Indian bean. I looked away.

Back into the sunshine, I would have loved to stay in the valley longer, to bask in the rustic ambience of farmhouses and cattle, and delight in the fascination of rosy-cheeked children with my binoculars, and the un-pretentious smiles of villagers. But we had a long way to go, and I had a mission to accomplish.

Joined up with the main road again, we headed toward Central Bhutan. Red rhododendrons bloomed well in the higher altitudes, and pines soon gave way to firs, spruces, and hemlocks. We crossed a couple of mountain passes, each marked with a small chorten and a colorful array of prayer flags. At each pass, Karma and Chimi called out "*Lha Gyel Lu!*" which Karma translated as "God wins!"

At three in the afternoon, we reached the town of Trongsa. Below the town, extensively spread out on the hillside, was Trongsa Dzong, with imposing white fortress walls and yellow roofs and the utse towering over all the rest, the complete ancient structure like a palace in Shangri-La.

We ate at an inn on the main street, the only street, it seemed, in the town. We were famished. Karma ordered several curries with rice and a heaping plateful of cheese momos for the three of us, and some emadatsi for himself and Chimi.

By the time we reached Jakar, the main town in the Choskhor Valley of

Bumthang, it was seven in the evening. We checked in at the Swiss Guest House, perched on an elevated level, with a good view of the imposing and somber Jakar Dzong across the valley. True to its name, the guesthouse had the trimmings of a Swiss chalet. My room had pine paneling, pinewood cottage furniture, and a bukhari stove for heat. A big wicker basket of dry wood stood beside the stove. The room was cold and damp, and I found myself replenishing the burning wood in the furnace every ten minutes.

After a small helping of buckwheat noodles, I decided to turn in early, to prepare for the long day ahead. The challenge of the trek to Jicho Goemba was the least of my anxieties. It was the thought of coming face-to-face with Marian's Lopen Pema the next day that kept me awake that night, assuming Lopen Pema Tshering was indeed Marian's monk. I was optimistic that this time I would meet him. What did he look like? Would he answer to Marian's description of him? How would he react when I told him I was Marian's sister? And the question that worried me most— where was Marian?

33

WE SET OUT FOR JICHO GOEMBA the next day, February 16, 1999.
The goemba, where Lopen Pema Tshering resided, could be accessed only on foot from Toktu Zampa, a small settlement in the Choskhor Valley. The trek would take a full day, through wheat fields and dense forests and up wooded slopes. Luckily, Karma had been there before on personal pilgrimages and would therefore be able to find his way without much difficulty.

Karma joined me in the dining room of the Swiss Guest House for an early breakfast of buckwheat pancakes and Gouda cheese. I was not hungry, consumed with nervousness at the thought of meeting Lopen Pema before the sun set again. What if Marian was in the vicinity of Jicho Goemba? Marian had not come home to Canada with Lopen Pema after Tibet, for reasons unknown to me, but if she was as in love with him as she said she was, she must want to be as close to him as she could. It wasn't all wishful thinking that I might find my sister before the day was done.

For the trek, I wore a fleece track suit over a thin cotton pullover and a T-shirt, and hiking shoes. Even though it was chilly in the morning, Karma had warned me that it could get quite warm as we trekked into noon, and it would be best to wear layers of clothing that I could take off.

Chimi drove Karma and me to Toktu Zampa, marked by a few stone houses and a dilapidated wooden shed. February was still too early for trekkers, but Karma thought we should manage without much trouble. We would follow the marked trail of the Bumthang Cultural Trek, one of the least strenuous treks, till we reached the village of Ngang. Beyond that we would go on a side trail that would take us to Jicho Goemba, reaching the monastery before dusk.

Karma and I each had a backpack. Karma said he would normally con-tract a cook and a horseman with his horse on treks, but he had not done so for us, since he was confident he would be able to get us accommoda-tion in a farmhouse close to the monastery for the night. We expected to be back at Toktu Zampa by sunset the following day, where Chimi would be waiting with his jeep.

That morning, I followed Karma across clear streams and small rapids on suspension and log bridges, and trod through flat fields of newly planted buckwheat. We passed a mani wall—a prayer wall, as Karma explained—piled with stones carved with Buddhist mantras. Karma circumambulated it—might as well squeeze in some merit on the way. We went up gentle forested slopes. Up till then, the trek was easy. My greatest challenge was avoiding the piles of dried horse manure that had been left along the trail by pack horses from the previous trek season. Karma made no attempt to go around them, calling them biodegradable matter healthy for the earth.

"At least there are no fresh ones. We are the first trekkers this season," he said, amused by my ballerina leaps over the horse dung.

By noon, we had reached a wooded plateau. We sat under a broad-leafed tree to eat the tuna sandwiches and hard-cooked eggs Karma had prepared that morning at the Swiss Guest House.

"There's a chance Lopen Pema Tshering is not the Lopen Pema I want to meet," I said, becoming more nervous as the day wore on.

"You'll know in just a few more hours, Miss Souza," said Karma, look-ing calm as ever. He handed me a mango juice box. "I guess our next place to visit depends on your meeting with this monk."

"Yes. At this point, I don't really know where else to go after this. I'll decide tonight, after I've met the lopen."

"That's fine, Miss Souza. February is low tourist season. We shouldn't have much trouble getting rooms at hotels."

Another hour's walk up and down forested slopes took us to a clearing in a valley and to the village of Ngang. We rested at a farmhouse, where the farmer's wife served us butter tea. A lama and eight gomchens, lay religious practitioners according to Karma, were chanting in the choesham, making an annual offering to the gods at the invitation of the farmer. We were invited to enter the choesham and observe. I was anxious to move on, but Karma said it would be a polite gesture for us to watch the chanting for a little while. We entered and sat on the wood floor, which was scattered with grains of rice sprinkled by the lama periodically as he chanted. The gomchens wore red capes over their ghos. They chanted from holy texts, thick stacks of loose paper between protective wood covers. They must be the kind of books Lopen Pema brought back from Tibet. At intervals, two of the gomchens blew long trumpets, two hit drums, and two played the dramyen. One young gomchen blew a *kangdu*, which, to my horror, was a human thigh bone, as Karma explained. It sounded like a horn. The chanting was rhythmic, with high and low notes, now a deep drone, now a quick succession of incantations, punctuated by the deep grunting sound of the trumpets and the sharper higher notes of the flutes, with the drums as a constant background beat. The younger gomchens, in no more than their mid-twenties, were distracted by my presence, and darted curious looks in my direction as they flipped the pages of their texts. After a while, we got up to exit the choesham. Karma put some ngultrums at the altar adorned with butter lamps, ritual cakes, and bowls of fresh fruit. I did the same, a gesture of appreciation for the host family, and a sign of respect for their practice.

Before we left the farmhouse, at my bidding, Karma asked the farmer and his wife if a woman with some resemblance of me had passed through in the last several weeks. They both shook their heads with a blank stare. If Marian had gone the way Lopen Pema Tshering had, the village of Ngang would have been a likely stop for her.

The next part of the trek was a test of physical endurance. It was an uphill climb all the way, and it was becoming harder as the afternoon progressed. We were no longer on the usual path of trekkers, but there was still a trail that Karma could make out, cutting through what seemed like virgin forests of hemlocks and firs, birches and rhododendrons. I was thankful for the bamboo cane that Karma had hewn at Ngang, chiseling it into a neat walking stick for me with his dagger, which he wore in a wooden sheaf at his belt.

"Now you see why Jicho Goemba is a monastery for monks who want to hide from the world and spend their time in prayer and meditation. It isn't easy to get to," said Karma, as we paused for breath.

"How long do monks usually stay in there?"

"It depends. There is a drubda, a meditation center, attached to the goemba. Monks go there for strict retreats, for three years, three months, and three days. During that time, they don't come out. They eat only the food passed to them by another monk."

"I hope Lopen Pema Tshering is not doing a strict retreat, else I won't get to see him," I said, adding extra weight to my already burdened mind.

The rest of the way was not as strenuous, except that, shortly before we reached the goemba, my sleeve was caught by brambles as I was weaving my way through the brush. Unable to extricate myself, I called to Karma ahead. Karma retraced his steps and managed to free my sleeve, but not without puncturing his own finger with the thorns.

Seeing him sucking the blood from his cut, I took a Band-Aid and some ointment from my backpack. As I tended to his finger, I could sense him first watching my act of ministering to him and then diverting his gaze to me. It made me uncomfortable, but I pretended not to notice.

We continued the rest of the way in silence until the last stretch, when Karma stopped in front of me.

"This is steep. Give me your hand," he said.

I put my hand in his, and he pulled me up, until we were on relatively level ground. But he did not relinquish my hand for a while after that, and I was too nervous to remove it from his grip as we trod alongside each other. Then we saw, about four hundred meters in front of us, a complex of five white buildings with brown window frames, the one in the center taller than the others, each with three levels, the broadest at the base. The top level of the tallest building was a square tower with a pointed golden rooftop.

"Jicho Goemba!" I called, finally freeing my hand from Karma's to point at the structure in the distance.

Karma nodded. He looked pleased at my apparent excitement, unaware that I was in fact having a nervous cramp over the prospect of confronting Lopen Pema Tshering. And added to that was my growing uneasiness over Karma's attention.

34

WE ENTERED A LHAKHANG in the center building at Jicho Goemba.
Four statues, two on each side, guarded the main entrance.

"The Guardians of the Four Directions," said Karma, "to protect us
from demons and all evil." Except for the Guardian of the East, who was
represented playing the flute-like dramyen, the rest looked rather wrathful and intimidating.

Inside the prayer hall, Karma performed his usual rite of veneration
in front of the center altar. We exited into a courtyard through a side entrance. Anxiously I scanned the place. The courtyard was deserted except
for two young monks, about ten or so, at a game of throwing stones. Karma approached them, and, at his bidding, they went looking for the custodian. We waited in the silence of the courtyard. After about ten minutes,
they came back with a monk who ambled leisurely toward us, making a
flip-flop sound on the concrete with his plastic slippers as he walked. He
would be in his fifties and had a wide middle spread.

Karma asked him about Lopen Pema Tshering. Without hesitation,
the custodian monk replied in Dzongkha, translated for me by Karma,
"Yes, Lopen Pema came here from Thimphu in December, but now he is in
Punakha, to attend dromche."

Karma noticed the disappointment written on my face. In fact, I was
close to tears. I was too distressed to speak, and for the first time since
arriving in Bhutan, I felt defeated. I was no longer the Ruth who could
find her twin sister. I had lost the intuition and the magic. I could go to
Punakha in pursuit of Lopen Pema Tshering, who might or might not be
Marian's lover, in my quest for a self-centered sister who had become

insensitive to the anguish she was causing. Or else, she could be dead.

While I wallowed in my dark thoughts, Karma must have been asking the monk whether Lopen Pema Tshering was returning to Jicho Goemba, and when.

"He says he's expected back here after the dromche, unless he decides to stay in Punakha longer. He says he's going to be honored in Punakha," Karma told me.

"Why?"

"For bringing back some holy books belonging to Bhutan from Tibet."

I covered my lips to suppress an involuntary gasp. Karma noticed my reaction. He thanked the custodian monk, and together he and I walked out of the goemba. Outside the goemba, I remained mute, too over-whelmed with emotion to speak.

"Ruth, we will go to Punakha. But tonight, you need some rest. I know the people at a farmhouse just ahead. We can spend the night there and plan for Punakha tomorrow." Karma sounded decisive.

"Lead the way," I said, smiling through my tears.

I followed Karma along footpaths across the buckwheat field to a farm-house about half a mile from the goemba. The farm folks there were very pleased to see Karma, who had stayed with them the other times he had been up that way. The head of the household, a tall, lean middle-aged man by the name of Ugyen, managed the farm with his wife, Ani, a fortyish stout woman with gold front teeth. The couple had two sons, the older in his early twenties, living with the family and helping his father on the farm. The younger son attended high school in Jakar as a boarding student but was home for the winter.

We were ushered into the house, passing two huge black Tibetan mastiffs in the yard with a don't-fool-with-me look on their faces. We found ourselves in the ground-level okhang. The floor was covered with straw and pine needles. Ugyen explained that animals were no longer kept in there but in an enclosed shed in the yard. A trunk ladder took us to the second level, a granary with bins all around filled with wheat. The third level was the living quarters. A good-sized bukhari dominated the center of the kitchen, whose walls had been blackened with soot before the installation of the stove. Copper pots hung on the wall above the old cooking area. A huge bin for water storage stood in a far corner, with ladles of all sizes hanging over it.

"This is a big house," I remarked to Karma.

"They are a rich family around here."

Karma helped Ugyen with the windows, shutting them by sliding panels across, to keep out the cold air of the night. The kitchen was lit by a dim bulb. Ugyen proudly explained that their home was the only one in the area with electricity, generated from a solar panel.

We sat on the floor around the bukhari, while Ani made buckwheat pancakes on the searing stovetop. A big basket of wood stood by, and every five minutes one of the sons would feed the furnace with more wood. Karma was completely at home and chatted with the family as though he were a part of it. He sat beside me on a mat, attentive to my needs, passing me the food prepared by Ani, the pancakes, buckwheat noodles, yak stew, and vegetables in a curry. Ani had prepared some chili for him, and a big piece of solid pork fat which seemed to be a favorite of his and which made me shudder. While I was given a fork and a knife, the others, including Karma, dug into the food with their hands. Ara was poured. I agreed to a sip, not wanting to be impolite. It tasted of wheat and warmed the stomach. Karma poured himself a full tumbler.

Dinner was a family affair, and we sat around the bukhari long after the food was consumed and the ara had been passed around many times. Mostly the family talked in Dzongkha among themselves and with Karma. Karma would translate for me some of the conversation. Occasionally they addressed me in limited English, but it was an effort for them to do so.

Finally, Karma hinted to Ani that I would probably like to rest for the night. Ani guided me with a flashlight to the toilet on the same floor.

"Liquid only," she said, pointing to the squat toilet in the floor boards. "Big things outside," she added, referring to the outhouse I saw on my way in. Nothing short of dire urgency could draw me past those Tibetan mastiffs to the outhouse in the night.

"This is your room," Ani said as we entered the choesham, smiling, exposing her gold assets. "Room for important guest."

The choesham contained an altar adorned with statues, butter lamps, fruit, and bowls of water. Thangkas of bodhisattvas and deities hung around the walls. I thanked Ani and said goodnight, recalling the time Marian slept in the choesham in Tashi's house, how scared she said she was. Was I walking in Marian's footsteps, reliving her every experience? I had visualized Marian on the streets of Thimphu, even *felt* her presence at the Memorial Chorten. I imagined her in her library, at the tsechu in the courtyard of Trashi Chhoe Dzong, in fact, everywhere in Thimphu that I had been. Surely Marian had to be somewhere close, perhaps within my grasp, if only I could reach out in the right direction. Unless she was dead, and it was her spirit that I was sensing.

To conserve the solar power, I turned off the light in the choesham as soon as I had changed. I kept a flashlight by the mattress on the floor, and covered myself with the blanket provided for me. Sleep overtook me in no time.

Daylight flooded in as I pushed aside the sliding panel of the window of the choesham. I inhaled the crisp mountain air, the fresh smell of newly turned earth mixed with animal manure. The sky was clear and blue. Another bright and glorious day outside. Quickly I changed into my golf shirt and safari shorts, and put on my fleece jacket.

I pulled aside the curtain hanging across the door to the choesham and emerged into the kitchen. Ani was toasting bread on the stove. I sat down on the mat beside Karma, who was already eating his breakfast of rice, spinach, and another thick piece of pork fat. He had on the same T-shirt and padded vest and river pants as the day before. I noticed how tanned he was. And robust. He must love going on treks when he could shed the traditional gho and dress with ease and freedom. Ugyen placed a bowl of warm butter tea in front of me. I was thankful when Karma offered to finish it for me. I was glad for the slices of buttered toast, though, and a cheese omelette that Ani made especially for me.

"So you're glad you came even though you didn't see Lopen Pema Tshering?" Karma asked, squinting at me, when we were on our way again. He must have sensed that the knowledge imparted by the monk at Jicho Goemba, of Lopen Pema Tshering bringing back some holy books from Tibet, was of vital importance to me.

"Yes, I'm glad I came," I said simply. Even though I trusted Karma, I could not divulge my sister's secret to him or anyone.

"I'll make arrangements for Punakha as soon as we get back to the Swiss Guest House," said Karma.

"Thank you, Karma," I said. "By the way, you said my name beautifully yesterday."

35

THE TREK BACK TO TOKTU ZAMPA was effortless compared to the outward journey. By mid-morning, we had reached Ngang. To save time, we pressed on without stopping at the village, because Karma wanted to return to the Swiss Guest House as early in the day as possible, to reserve accommodations for Punakha. Even though it was low tourist season, Punakha would be busy, he said, on account of the dromche.

We rested at the same spot where we had lunch on our way out. Ani had prepared a hot lunch stored in tin canisters that Karma carried in his backpack. I was hungry, and rice and curry never tasted so good. As usual, I opted out of the chili. Karma savored every bite of it.

After lunch, Karma packed away the utensils while I sat on the ground nursing my overworked legs. He then came over to me.

"May I?" he asked, gesturing at my legs.

I was too stunned to answer or show any sign of objection. He took my silence as consent. He knelt down in front of me and started massaging my right calf. He had big strong hands, with dirt-encrusted nails. He kneaded and squeezed with a gentle, relaxing firmness.

"I didn't know you were such a good masseur," I said, embarrassed at our physical proximity and wanting to break the silence.

"Only for my favorite customer," he said in a tone of joviality.

After a while, he gently let go of my right calf and performed the same treatment on my left. I felt the coarseness of his calluses, the warmth of his hands, but tried to concentrate on the therapeutic effect of the massage.

"Feeling better?" he asked, looking up at me after a while.

Our eyes locked for a good ten seconds, as his hands gradually slowed down their movement, until they rested gently on my calf. It was a moment when massage turned to touch, and the contact of skin carried with it emotional repercussions. I gave a delayed nod to his question. As if awakened from a stupor, he removed his hands quickly, and got on his feet.

We were quiet for the rest of the way till we reached Toktu Zampa. Neither of us made any attempt at small talk. Chimi was happy to see us, wanted to know how the trip worked out, and seemed puzzled about our reserve. He was pleased, however, about going to Punakha for the dromche.

Back in the privacy of my room at the Swiss Guest House, I wasted no time in taking a much-needed shower. I kicked off my walking shoes and socks, cast off my shirt and shorts and my underwear. My eyes wandered to the mirror, and rested on the reflection of a petite woman with high pointed breasts, a flat stomach, narrow hips, the figure of one who had never borne a child. It had been a while since I had shown such an interest in my own body.

I turned on the tap, adjusted the water to a comfortable temperature, and stepped into the shower. I felt the warm satiny flow of the water. Soothing. Relaxing. I ran soap over my neck, my shoulders, my breasts. I felt my hardened nipples. Gradually, my soapy hand reached down to my thigh. I felt a stir in my groin. Slowly I moved my hand up until it rested between my legs. My head throbbed as I closed my eyes and concentrated on the slow compulsive motion of my fingers, until my entire body pulsated with irrevocable pleasure and release.

36

FROM MY WINDOW AT THE SWISS GUEST HOUSE, Jakar Dzong loomed behind a morning mist, enigmatic and mysterious. In ordinary times, I would have wanted to enter it, if permission could be granted. But my heart was not in it, or in the many other fascinations the kingdom held. I only wanted my sister back.

Breakfast was a bowl of warm oatmeal with bread and Gouda cheese. Karma, in blue jeans and a T-shirt, came into the dining room to look for me. He had cast off his moodiness from the day before and looked his usual self, pleasant and conversational. I was relieved that we could put the previous day behind us.

"I have reserved a room at the Meri Puensum Resort for you, one of the best hotels," he said with great enthusiasm. "You'll like the view from there. I've booked it for seven days, until the twenty-fifth, so you can attend the dromche, and the Punakha serda, the highlight on the last day of the festival."

"That's wonderful," I said, not paying much attention to what the festival promised. What mattered was that I would have plenty of time to find Lopen Pema, and possibly Marian.

The road to Punakha took us through Trongsa again, but our first stop was the Yatra Factory off the highway, where women sat in front of storefronts weaving beautiful fabrics of intricate designs with yak hair and sheep's wool.

"When in Bhutan, you've got to see our textiles," announced Karma.

Knowing we would be in Punakha by nightfall, I felt I could be justified in setting aside my hunt for Marian for an hour to indulge in one of my passions, collecting weavings from around the world. The woven products were displayed inside the few stores as well as hanging outside—multicolored coats and jackets, carpets, wall hangings, shoulder bags.

"How did you know about this weakness of mine?" I asked Karma, my spirits perked up. "I love handwoven products, and these are simply amazing."

Karma looked pleased. Perhaps this was the first time since my arrival that I had shown some genuine interest in things around me. I picked out a piece of woven fabric of yak hair, in a geometric design of vibrant colors of green, orange, red, and blue.

"I could use it as a wall hanging, or make something out of it," I explained to Karma.

Karma also made a purchase. It was a beautiful shoulder bag of soft lamb's wool with a maroon design on a white background.

"This is the endless knot, one of our auspicious symbols," Karma explained, referring to the symmetrical pattern resembling a maze with no exit. Then, looking shyly at the bag, he added, "It's for you, Ruth."

"But I can't accept a gift from you," I protested. Seeing the hurt look on his face, I added, "I mean, a guide shouldn't be buying his customers presents, else he'd go broke in no time."

"I only got it for you," Karma said in a quiet voice, rather defensively.

"I'll treasure it then. *Kadrinche la*." My Bhutanese probably didn't sound too bad after all, for Karma looked pleased.

We checked in at the Meri Puensum Resort in Punakha after dark. The hotel consisted of a main two-story building and a separate five-room unit on a downward slope, where my room was situated. After freshening up, I walked up some stone steps and crossed the front garden to the main building, which housed the dining room. Marigolds, geraniums, and, to my surprise, red poinsettias were growing in stone planters along the path lit by multicolor paper lanterns. The nice cool evening breeze was balmy and soothing, and I could smell the sweet scent of subtropical air, without the humidity of Phuentsholing. No wonder Punakha, at a much lower altitude than Thimphu, was the winter residence of the Central Monastic Body. Since the trek to Jicho Goemba, I had become more aware of my surroundings. The likelihood of finding Marian's Lopen Pema seemed to have relaxed me a bit for the moment, even though the thought of what he might tell me about Marian was putting me on a new level of anxiety.

Karma, changed back into a gho, greeted me in the reception hall. Suddenly, he was my guide again, hired to take me places, a fact I had forgotten the last few days.

"You look very nice," Karma said, staring at the red and black Chinese brocade jacket I was wearing over my black dress pants. I felt heat in my cheeks. Was I subconsciously trying to impress him with what I wore?

"Aren't you going to eat with me?" I asked, having grown accustomed to sharing his meals.

"I'll eat with Chimi and the other guides," he replied quietly. "There will be other guests dining with you tonight."

"I'll see you later then," I murmured, troubled by my disappointment.

Feeling strangely alone, I entered the dining room and sat at a table for four. I was soon joined by a tall, middle-aged couple from Texas, Dan and Marge Summers, both brazen and loud. Throughout dinner, they raved about the temple they had visited that afternoon, Chimi Lhakhang, built by a lama nicknamed the Divine Madman in the fifteenth century. The lama was known for stories of how he subdued demons, spread his teachings by indulging in alcohol and sexual liaisons, and answered the prayer of childless women to become pregnant with his blessing.

"As soon as I walked in, this young monk touched my head with an ivory phallus, then a bamboo one," Marge said, breaking into a brassy chuckle. "At my age, it will take a lot more."

"He hit me with them too. I bet they're more potent than Viagra. I feel I can carry on till I'm ninety," her husband cackled.

"Don't flatter yourself," Marge drawled. Turning to me, she said, "Tell your guide to get you out there, honey, if only to see the temple and all around."

"And don't forget to get your blessing while you're there," Dan said. "Do whatever is humanly possible," he winked, "and leave the rest to the Divine Madman."

The dinner was decent. I was glad for the Chinese noodles and stir-fried vegetables, which were a refreshing change from the curries I had been getting. Marge and Dan invited me to join them for an after-dinner drink and a game of cards in the guest sitting room. I declined, citing a strong need for rest.

I left the dining room soon after and went looking for Karma. I found him with Chimi and several other guides and drivers, lounging by the side of the main building, enjoying drinks and betel nuts. As soon as he saw me, he got up and came over.

"How was dinner?" he asked.

"The food was good, but the company was not. I'd rather eat with you," I said, and added quickly, "and Chimi."

"The hotel usually gives the guides different food."

"You have different quarters too, I suppose."

"Yes," he said, "but they treat us pretty well, 'cause we bring them the business." After a pause, he added, "Actually, we're just chitchatting over some drinks. Want to join us?"

"Ara?" I asked, buying time to decide.

"No, ara is a homemade drink. We're having beer, and some harder stuff."

It was only nine. There was no television in the room, or anywhere for that matter, no reading lamp by the bedside, and I wasn't really tired, since I had slept a lot on the way to Punakha. I asked for a local beer, which Karma brought. After acknowledging me, the other guides and drivers settled back to talking in Dzongkha, leaving Karma to entertain me. Other tourists passed us and gawked a little. Marge and Dan saw us on their way back to their room. I didn't care.

"Tomorrow morning, I will go with you to Punakha Dzong to inquire about Lopen Pema," said Karma. "I hope you'll enjoy Punakha, Ruth. The festival is the main attraction, but there are lots of wonderful things around here to see."

"Like Chimi Lhakhang?" I asked, not meaning to be serious about seeing the temple where monks blessed visitors with wooden phalluses.

"Like Chimi Lhakhang," Karma said, seriously.

After a while, I got up to return to my room. Karma walked with me, his hands behind him as I had seen them many times since the first day at the airport. He took my key, opened the door, and stood on the threshold to keep the door open for me. I could feel his closeness and his warm breath smelling of alcohol as I brushed past him to enter the room. He handed me the key. Our hands touched.

"Good night, Karma."

I couldn't hear his response, as he turned to go.

"By the way," I said hurriedly, "I like the shoulder bag, the endless knot, very much. Thank you."

"You're welcome," he said, looking back at me, but I could not see his face in the shadows as he slowly started up the steps to the guides' quarters, his hands behind him.

37

DAWN UNRAVELED for me the paradise I had come to. All around, golden terraced mustard fields, scattered with farmhouses and prayer flags, sloped gently down to a river valley. In the further distance were hazy layered foothills ranged across the blushing sky like a dream. A majestic chir pine decked with a white prayer flag at its top trembled by my balcony. From the valley below came the sweet melody of a lone flute, enhancing the idyllic atmosphere. The quietude was broken by the excited yelping of some dogs coming from the hillside houses. Soon it was calm again. For a moment, I was in heaven with all that confronted my senses. Was this a conspiracy, that I was being drawn to the place just as Ulysses was tempted by the Sirens or retained in the Land of the Lotus Eaters? I had a mission here to find my sister and make my exit with her. This was not my world, and I didn't belong. Neither did Marian.

Karma came into the dining room looking for me after breakfast, dressed in a fresh red and blue striped gho. He usually wore knee-high socks reaching up almost to the hem of his gho, but that morning he had on white tights. He was indeed a Ming Dynasty hero out of the pages of a Chinese classic novel. We soon left in Chimi's jeep for the dzong, going down to the valley, then along the bank of the Punak Chhu to the confluence of the Mo Chhu and Pho Chhu. Punakha Dzong soon came into view, framed by sprouting willows and rising out of the water from the two rivers that joined to become the Punak Chhu. High white walls stretched up to decorative framed windows, higher towers, and multi-leveled white tiled roofs, dominated by an utse with a rounded golden top.

"Ruth, I have to go in first to look for Lopen Pema. You can enter the dzong when the dromche begins tomorrow, but not today, unless Lopen Pema gets you permission to see him inside." Karma picked up his kabney which was on the back seat beside me. "Wait here with Chimi."

Chimi parked the car by the riverbank. We all got out. I watched Karma putting on his kabney. With a wave, he walked toward the cantilever bridge, and went across. He climbed up a steep, wide flight of stone steps and then a wooden staircase to the front entrance of the dzong, which was guarded by two policemen. He stepped over the threshold and disappeared from view. Chimi crossed the street to a row of stores. I waited anxiously by the car, my eyes fixed across the river on the entrance to the dzong. Every time a monk appeared in the grand doorway, I hoped it was Lopen Pema, and my heart beat faster.

I felt a tug. I turned and gave an involuntary shudder. A witch woman was looking intensely at me from out of chilling, beady eyes. A vision of darkness, she was dressed in a black jacket and skirt, silver ornaments hanging from her neck, a bamboo cone of a hat pointed at the top, over long stringy black hair. She smiled, exposing a gap in her front red-stained teeth. Instinctively I stepped back. She put out a wrinkled hand and beckoned. Seeing that I was cringing from her, she extended her claw-like appendage and grabbed me by the wrist, much to my alarm, pulling me after her.

Chimi's voice rang out just then. The witch woman dropped my hand, frightened by Chimi's apparent reprimand. She backed, gave me a last look, turned and crossed the street, disappearing behind some shops.

"What was that all about?" I asked Chimi, much shaken.

"Laya woman. From northwest. Want to sell you things. I tell her go away."

"Thank you, Chimi. I was really scared for a moment."

"Laya people okay, no harm. They work hard. They come long way to dromche. Sell to tourists jewelry and bamboo hats like what they wear."

The episode distracted me from the dzong. I watched Chimi as he carefully wrapped a quarter of a betel nut made into a creamy paste with crushed lime in a betel leaf, put the concoction into his mouth, and chewed. It must taste paradise to him.

"Our cigarettes," he smiled, more open to conversation than he had ever been since we met. "Not good for us, but can't stop."

"We indulge in things that are not good for us sometimes, don't we."

"You have bad habit?" Chimi asked.

I pondered, and finally answered, "I try very hard not to. In fact, all my life, I've tried to do the right things."

"Very good." Chimi nodded approvingly.

"I don't know. Sometimes I don't even know what the right things are anymore."

Karma returned not long after, alone as I had guessed. That Lopen Pema would come with him to talk to me was just my wishful thinking.

"He's at the dzong. I asked. But I couldn't see him because he is with some visiting monks today. Tomorrow I should be able to find him for you."

"I've looked for him for so long. I suppose another day is not going to make a big difference," I said, biting my lip in disappointment. Then, moved by a sudden impulse that surprised myself, I said to Karma, "Since we won't be seeing him today, why don't we go to Chimi Lhakhang?"

38

"LAMA DRUKPA KUNLEY SUBDUED A DEMON of Dochu La and trapped it in a rock at the site where he built Chimi Lhakhang," Karma explained, as we stood to the side of a narrow dirt path to let a herd of cattle pass.

Chimi had driven us to a spot about ten kilometers from Punakha, from where we entered fields of yellow mustard blooms, pretty and shivering in the breeze. We trod along narrow footpaths bordering the fields, passing a few small villages. After mustard would come rice, Karma said, two crops a year. We hiked across more fields and up a hillock that stood out of the valley. At the top was Chimi Lhakhang, visible from a far distance below, with prayer flags fluttering all around.

For all the reputation of its founder, the lhakhang was but a temple of modest size, with a row of small prayer wheels and some exquisite slate carvings of saints along its exterior walls. A small chorten not far from the main building marked the spot where the demon was trapped. The interior of the prayer hall was decked with Tantric paraphernalia, thangkas, bells, dorjis, drums, horns, even a kangdu. Sitting in a reclining posture, his ceramic dog beside him, and with a face that could belong to one given to a life of pleasure but for his monk's robe, the statue of Lama Drukpa Kunley, lovingly dubbed the Divine Madman, dominated the center of the altar.

"He's different," I observed.

"Different?"

"He doesn't look like the other saints. He's like one of us, that human look, if you know what I mean."

Karma laughed.

"Yes, he's very very human. In fact, he was said to have known quite a few women in his lifetime."

I smiled at Karma's euphemism, used intentionally or otherwise.

While Karma prostrated, a young monk in his early teens hit my head gently with the ivory and bamboo phalluses that Marge at the hotel had boasted about. He offered me water from a brass bumpa for purification, which I ceremoniously took with cupped hands and splashed on my hair.

Outside again, Karma showed me the nearby linden tree, nicknamed the buddha tree, because the Buddha, Sakyamuni, gained enlightenment under one, he said. I asked Karma to stand under the tree so I could take a picture of him getting enlightened.

While I squinted behind my camera at Karma, adjusting the focus, suddenly I was not looking at Karma alone, but at someone else who had appeared within my range of vision, a good distance behind Karma. I froze. It was a monk, thirtyish, looking at me with cold eyes, his lips wearing a smirk. I looked up from my camera and he was gone, vanished like an apparition.

"What's the matter?" Karma asked. I had turned pale as I looked past him, my hands holding the camera without snapping a shot.

"I just saw a monk behind you, and now he's gone." I must have sounded ridiculous, to be frightened at the sight of a monk in a land where there were more men embracing the monastic life than other professions. "It's the way he looked at me, Karma, with piercing eyes," I added.

Contrary to my expectation, Karma seemed concerned and immediately scanned the grounds around us. Not seeing anyone who might answer to my description of the monk I had seen through the camera, he finally said, "Come, Ruth, take a picture of me under the buddha tree. I want to be enlightened."

We walked down the hillock by another path, and cut through more fields and villages, passing a stone hut enclosing a water-driven prayer wheel. I was enjoying the fresh air, the bucolic surroundings, and Karma's company, and soon put the image of the steely-eyed monk out of my mind.

"You have a beautiful country, Karma, so unspoiled. I would say God created this land and lives in it." We sat on a gentle slope overlooking the golden valley with Chimi Lhakhang in its center, perched on its isolated hilly pedestal.

"In Bhutan, we believe in treating everything with respect and living in harmony with the environment, with the earth, and all its blessings."

"I cannot agree more with you. I wish the rest of the world would think and act this way."

"Our attitude toward nature comes from our traditional beliefs. We respect the mountain gods who protect us. We think if we disturb the earth, its blessings will go away. That's why many of our mountains are not climbed, and most of our virgin forests are preserved."

"No matter what motivates your conservation, the outside world has a lot to learn from you."

"But people who want to climb our mountains and conquer their peaks would accuse us of superstition. Those who think leveling forests for land development is progress would say we are still living in the Dark Ages."

"The world should know better—that only when we protect our natural resources and use them with care can we continue to enjoy them for a long time." I smiled at myself, for sounding didactic.

"Still, we must seem quite backward to other nations."

"That's part of your country's charm. I don't mean just the natural beauty, although that is an essential part of it, but also the beauty of your people, and their way of relating to the world." I sighed. "Too bad I don't belong here."

"Why not?"

"Wouldn't your government ask me to leave once my visa expires?" I asked lightly. "But frankly, I don't *feel* I belong. For one thing, I am not a Buddhist, let alone your Tantric Buddhist. You don't even have a church of any kind here."

"I am very sorry about that," said Karma quietly.

"I can't live in a place where the basic freedoms are compromised."

"We may not have the democracy people elsewhere enjoy, but our people are generally happy. We trust the king, for he cares about us." Karma looked thoughtfully at me, then added quietly, "Ruth, I hope you will stay longer, to see the country, after you've found your sister."

"And you'll still be my guide?" There was a hint of flippancy in my tone.

"Yes, I'd like to show you more of Bhutan. So far, you've been too busy looking for your sister to really enjoy yourself."

"I won't be able to afford you."

"I'm not thinking of getting paid. You will be my guest." He looked earnest and flushed. "I like you very much, Ruth. I want you to stay a little longer, for me."

At last, we were no longer sending signals with looks and touches like high school boys and girls. We were talking. Somehow, the practical aspect of words seemed to have cured me of any romantic fantasizing about my guide I might have foolishly allowed myself to relish. He was not asking me to stay forever. He knew how different we were, and those differences were hard to reconcile. Marian would have said yes, live for the moment, for a moment. How could I, when there was no future for us? When we belonged to two worlds so far apart, not only in physical distance but also in our upbringing, way of life, and personal beliefs?

"I don't know, Karma. Thank you for asking, but right now, I only want to find Marian." Hurting his feelings and ruining our good relationship were the last things I wanted, yet I had no right to lead him on.

"I understand," he said, forcing a smile. "Come, let's not keep Chimi waiting."

We got up, and I followed him down the slope in silence, across the fields to where Chimi was standing by his vehicle by the side of the motor road. The clouds that had gathered since we were at the temple had started to yield a few drops. I climbed into the backseat behind Chimi and Karma. All the way back to the Meri Puensum Resort, Karma and I were quiet, probably leaving Chimi wondering what had happened on our outing to Chimi Lhakhang.

39

I HAD SEIZED EVERY OPPORTUNITY TO READ *The Jesuit and the Dragon* since Sonam at the Thimphu Public Library lent me the book. I read at the Hotel Druk in Thimphu, the Hotel Druk in Phuentsholing, and sometimes on the road as I bumped along in Chimi's jeep. And now I had come to the last pages. It was an engaging and lively account of the life of Father William Mackey, in the Kingdom of the Dragon, Bhutan. With fervour I read it, for its own merit, and for its connection with Marian. As I read on, I imagined what was going through the minds of my sister and her monk as they were reading it.

I was finishing the book in the guest sitting room at the Meri Puensum Resort the evening after the visit to Chimi Lhakhang when Karma came in. He had cast off his earlier gloom. Like most Bhutanese, he knew about Father Mackey and his contribution to Bhutan.

"What impressed me most was that Father Mackey had not attempted to convert a single Bhutanese to Christianity in all his years in Bhutan," I said. "He only wanted to help the Bhutanese people build their school system, and he did that with very limited resources. He had no ulterior motive of evangelizing."

"And that was why the Bhutanese appreciated and trusted him, including the late king. Father Mackey respected the Bhutanese people. He did not try to change us."

"That was because he saw goodness in all people," I said, busily looking for passages in the book. "He said in the book that Bhutan had taught him how to pray, and he was a better priest and a better human being because of his years in Bhutan and India."

"Doesn't his story prove to you that your own faith will not suffer in Bhutan even though there is no church to attend?"

"His case was a little different, Karma. He was allowed to say Mass in his own residence, although not publicly. I may find it harder here."

In a sense, though, Karma was right. Just as Marian was right when she said, "I don't need to get physically inside a church to do my bit of worshipping, under adverse conditions."

"So you agree with everything Father Mackey did in Bhutan?" asked Karma, as I got up to return to my room.

"Except for one. In the book, Father Mackey considered the biography of Drukpa Kunley, your Divine Madman noted for his sexual liaisons among other things, to contain spiritual teachings. Well, he was a little more accommodating than I could be—I'm afraid I don't get the carnal-spiritual connection." With that, I bade a bewildered Karma goodnight.

40

Febru ary 20th, the first day of the Punakha Dromche. The day of confrontation I had nervously anticipated, when I would come face-to-face with Lopen Pema Tshering, the monk who in all likelihood was the reason why Marian had not come home.

Karma and I crossed the Mo Chhu over the cantilever bridge, our first step into Punakha Dzong. The grounds outside the dzong were bustling with people, mostly Bhutanese in colorful ghos and kiras, but also tourists, and monks in flowing rust-colored robes. At the top of stone steps and a flight of wide and steep wooden stairs was the front main entrance guarded by a giant prayer wheel on each side of the doorway. As I paused for breath at the top of the stairs, looking at the myriad mantras painted on one of the prayer wheels, a Laya woman brushed past me and quickly grabbed the handle at the base of the barrel, turning it as she walked briskly clockwise, oblivious to me or anyone around. To my relief, she was not the woman who had accosted me the day before but a younger one, with tighter but nonetheless weather-beaten facial skin and wearing a conical bamboo hat decorated with lots of colored beads.

The first courtyard was relatively deserted. An older monk, a discipline master, according to Karma, with a well-groomed mustache and holding his whip—a cat-o'-nine-tails—playfully cracked it on the ground, as he gave orders to junior monks who were carrying wicker baskets and brass bumpas on missions of delivery. A few older men, apparently lay workers inside the dzong, were sweeping dust off the concrete grounds with dried branches of dwarf willow.

We crossed the smaller first courtyard to the spacious second courtyard which was bursting with noise and color. An army of warriors of all heights and sizes in red and black cloth uniforms, complete with red cloth caps and black cloth ceremonial boots, were marching in a circular path in the center of the courtyard. Karma explained that they were local residents dressed up as warriors of the seventeenth century. The Punakha dromche commemorated the victory of the Shabdrung Rimpoche's army over the Tibetans who invaded Bhutan in the seventeenth century. The mock army waved swords and shouted army slogans. They were obviously enjoying their role-playing and the attention of the throng of onlookers, themselves dressed in their festive best.

Like strutting peacocks displaying their plumes, the women, young and old, some with babies strapped to their backs, paraded in their richly woven kiras among the crowd, although their colors in matchings of purple and red, pink and turquoise were not exactly fashion statements by many standards outside of Bhutan. To my relief, I was not the only female not wearing a kira, for there were some foreign women dressed in tourist garb among the onlookers.

Karma took me to the main chapel, open to foreigners for the festival, and up some steps to the viewers' balcony from which I looked down to the main altar and assembly hall. Colorful ritual cakes and flickering butter lamps adorned the altar. Barefooted monks were practicing a dance on the center wood floor, their red skirts forming wide flaring circles as they turned.

"They are practicing the Black Hat Dance which will begin in an hour's time," said Karma.

Could Lopen Pema be among the dancers? He participated in the dance at the Thimphu tsechu, the dance that robbed Marian of her senses. No, he could not be performing this time. This time, he was a visiting monk, and an honored one because the Je Khenpo, the Chief Abbot of the Kingdom, had asked for his attendance at the dromche.

As if reading my thoughts, Karma said, "This is not the best time to look for Lopen Pema. Wait till the dance is over. I'll inquire then."

Karma found me a spot on the balcony, commanding a good view of the assembly hall below. The crowd had shifted from the courtyard to the chapel and hovered around the balcony. I was pushed and jostled but managed to keep my place at the rail. Meanwhile, Karma had wandered off.

The ceremony began, first with monks seated in rows on the floor of the assembly hall below, hitting drums at regular intervals and blowing trumpets and flutes. Then the dancers emerged, wearing flowing purple brocade robes with colorful, elaborate designs. On their heads were pointed, broad-brimmed black hats festooned with colorful ribbons hanging from the rims.

I was Marian, watching the Black Hat Dance, feeling the pounding of her heart as it vibrated to the beating of the drums. I was Marian, romantic and vulnerable, about to lose her heart to the best of the dancers out there, the dancers, as Karma explained earlier, assuming the roles of yogis who subdued demons and recreated life. I looked across the void above the assembly hall to the opposite side of the viewers' balcony. And, for a moment, I thought I was staring at the dreaded monk I saw at Chimi Lhakhang, smiling a sinister smile at me. I shivered. I blinked. He was gone. Probably my pumped-up imagination was tricking me again. I looked further down the rail on the opposite side and saw Karma watching the dance. His presence was reassuring.

When the dance was over, Karma came to me and together we made our way down some stairs to the courtyard outside the chapel. He told me to wait there while he looked for Lopen Pema. The crowd had thinned considerably by then. I was nervous and fidgety as I stood in the rapidly emptying courtyard, surrounded by closed doors and open entrances to passageways that led to dark recesses. Above, the balcony was deserted, with doors and windows opening into the monks' quarters. Images of the steely-eyed monk and the witch-like Laya woman clad in black crept to the forefront of my mind, giving me gooseflesh. Every footstep in the almost vacant courtyard startled me. Every creaking of a door made me cringe.

Karma returned after a long ten minutes, alone.

"I met the discipline master we saw earlier. He said Lopen Pema would be busy all day. He didn't say, but I think Lopen Pema's popularity has to do with the treasure he brought back."

"What shall we do, Karma?" Disappointed once again, I let tears flow freely from my eyes. Karma put an arm around me, and, this time, I put my head on his shoulder and cried. "I must see him, Karma. I've come this far. I'll not give up until I've talked to him."

"I know, I know," comforted Karma. "We'll come back this afternoon. We still have tomorrow, and the day after, and then the last day of the dromche, when all the monks at the dzong will parade for the serda. We will catch his attention somehow. Let's go back now to the hotel for some lunch."

I let Karma hold my hand, and we walked in the direction of the front entrance, cutting through the first courtyard enclosed by administrative buildings. There we met a monk walking toward us. He was short and stocky, walking with a sway. When we were within recognition range, he looked in my direction, and broke into a smile.

"Hello! I am happy you have come for Punakha dromche," he said in a high-pitched voice.

I studied his face for a moment, the overbite, the smile, then recalled where I had seen him.

"The airport in Bangkok! Good to see you again, Lopen," I said, puffy-eyed. "Yes, I've taken your advice."

I introduced Karma, and the monk told us he was Lopen Jamphel Rinchen. Before we went our separate ways, pushed by a sudden impulse, I asked, "By the way, Lopen Jamphel, do you know Lopen Pema Tshering?"

"Pema Tshering?" He laughed. "I've known him most of my life. We went to monastic school in Dechen Phodrang together, before he went to India. Why do you ask?"

I was heartened by my unexpected break. I told the age-old lie about meeting Lopen Pema on a train while I was traveling in India. To avoid giving Lopen Jamphel time to question for details, I quickly continued, "I heard he would be here for the dromche and was hoping to see him again."

"If you really want to see him, I can arrange meeting, no problem."

Karma and I exchanged quick glances.

"That would be excellent. I don't know if he still remembers me, but if you tell him I am Ruth Souza from Canada, he may know who I am," I said, hoping Lopen Jamphel did not detect my nervousness.

"Come back at three, and meet me here," he said. "The warriors are parading at that time. That may be best time to catch Lopen Pema."

41

K ARMA AND I CROSSED THE CANTILEVER BRIDGE AGAIN at a quarter
to three in the afternoon of the first day of the dromche. We climbed
the steps and walked through the front entrance into the first courtyard,
my eyes scanning the entire compound for Lopen Jamphel. We were a little
early, and he was not there. The courtyard was again quite deserted, for
most of the crowd were in the second inner courtyard watching the ancient
warriors parade. I could hear war chants and shouts of command. Karma
and I stood at the same spot where we had talked to Lopen Jamphel.

Three o'clock arrived by my watch. A minute passed, then two, then
five. I tapped the ground with my shoes. Twelve minutes had passed
before Lopen Jamphel appeared from a passageway at the opposite end of
the courtyard. I smiled and waved nervously to him. Behind him was another monk, a couple of steps behind him. They approached. The second
monk was tall, lean, with arresting bony facial features and a tanned complexion. I was gazing on Lopen Pema Tshering.

Lopen Pema looked in my direction. I was trembling all over, filled
with a surge of mixed emotion, a sense of accomplishment and relief that
I had found him at long last, and anxiety to hear what he could tell me
about Marian. I had a natural curiosity toward him, the monk with whom
my sister had fallen in love. But as we looked at each other in a moment of
instinctive mutual acknowledgment, all I could feel was warmth toward
the man and the consciousness of an unspoken understanding between us
that we shared someone very precious.

"Lopen Pema," I said rather formally, unintentionally bypassing Lopen
Jamphel.

"Ruth," he pronounced my name somewhat reverently, while bowing slightly in a gesture of greeting.

Tears started to form in my eyes. I was trembling. To hide my emotional outburst from Lopen Pema and Lopen Jamphel, I turned around to Karma who was standing quietly behind me, and introduced him to Lopen Pema as my guide. I had more control by then, and turned to Lopen Jamphel, who was watching us with intense interest.

"Lopen Jamphel, I do believe our meeting at the Bangkok airport was for a reason," I said with a grateful look. "It would have been hard for me to see Lopen Pema if we hadn't run into you this morning."

Lopen Jamphel wished me a pleasant time in Bhutan for the rest of my stay. He then gave Lopen Pema a friendly pat on the back and took his leave of us.

"I will watch the parade while you talk to Lopen Pema," said Karma.

I cast him an appreciative glance. I then looked enquiringly at Lopen Pema, who suggested we talk on the upper level balcony outside the monks' quarters, overlooking the second courtyard where all the festivities were taking place. It would be quiet enough up there, he said. And open enough as not to arouse suspicion, I thought.

I followed him in silence through a dark passage between the two courtyards and up a flight of stairs emerging into the balcony above the second courtyard. He stopped at a bench beside a door to one of the rooms. We could hear each other distinctively above the noise of the warriors and crowd below. We sat down awkwardly. Stripped of his initial confidence, he looked anxious. The cheerfulness that was so much a part of him in Marian's memoir was not there. He waited for me to begin.

"Lopen Pema, I'm here to look for my sister Marian. I haven't heard from her since she called me late in November from Bhutan."

"You confirm my suspicion that Marian has not gone home. At least, I am relieved that she got back to Bhutan, since she called you from here. I don't know where she is now. What did she say when she called?"

"That she would come home as soon as she could, but I don't see how she could travel without her passport. She's left it with her luggage in Thimphu." I paused. "I was hoping you could help me find her." My voice must have betrayed deep disappointment and despair.

"I wish I could. I want to find her, too," he said in a low thick voice. "I don't know why she disappeared, why she left me as she did. I am very worried about her."

So Marian left him. He hadn't changed his mind about giving up the monastic life for her.

"Marian wrote me, about you," I said.

He nodded and looked gently at me. "She told me about you, too. You're very special to her." His words brought fresh tears to my eyes. "Did she write to you about Tibet?"

"In a sense, yes. You see, she had sent me the memoir she was writing of all that happened. I found the latest chapter in the luggage she left at the guesthouse in Thimphu. It was in an envelope addressed to me, but never mailed. It was about your plan to go to Tibet to reclaim some volumes of a sacred sutra. It ended there. But I have since met the guide who took her to Tibet to look for you." I paused. He looked at the void in front, his gaze at once sad and passionate, his taut facial muscles wrought with a consciousness of deep loss. I asked, "What happened in Tibet?"

Two young novice monks and an older one walked toward us. They looked curiously at me and waved to Lopen Pema. He acknowledged them with a tight smile and said in Dzongkha, "Interviewing. Writer doing research," which he translated for me after they were gone.

I took from my purse a note pad and a pen, to look authentic. He nodded in approval.

"The trek from Paro to Phari is a difficult route. It has been closed and the Bhutanese government forbids our people to cross to Tibet. It wasn't easy for me, and I still don't know how Marian managed it, even though she had a guide. I will not talk about my experience on the trek. It's enough to say what kept me going was Marian.

"It was on the fourth day after I left Paro, before I reached the top of Tremo La, that Marian and her guide caught up with me. I could hardly believe my eyes when I saw her. I was overjoyed, but at the same time worried about her. I felt I was the luckiest man on earth, that she should risk her life to follow me. She told me the danger I was in as a monk traveling to Tibet. Dechen the guide had told her the Phari border was heavily guarded by the Chinese, and they were especially strict on monks and nuns.

"Marian asked me to change into clothes that belonged to Dechen. Her knowledge of Mandarin would be useful if we were caught by Chinese border guards, she said. She would tell them she was a Chinese originally from Guangzhou working in Bhutan and I was her Bhutanese husband." Lopen Pema gave an embarrassed smile. "She would say we crossed Tremo La from Bhutan to buy horses in Tibet, because Tibetan horses were very good, and we wanted to start a horse contracting business in Bhutan.

"Dechen led the way, and we bypassed the Chinese army post by taking a longer and harder route, overshooting Phari by about three kilometers north of the town. By then, it was almost dark. Since I would be heading further northwest to Thumpsing Goemba the next day, I decided not to backtrack to Phari for the night. Instead, I would look for somewhere close to camp. I asked Dechen to take Marian to Phari for the night. Near where we stood was a heap of rocks with small prayer flags strung between two poles at the top. I told her I would meet her again at that spot at sunset two days later, after I had obtained the holy books. Marian was upset that she could not go with me, but we both understood there was no way she could accompany me to the monastery.

"We said good-bye. I then went on my way and soon reached a field where I could pitch the small dome tent a trekking company lent me. Some nomads had camped not far from me. They must have seen my torch, for a yak herder came over and offered me a dung-fueled stove to warm my tent. He also brought some warm mare's milk. It was a cold night, and I was grateful for the stove and milk.

"When I awoke, the sun was already in the sky. I had slept longer than I intended. Before I set out for Thumpsing Goemba, I changed back into my monk's garments. I had walked some distance along an unpaved road at the edge of a grazing meadow when I saw a Tibetan fellow who had stopped his old jeep by the roadside to relieve himself. I approached him. I told him that I wanted to go to Thumpsing Goemba. He was happy to drive me there for fifty yuan. It was almost noon.

"At two in the afternoon, I reached Thumpsing Goemba. It was made up of three whitewashed buildings which seemed to have been built into the mountain. I saw a monk outside and introduced myself in Tibetan. I asked to see the lama in charge. He took me into the middle building. There, I was received cordially by Lama Ngawang Nudup.

"As we were talking, there was commotion outside. Then a monk came in with a young man carrying a backpack. To my surprise, the young man was wearing a gho. The monk told Lama Ngawang that he caught the man standing on a flower pot outside, peeking into a window of the monastery, and when the monk confronted him, he got frightened and fell, and broke the pot. The monk asked him who he was and why he was there, but he did not answer.

"I looked more closely at the fellow. If indeed he was Bhutanese, I could talk to him in Dzongkha. Then, to my utmost shock, I realized the man was in fact Marian in disguise! With her short haircut and wearing a gho, she really looked like a young Bhutanese man. I was frantic. I had no time to think. The minute she started to speak, she would betray herself. I had to make up a story in a split second. Immediately I said the Bhutanese man was my page who had accompanied me on my journey. I had left him to wait outside for me. I apologized for the broken flower pot. I explained my page was deaf and dumb as a result of a serious childhood illness. I gave my page the name Tenzing Dorji. To my relief, Lama Ngawang believed me, and told the monk who brought my page in to take him to the kitchen to get some food.

"That afternoon, Lama Ngawang presented me to the monks of the goemba at their prayer assembly."

"Was—Tenzing Dorji—with you?"

"Yes, my page was asked to be present in the assembly hall during prayer. Lama Ngawang said it would be good for him to observe the rituals, for the eyes were the gateway to the mind, especially in his world of silence. The monks were very sympathetic toward Tenzing Dorji because of his condition. We were given a room for visiting monks. There were two mattresses on the floor, for Tenzing Dorji and me.

"I had a letter from Yeshey Tulku Rimpoche requesting the monks of the goemba to give me the three volumes of the sutra to take back to Bhutan. That evening, I asked for a private meeting with Lama Ngawang. He saw me in his room. I showed him the letter from his Abbot. You should see the expression on his face, changing from warm hospitality to deep concern with some distrust. And yet, the Abbot's personal seal was there, which he could not deny.

"'Lopen Pema, this is an order of the gravest significance,' he said finally, after reading the letter several times, and deliberating over it in his mind. 'It is my duty to obey the rimpoche, who is our Abbot, and return the sacred volumes to Bhutan. This irreplaceable treasure had escaped the terrible fate that had befallen many other sacred Buddhist texts and relics during the Chinese invasion and the Cultural Revolution. However, if I hand it over to you without proving to the members of our community here that I am placing it in the hands of one who can guarantee its safe return to Bhutan at the order of their Abbot, I am not worthy to be the custodian of the treasure, or of the goemba. Therefore, Lopen Pema, I will have to submit you to a test on Buddhist philosophy. We will meet in the assembly hall at four tomorrow morning. At that time, members of our community will ask you questions to prove yourself.'"

"It must have been unnerving to be tested."

"Yes, I was very nervous about the test, and also worried about Marian's disguise. That night, when we were alone, Marian told me the reason she followed me to Thumpsing Goemba. She said she couldn't sleep the night before, after she and Dechen went into Phari. In the middle of the night, she saw from her hotel window a truckload of Chinese soldiers entering the town. She went to ask the hotel night attendant why the soldiers were there, and she was told that whenever a reinforcement of Chinese soldiers arrived in town, it meant they were on a mission to search the surrounding area, including monasteries, for anything regarded as incendiary toward the Chinese government, anything that would be considered supportive of the Tibetan independence movement against the Chinese. Marian feared for me, if I ran into the soldiers, and they found out I was a Bhutanese monk who had sneaked into Tibet. She recalled what I told her about a Bhutanese monk who went secretly to Tibet many years ago to reclaim the volumes of the sutra, and was caught by the Chinese and had disappeared since. She had to warn me, the sooner the better."

"I thought she was very impulsive and reckless to follow you from Phari when Dechen first told me about it. She didn't tell Dechen why she decided to go after you, but just sent him back to Bhutan," I said. "I guess she didn't want to detain him longer, since he was also a Bhutanese who had entered Tibet illegally. What Marian did, I could never do." I shuddered at the thought of her going after Lopen Pema alone in a strange land. "She must have arrived at the monastery soon after you got there."

"She told me she had in fact arrived at Thumpsing Goemba before me, for the bus she was on left early that morning, and dropped her off two kilometers from the goemba. The bus driver directed her to the goemba. First she changed into the gho that Dechen had left in her backpack, so that it would not seem inappropriate if she was seen with me. Then she walked to the goemba. She did not know if I was already there. She waited outside the buildings, hiding in a wooded area. She saw me arriving in an old jeep, but could not approach me then, as I talked to a monk outside the goemba as soon as I got off the jeep.

"Her plan was to wait outside for an opportunity to get close to me, to warn me about the soldiers on a search. She would then find accommodation in nearby Gyantse for the night and meet up with me at the rocks where we parted the day before. As it turned out, she was caught, but apart from the risk of being exposed by the monks at the monastery, we were happy to be together. I could not sleep that night. While I paced the floor with my beads, Marian took hers out and prayed silently with me. She stayed up with me into the morning hours. I told her to get some sleep, promising that I would wake her for the assembly. Reluctantly she lay down on her mattress, and before long she was sound asleep."

By then, it was late afternoon. The warriors' parade was over in the courtyard below. The crowd was dispersing, going home for the evening.

A child monk ran up the stairs to our balcony and spoke in Dzongkha to Lopen Pema in a breathless voice.

"I have to go, Ruth. Can you be back tomorrow?" Lopen Pema asked.

I told him nothing could keep me away. We arranged to meet again the next day.

42

L OPEN PEMA COULD MEET me only for an hour late in the morning of the second day of the dromche. We sat at the same bench on the balcony of the monks' quarters. I held my pen and notebook. To everyone who passed by, I was an author interviewing for my book on Buddhism in Bhutan.

"The test," I prompted, as soon as we had settled down.

"Yes, the test. The monks were already seated in the assembly hall when we arrived. Tenzing Dorji sat in a far corner behind Lama Ngawang across from the altar. The monks shot questions at me in all directions, on my perception of Dharma, my insight into the principal Mahayana sutras, my understanding of the Tantras. It was the toughest exam I had ever taken, harder than all the tests I took before my final commitment as a monk.

"Tenzing Dorji's presence kept me going when the questioning was hardest. She was my motivation and my inspiration. I told myself I must bring back the sacred volumes. The more determined I felt about my mission, the more it seemed the monks of Thumpsing Goemba wanted to foil it, by trying to demoralize and defeat me, to prove me an incompetent fake, to whom they could not entrust the sacred text. But to every one of their questions, I returned an answer that satisfied them. Gradually they changed from harsh examiners to approving peers, at least most of them."

"So they handed the sacred books to you?"

"Not yet. The final and perhaps greatest challenge was from a younger monk. He looked directly at me with threatening confidence, his eyes sharp as blades. First he spoke in Tibetan. 'Lopen,' he addressed me in a clear stern voice as he stood there with his arms folded, 'you've made a difficult and risky journey to take back to Bhutan this sacred text by an illustrious lama and wise scholar of the fifteenth century. What is your ulterior motive, as I assume there is one?'"

"That was so mean. He was attacking you personally."

"For a moment, I thought he could see through me and look into my mind and my heart. I thought he was about to expose Tenzing Dorji's disguise. But I soon regained my composure. He could not have known about Tenzing Dorji and me. I stood in the midst of all the monks present, quietly contemplating an answer. It was the ultimate test, for I wanted to speak the truth, without giving Marian and myself away. There was silence in the assembly hall. My challenger looked pleased, perhaps because he thought he had finally asked a question that would trap and discredit me, simple though it sounded. He stood up again, and in my dialect Dzongkha, which he spoke with a stiff accent, asked the question a second time, this time with a faint smirk on his face, and a penetrating look in his eyes that seemed to cut to the depth of my being.

"I looked in the direction of Tenzing Dorji sitting mutely in a corner, like a scared deer about to be hunted down by a predator. True, I had deceived the monks of the goemba about the identity of Tenzing Dorji, but I had no choice under the circumstance. However, I would not lie on a question that concerned my faith. Finally, facing my questioner, I answered slowly and deliberately, 'Whatever turn my life journey may take in the days ahead, my ulterior motive is to have served the monastic community and the people of my country the best I could, as I, guided by the teaching of the sacred sutras, continue to strive for the wisdom and compassion of the heart, the heart of the Buddha.'

"There was a minute of absolute silence. I was afraid to breathe. I looked at my challenger who had sat down again. His expressionless face was not betraying any emotion, such that I could not tell if my answer satisfied him or not. Then Lama Ngawang got up and went into an inner sanctuary.

He returned with the three volumes, each wrapped in a fine piece of gold brocade, and presented them to me.

"'Lopen Pema, will you do us the honor of reading the enlightened prayers of the illustrious fifteenth-century high lama?'

"The test was not over yet. He wanted to hear me read from the sutra. Carefully I unwrapped the top volume, turned over the front engraved wood cover, and proceeded with the chanting of the text in Choekey, the language of our holy books. I started out nervous, unsure of myself. Gradually, I could hear my voice becoming stronger and clearer, rising up to the second level balcony, to the four high walls of the assembly hall. As I chanted on, flipping sheet after sheet over, I was overpowered by the prayers to the Buddha and the saints, presented in the form of aspirations, and dedicated to all sentient beings. Such poetic and high-spirited outpourings from a wise and highly accomplished one. As I chanted, I felt transported to the celestial abode of the Buddha. I was carried to the ends of the universe, the limits of the heavens. I was brought to the infinite realms of the saints from where they bestowed their blessings on all sentient beings. I was filled with gratitude for having made the journey. The treasure made it all worthwhile."

As he spoke, Lopen Pema seemed to be reliving his sublime experience in the assembly hall when he chanted from the treasured volumes. "Too bad Marian couldn't understand a word. She would have loved to know what you were chanting," I said, awed by his eloquence.

"She would indeed. When it was time for the morning assembly to end, Lama Ngawang stood up and said in the presence of all the monks, 'For over three hundred years, we have been the proud and honored custodian of a very important Buddhist treasure. At the order of our venerable Abbot, Yeshey Tulku Rimpoche, we will now return to Bhutan what was once Bhutan's. We will entrust the sacred volumes to you, Lopen Pema, as the carrier of this treasure back to Bhutan, for you have proven yourself worthy today.'"

"And so the monk who questioned you last was satisfied?"

"Satisfied or not, there was nothing he could do about it, since Lama Ngawang entrusted me with the holy books. Many monks saw us off later that morning when we boarded a lorry for Phari, but he was not there."

"You were lucky the Chinese soldiers didn't show up to search Thumpsing Goemba."

"Yes, we were lucky," said Lopen Pema.

The blare of trumpets coming from the main temple signaled to Lopen Pema that he had to go. He and I arranged to meet again on the third day of the dromche.

43

"I MUST ADMIT I WAS IN THE BEST STATE OF MIND, having accomplished a task that was very difficult," Lopen Pema began, soon after we sat down above the courtyard and all the noise from the crowds and the mock army below. "As the lorry headed in the direction of Phari, I recounted to Marian how I answered the monks' questions, especially the final one. I told her she was the inspiration for my success. Seeing her in the assembly hall kept me going even when the questioning was toughest. We were sitting in the back of the lorry, so the driver could not hear us.

"'Your success meant the world to me,' she said.

"I asked the driver to let us off near the rocks with the prayer flags. Marian and I went into the brush. She changed back into her trekking clothes, and I took off my monk's robe and put on Dechen's jacket and pants. We also wore our winter coats and hats. The hats served to cover up our unusual hairstyles. This time, I put my monk's robe in a plastic bag, dug a hole in the earth with a small garden spade Marian had brought with her from Bhutan and buried the bag. She really thought of everything, even a spade. It was too late to start the trek up the mountain, so we went into Phari."

"Did you see a lot of Chinese soldiers in Phari?"

"We saw some, but they left us alone."

"They probably thought you were Tibetan. Your facial features are so similar to Tibetans'. And Marian looks all Chinese."

"Yes, they must think I was Tibetan. Still, we tried to avoid them. We got a room at the Phari Inn for the night. The manager at the inn heard me speak Tibetan and asked if I was foreign. I admitted I was Bhutanese, but told him to keep quiet about it, lest the Chinese soldiers find out. Marian brought food up to our room for dinner that night, as we wanted to avoid being seen in public as much as possible. She also bought bread and water for our journey back to Bhutan. Later, I found her crying silently as she sat on her bed. I sat down beside her, and asked her why she was sad. She just shook her head. I comforted her for a long while. We then turned in for the night, each in our own bed. We slept in our trekking clothes.

"When dawn broke, Marian looked somewhat refreshed, though swollen-eyed. We left Phari without delay, to start on our trek back to Bhutan. Dechen had left two days earlier. We were on our own. We would reverse the route we took with Dechen, taking the longer way to bypass the Chinese army post. We planned to cross Tremo La into Bhutan on the first day and camp as far below the mountain pass as we could reach before sundown. Since it was a downhill trek the rest of the way, we could probably make it to where the side trail to Tremo La joined the main route of the Jhumolhari trek by sunset of the second day. From there, the trek back to Paro would be relatively easy on the third day.

"We were going up the mountainside below the tree line the morning we left Phari when we had a close escape. We had decided to take a toilet rest at mid-morning while we were still in the wooded area. We each went in an opposite direction. I was just about to retrace my steps to where I would meet up with Marian again when I heard rustling sounds, and then I saw about thirty meters from where I was standing several Chinese soldiers walking in the direction we had come from. I was hidden behind some trees. I stood motionless. I was so afraid they might see Marian, who could not be too far from their path. But they moved on without seeing her. When they were out of sight and hearing, Marian stood up from her crouching position. She was only ten meters from where they had been. Lucky nature called at the right moment, for otherwise we would be walking directly into the path of the soldiers. They would question where we were going and might search our bags and find the sacred books."

"I'd say your guardian angels were watching over you."

Lopen Pema smiled at my interruption, and continued, "Because of my added load with the volumes, Marian was carrying the food and water in her backpack." Lopen Pema paused. "We were at the top of the mountain pass by mid-afternoon of the first day. In spite of the cold air, we were warm from the trek, feeling the heat of the sun at forty-seven hundred meters. We took a break of bread and water. It was then that Marian made the fearful discovery that she did not have her rosary beads with her. She searched her backpack frantically, but her rosary wasn't there.

"'What if I left it at the goemba?' She turned pale. 'The rosary is so Catholic. They would know we cheated them if they found it.' She was in tears.

"I comforted her, saying she could have left it at the Phari Inn, although secretly I was worried too that someone at the goemba had found it. Yet, I had to be strong, for both of us. I said to her, 'Don't worry about something we have no control of. In any case, we are leaving Tibet.'

"After that, she was calmer. We proceeded downhill, using the map Yeshey Tulku Rimpoche gave me to guide us. By dusk, we had reached a flat space about nine hundred meters below the mountain pass, which would be a good place to camp. We were already in Bhutan. I pitched the tent and lit a fire, and after another simple meal of bread and water, we crawled into the tent, into our sleeping bags.

"I stayed awake for a long time. I was still excited over my success at Thumpsing Goemba and feeling triumphant over the monks' approval. I had no idea when Marian fell asleep. I probably drifted into sleep before she did. It was the seventh day of November, and another cold night."

A young monk came up to Lopen Pema, and said the Lam Neten from Wangdue Phodrang Dzong had arrived and would like to see him. Lopen Pema told the monk to say he was at an interview and would be honored to meet with the Lam Neten that afternoon. Their conversation conducted in Dzongkha was again translated by Lopen Pema after the monk had gone on his way.

"Word gets around. Everyone wants to know what happened in Tibet. It's become an open secret with the monastic community. On one hand, it is illegal to go to Tibet. On the other hand, the monastic community is very excited about the recovery of the missing volumes. The government is not asking questions."

"You've given something very valuable to the monastic community in Bhutan. I understand they are going to mention your achievement formally in the dzong."

He shrugged his shoulders.

"I don't care for the honor in others' eyes. But my motivation was in part a selfish one nonetheless. I did it not just for my karma, but for the self-gratification of having accomplished something worthwhile. My sin is pride, and I am paying for it. If I hadn't gone on this mission, I wouldn't have lost Marian." He paused and sighed. "Going back to my story, we had plenty of time the second day of our journey back. About five hours of downhill hike would take us to somewhere near the junction of the side trail and the Jhomolhari main trail. Marian woke up looking flushed and forlorn, and beautiful. I asked if she was ill. She said she was not.

"I told her when we got back to Thimphu, I would ask for permission to leave the monastery. Then I would apply for my passport and my no-objection certificate to leave the country. I was determined to give up the monastic life for her.

"Marian said when we returned to Thimphu, she'd look into the technicalities of getting me to Canada. She was soon herself again, and I was happy to see her so. We took our time that day. We were like a pair of butterflies fluttering free in the wilderness of nature. We had the whole space to ourselves, up there on the slopes of the Himalayan foothills. We joked and laughed as we made our way downhill, pausing to rest and eat the bread and crackers that were all we had for food. That day was the happiest day of my life.

"I was glad for the trekking clothes Marian brought along for me, for even though we were in Bhutanese territory again, it wouldn't look right for a monk to be in the company of a female traveling companion."

"The time you were together must have meant so much to Marian."

Lopen Pema nodded. "To us both. She said, 'If only we could stay up here longer, if only we could capture this moment for eternity.' I told her in Buddhism we believed nothing was permanent. She said, 'Then we should live from moment to moment and enjoy every second we have together.'" He laughed. "She then told me Christians too were taught not to place too much importance on things of the world, for they were impermanent. 'It's all about first things first, and about letting go,' she said."

Another monk came by and spoke to Lopen Pema in Dzongkha. The monk cast a curious glance at me. The sight of me scribbling seriously told him we were on official business.

"He was reminding me about the briefing for the serda at five this evening," Lopen Pema said, turning to me. "I hope you are coming to the Punakha serda tomorrow. It's a unique experience."

I asked him what it was. He said the Punakha serda was the highlight, the grand finale of the Punakha dromche. On the last day of the dromche, after a re-enactment of the Bhutanese army's strategic deployment which defeated the Tibetans as they laid siege to Punakha Dzong, a procession of the monk body to the riverbank would follow. There, the Je Khenpo would throw oranges into the river, to commemorate the Shabdrung's act of throwing a sacred statue, which was a much-coveted relic, into the river, to stop the Tibetans from further invading Bhutan for the relic.

"We finally reached the paved trail that led to Tremo La from the main trek route. We walked easily along the trail until we reached its junction with the main trek route. To avoid any group that might be catching the tail end of the trek season, we crossed several shallow streams over log bridges and rocks and finally came upon a small clearing, with a flat space just enough for the tent. Marian liked the spot.

"That night, in the tent, Marian ran her fingers over my face. I remember distinctly what she said: 'I want to feel your face in the dark. I want to see you in my mind's eye, so that in years to come I will remember how you look now.'

"It was strange that she should say those words to me, as if she would not be seeing me more. But at the time, I did not give it much thought. I was overwhelmed by the physical and emotional intimacy we enjoyed that night. But I remained faithful to my vows." At this point, Lopen Pema covered his face in his hands. When he finally raised his head, I noticed he was crying. "I must have fallen asleep some time in the night. When I awoke, it was broad daylight. I opened my eyes, and stretched my arm to gather Marian to me, but all I could feel was emptiness. I called her name. There was no answer. My first thought was she had gone out into the woods to relieve herself. I looked up contentedly at the domed ceiling of the tent, while I waited for her return. Ruth, if I had gone out to look for her then, I might have found her. But I was not alarmed by her absence. Because we had unzipped our sleeping bags and spread them over us the night before, I was not conscious while I was lying down that hers, which had been on top of mine, was missing. I waited for some twenty minutes before I sat up. It was then that I realized her sleeping bag and backpack were gone. Where the backpack had been were some biscuits and water.

"I was frantic. I took my backpack, which held the holy books, and went looking for her, calling her name the whole time. I was like a wild animal that had lost its senses. My first thought was that something bad had happened to her. But if so, would she have taken her backpack and sleeping bag with her? I combed the hillside, cutting through mud paths and dense forests. After about two hours of fruitless search, I returned to the tent. I sat down inside the tent, trying to gather my thoughts and keep a cool head. I then noticed a piece of paper left on the floor of the tent, near where her head had been."

Lopen Pema pulled out from an inner pocket of his vest a folded piece of paper, and handed it to me. I looked at the words which were in Marian's handwriting. I read them aloud:

"Now we see but a poor reflection as in a mirror; then we shall see face to face. Now I know in part; then I shall know fully, even as I am fully known." I looked up at the Lopen. "It's from Corinthians, on love."

"Corinthians, on love?"

"This is a verse in St. Paul's Letter to the Corinthians in the Bible," I explained. What Marian left him was one of the three verses she had marked in the Bible I found in her luggage at the guesthouse.

"I have thought of those words often, her last words to me," said Lopen Pema. "I have kept them here, close to my heart." He patted his breast pocket. "They have sustained me through this ordeal of losing her. She was so affectionate up to the moment before I fell asleep on our last night together. She had wanted me to leave with her all along. She loved me."

"The workings of the heart are often beyond reason. Marian has always been ruled by her heart. No matter what triggered her to leave you, she still loves you, perhaps more than you know."

"I hope I will find her."

"And if you find her, what will you do?"

"I'll give up my life as a monk and go with her."

"Maybe she doesn't want you to do so."

"But she told me she loved me. She had wanted me to go with her to Canada. She is one treasure I will not give up." Looking at me, he asked, "What will *you* do if you find her, Ruth?"

I thought for a few seconds, then replied, "Before I came to Bhutan, I would have said that if I found her, I would handcuff her and not let her out of my sight until I had her home. Now that I have seen your country and its people, and met you and heard your story, I am tempted to let her be. She should do whatever her heart dictates. Your account has told me that her disappearance was a conscious act of her own will. She must have a very good reason to go into hiding. Still, I'm worried about her, even though her phone call in November proved she made it back to Thimphu. Why hasn't she written or called again?"

It was late morning. The warriors below were lined up in rows in the courtyard, with great variances in height, like a makeshift militia, while their generals walked up and down to inspect. The crowd was enjoying the ceremony. After all, no sons and husbands were really going to war.

Before we parted, I asked Lopen Pema if he knew a man by the name of Tenpa Norbu. At the mention of his name, Lope Pema flinched.

"Tenpa Norbu is the monk at Thumpsing Goemba who asked me the last question. Why do you ask?"

His revelation was most upsetting. "Tenpa Norbu called me in Toronto from Bhutan, and he was most likely the Tibetan monk who went to the Thimphu Public Library and the Pelri Guesthouse, asking about Marian in November."

Lopen Pema looked worried. "I haven't told you this, but he found Marian's rosary at the goemba, on the floor under her mattress, the day after we left Thumpsing Goemba. I knew he came to Bhutan. He went to see Yeshey Tulku Rimpoche at Trashi Chhoe Dzong. I also ran into him in Simtokha Dzong. That was when he told me he found the rosary."

"My God!"

"He said after he found the rosary, he told Lama Ngawang his suspicion that we were frauds. Lama Ngawang sent him to Phari to look for us, but luckily we had already left. He must have asked about us in Phari. The manager at the Phari Inn, seeing he was a monk and presumably to be trusted, might have told him there was no Bhutanese monk with his deaf-mute page, but a Bhutanese man with his Chinese wife, which would further rouse his suspicion. He is a sharp fellow. In any case, not finding us, he returned to Thumpsing Goemba and asked for permission to go after us and the treasure in Bhutan. He was afraid to cross the Tremo La on his own without a guide, so he took a longer way south, crossed a different mountain pass into Bhutan's Haa district, then made his way to

Thimphu. He arrived in Thimphu on the eighteenth of November.

"He went to see Yeshey Tulku Rimpoche at Trashi Chhoe Dzong. Luckily I happened not to be at the dzong that day. The rimpoche told me about it afterwards. Yeshey Tulku Rimpoche is still the Abbot of Thumpsing Goemba even though he no longer resides there. The rimpoche told him the three volumes of the sutra had been safely returned to Trashi Chhoe Dzong."

"At least he knew you weren't a fake then."

"You'd think he would be satisfied, as long as the volumes of the sutra were safely returned to Bhutan. But not Tenpa Norbu. He wanted to expose my page—and me."

"It looks like a case of personal vendetta," I said. "Did he tell Yeshey Tulku Rimpoche about his suspicions concerning your page?"

"I think he did, but the rimpoche did not tell me the details. The rimpoche simply said he dismissed any suspicion of his as far-fetched and ridiculous."

"I think the rimpoche is behind you all the way. To him, all that matters is that you brought back the holy books," I said. "By the way, is the rimpoche here for the dromche?"

"No, he is at Trashi Chhoe Dzong in Thimphu. His health is not good, and his advanced age makes it difficult for him to travel."

"When did you see Tenpa Norbu at Simtokha Dzong?"

"The twenty-second of November, a few days after he went to see the rimpoche."

"That was the day he called me in Toronto the first time, asking for Marian."

"He must have called you after our unpleasant meeting that day."

"What happened?"

"I was shocked seeing him at Simtokha Dzong. First, he told me how he got into Bhutan. Then he dangled Marian's rosary in front of me and said, 'I have lived by the rules of the sangha all these years. I have fought successfully against temptations of the flesh. But you came into our monastery with someone whose identity was questionable, made a fool of me and all my fellow monks at the goemba, took a treasure that had been in our safekeeping for centuries to Bhutan, and now they are honoring you as a hero here.'"

"He's jealous."

"Whatever the reason, Tenpa Norbu would not let me off so easily. I denied all his accusations, and left him rather unceremoniously that day."

"It's obvious he suspects Marian to be Tenzing Dorji, and he's determined to catch her in order to expose your relationship with her." Just then, I was more fearful for Lopen Pema than for Marian. "That was probably one of the reasons Marian went into hiding."

"Soon after my unexpected meeting with Tenpa Norbu at Simtokha Dzong, I asked for permission to go to Jicho Goemba in Bumthang, on the excuse of preparing to go into a strict retreat, but more to avoid further confrontations with him. He told me he was staying at a goemba near Simtokha Dzong." Lopen Pema was thoughtful. "Actually, I shouldn't be worried if Tenpa Norbu finds Marian in order to expose me, as long as he doesn't do her any personal harm. In fact, I should then thank him for finding Marian. I love her and I am ready to submit myself to the humiliation and punishment, as long as I can eventually be with her."

"Marian would never want you humiliated and punished for loving her. She loves you more than you can imagine." Then, a chilling thought came to mind. "What does Tenpa Norbu look like?"

"He's about my age, tall, lean. He has an intelligent but severe face. But it's his eyes you cannot forget, the way he looks at you in a sharp, cutting way as to make you very uncomfortable."

"That's our man," I murmured, shuddering involuntarily. "He's here."

"Pardon?"

"The Tibetan monk I've spotted watching me a couple of times since coming to Punakha is Tenpa Norbu. He's in Punakha."

"To be expected," Lopen Pema said, nonetheless looking disturbed, but soon regaining his composure.

"Do be careful, Lopen." I extended my hand and he shook it. "I am very glad to have met you. Whatever happens, I wish you peace and fulfillment. May you always make the right choice."

"Thank you, Ruth. When you see Marian, as I know you will, tell her I love her. Tell her I still want to leave my monastic life to be with her. Tell her to give me some sign."

"I will convey your message if circumstances allow."

"Goodbye, Ruth. *Tashi Delek.*"

"*Tashi Delek.*"

I walked down the stairs to the courtyard below, filled with a strange sense of gratification. After all, how often does anyone get to share with a Buddhist monk a deep dark secret of forbidden love? Not once in most lifetimes.

44

MARIAN'S DISAPPEARANCE was in all likelihood a self-imposed exile. Still, I worried about how she was surviving out there, hiding from the immigration authorities, from me who wanted her home, from Tenpa Norbu who in all likelihood wanted to use her to bring down Lopen Pema, and from Lopen Pema who would give up his monastic life for her. There was also the mystery of her sudden change of mind. What happened in Tibet that caused her to leave Lopen Pema when she had wanted him so desperately? Without her passport, she could not have traveled far. And always, there was that gnawing fear that something had happened to her since her last phone call to me in November.

Karma ushered me through the crowd to a good viewing spot by a flag-pole at the bottom of the steps leading to the main entrance of the Punakha Dzong. Before long, the warriors emerged from the dzong through the double doorway and marched down the red-carpeted steps, followed by the generals, distinguished by their fancier outfits and hats, who mounted horses waiting at the bottom of the steps and rode off down a road leading away from the dzong. A commotion was caused when one of the generals fell off his horse as it galloped away.

After the last general had mounted his horse, the jarring sounds of trumpets and drums heralded the procession of monks. Monks filed out of the dzong and descended the center steps. A path was cut out for the monastic procession down the road to the river bank. Trumpets and drums continued to be played by monks coming out of the dzong. Those holding more important positions wore ceremonial robes of rich bright colors, complete with golden feather-crested hats. Child monks carried ornamental chests and vessels, which Karma said held important relics. He pointed out the Je Khenpo in his saffron robe under a yellow canopy held over him by a monk. Colorful victory banners decked the line of procession.

I recognized Lopen Jamphel Rinchen and the discipline master whom Karma and I had seen the first day of the dromche. Then I saw him, Lopen Pema Tshering, in his red robe and shawl, taller than most of his peers around him, imposing as a monk, handsome as a man. Excited, I waved to him and was disappointed that he did not see me in the crowd, so strong was my sense of kinship with the man my sister loved. My eyes followed him until I lost him in the rest of the procession.

When the last monk had left the dzong, the crowd followed the procession down the road. Many crossed the suspension bridge. Karma held my hand, and I was glad he did, for I was anxious not to lose him. We crossed the bridge and walked along the riverbank to a sandy beach across from where the Je Khenpo would throw oranges into the river.

Karma and I sat on the beach by the water's edge. As the Je Khenpo threw oranges into the river, some young boys, naked to the waist, dived into the cold water to retrieve them. I felt Karma's arm around me, and I leaned against him, finding comfort in his closeness.

With the conclusion of the Punakha serda at noon on February 24th, the festivities of the Punakha dromche came to an end. The crowd that had watched the casting of the oranges into the river dispersed. Karma and I walked along the riverbank in the direction of the busy intersection. We did not see Chimi or his jeep in the parking field across from the dzong. Karma told me to wait there while he looked for Chimi.

This time I saw the Laya woman coming toward me, grinning and exposing her blood-red teeth like a predator's that had just made a kill. On my own, I stood my ground, ready for a confrontation. Instead of beckoning or tugging, she handed me a piece of paper folded twice. I took it reluctantly, not wanting to look inside. She pointed a long dirt-trimmed nail at the paper. Was she trying to tell my fortune with some cosmic symbols drawn on the paper? I unfolded it with suspicion but not without curiosity. My heart beat faster and my head throbbed. Inside the folds was a seed from an Indian bean. Other than Lopen Pema, there could only be one person who would speak through the seed of an Indian bean. Instinct told me it wasn't Lopen Pema.

"Where is she?" I asked the Laya woman.

As if she understood me, she started walking away, giving me a hand signal to follow her. Briskly she walked, and closely I followed at her heels. Soon we had left the busy parking area by the river. We went behind the stores facing the river and the dzong, and came to a mule track skirting the hillside. *Marian, at long last.* Just when I least expected to see her. The Laya woman led me on, to a decrepit shanty off the path. She stopped a few meters from it and indicated with her thumb for me to approach it, grinning complacently. Stealthily, my heart pumping and my head pounding, I walked up to the shanty and knocked on the half-shut door. No answer. I pushed it open. The door hinges gave a nerve-wrecking creak. It was dim inside for the lack of a window, but my eyes soon adjusted to the faint lighting, and I found myself staring at an empty space.

"Marian!" I shouted, hoping that she would materialize before me. But all was silent and vacant.

Frustrated and disappointed beyond measure, I turned and faced the Laya woman who had followed me to the door.

"Where is she?" I asked, gesticulating with my hands.

The Laya woman gave me a baffled look. She pointed to the interior of the hut and started talking in her dialect, gesturing and shrugging her shoulders. After a while, I came to the conclusion that she had expected the person who told her to take me there to be waiting inside, and she could not understand why the shanty was empty.

Pointing to the hut and then to my face, I was able to ask the Laya woman to describe the one who was supposed to be in the shanty. I gathered that it was a woman, about my height, with short hair just reaching to the ears. She then pointed at my face and nodded. So she looked like me. I needed no more proof that it was Marian.

I thanked the Laya woman. Feeling let down though I was, I gave her two hundred ngultrums for her trouble. My greatest consolation and relief was the knowledge that Marian was alive. I soon found Karma and Chimi waiting for me at the parking area beside the car.

"Karma, she's alive! She's close by!"

I told Karma about the Laya woman and the empty hut. We went back to look again. We scanned the ground near the shanty. Not a sign of Marian. She had obviously intended to wait for me in that hut, but someone or something must have scared her away.

45

KARMA AND I HAD REACHED an unspoken understanding, since our outing to Chimi Lhakhang, that I was not about to let our relationship go beyond that of friends. We must also have recognized that the attraction was there, the stirring of the heart to cross over to the realm of lovers, however loose that definition might be.

That night, when Karma walked me back to my room in the separate complex of the resort, he did not take his leave after we had said goodnight at my door. Perhaps he was hoping the recent developments in my hunt for Marian had softened me and changed my mind about him and me. Indeed, Karma was a physical presence I found hard to resist, a threat to my judgment that could not be denied. But soon I would have to leave Bhutan. Nothing could come of any attachment we might allow ourselves to develop. He must have had a few romantic liaisons with his clients in times past. I was probably not the first on his interest agenda. Nor would I be the last. Slowly I turned my back on him after removing the key in the lock, avoiding his eyes, not to reject him but to protect myself from letting hell break loose. I went into my room, leaving him standing outside. Gently I closed the door on him.

I couldn't sleep that night. I kept thinking of my recent near encounter with Marian. Why had she not met me in the shanty? Was there fresh danger that kept her from me? I planned to stay in Punakha a couple of days more, for Marian might try to connect with me again if she was still in the area.

I was proven correct soon enough. The morning after the Punakha serda, as I was finishing breakfast of hot oatmeal and toast, Karma came into the dining room with a packet, a white nine-by-twelve-inch envelope. There was no sender's name or address. But as soon as I saw my name scribbled on the envelope, I knew it was from Marian.

"Who delivered this, Karma?"

"A young fellow left it at the reception desk early this morning. I didn't see him."

"This may lead me to Marian." My voice trembled with excitement.

I returned to the privacy of my own room. On the balcony facing the terraced mustard fields and farmhouses on the slopes, I sat down in a wicker chair, opened the sealed envelope, and took out its contents.

46

Near Punakha
February 24, 1999

MY DEAREST RUTHIE,

Most sisters and friends would begin their letters by inquiring into each other's health, when they have not been communicating for some time. Mine will not be different, especially since I have been thinking of you and Dad every day, although it may be hard for you to imagine with my long absence. I hope this thesis of a letter will set your mind at ease as far as my well-being is concerned.

I have been staying in a farmhouse on the outskirts of Thimphu for some time. The first time I saw you was February 11th, when you went to the Memorial Chorten with your guide. I had gone to the Memorial Chorten a few times lately, but never on auspicious days. I felt especially close to Pema when I was there, although I was always careful not to run into him or Tenpa Norbu, who was looking for me. The day I saw you, I wore a kira like I usually do, so as not to stand out. I went up to the third floor. I got scared when I heard footsteps coming up and hid behind an altar at the far end. Whom did I see but my own sister! I was shocked and happy. I wanted to run to you, hold you in my arms, and cry my heart out. But your guide was there, and I had become very distrustful of strangers lest they betray me to Tenpa Norbu. He probably already knew you were in town, since word gets around easily when a foreigner arrives. He could be trailing you, in the hope of getting through you to me. Nothing misses that hateful creep. My hasty appearance before you could mean running right into Tenpa Norbu's trap. So I stayed hidden where I was, while you descended the stairs and left the chorten. I figured as long as you were in

Thimphu, I could get in touch with you somehow.

The rest of that day, I remained in Thimphu. That evening, I waited near the Hotel Druk, hoping to see you going in or out, as that's the hotel where most visitors stay. Sure enough, I saw you and your guide hauling my two suitcases into the hotel! I knew then that my belongings were in safe hands. Still, I refrained from going to you at the hotel that night, for fear Tenpa Norbu might be lurking somewhere close by, using you as a bait to catch me.

I went into Thimphu again two days later, on February 13th. I called the Hotel Druk from a phone booth, asking for you, but was told you had left with your guide for an undisclosed destination.

I suppose, having read the last installment of my story that was in my luggage, you would know about Pema's intent to cross Tremo La into Tibet to claim the missing volumes of the sutra. Why hadn't I mailed that chapter? It was an honest oversight on my part. I had run out of stamps and intended to mail it at the post office. Knowing you, I am sure you must have talked to Tashi Campbell and learned from her that I followed Pema to Tibet the day after my work contract ended. I realized the night before I left for Tibet that I had forgotten to mail the last installment. I decided not to mail it after all. I would be back in Thimphu in ten days, hopefully with Pema and the sacred books, and would tell you the whole story then.

Tashi must have also led you to Dechen, my trek guide. He must have told you we caught up with Pema before crossing Tremo La, that we got safely to Tibet. The next link in the story must have come from Pema himself, whom I know you interviewed during the Punakha dromche. I came to Punakha for I heard from the family I was staying with that Pema would be honored at the dromche for bringing back the holy books from Tibet. I also figured you would be here for the festival—one of the big events of the year. I needed to see you. With the thick crowds at the dromche, it would be harder for Tenpa Norbu to catch me with you, even if he had followed you here. I blended well into the crowd in a kira. I saw you and Pema talking on the balcony. You would never dream I was watching you both as he probably related to you how he retrieved the sacred books. Ruthie, how I wanted to appear before the two of you, the two persons I love more than myself, and to tell you both so. Several times, I had taken a first step toward you from the crowd in the courtyard, but every time I pinched myself to remind myself why I had left Pema. I was able to hold back.

In order for you to understand why I left Pema, let me tell you my side of the story from the time we were at the monastery in Tibet.

Pema had not slept a wink the night before the test. I stayed up with him for a long time and prayed. His eyes were wide with fierce concentration the next morning. There was an intensity on his face that I had not observed before. It scared me.

He said before we left our room that all depended on the outcome of that morning, all that mattered to him. To us, I corrected him. His face softened, and immediately I kissed him for luck. He squeezed my hand firmly, and we walked out of our room as a monk and his deaf-mute page. We entered the assembly hall. I was as nervous as Pema, perhaps more so, for he looked calm and composed, although he must have been feeling a strong turbulence inside.

Pema must have told you all about the test, but I want you to see the whole picture from my vantage point. After group chanting for some twenty minutes, the head lama spoke. Then the monks bombarded Pema with questions in turns, each standing up and gesturing with his hands as he spoke. My heart ached for Pema. How I wished I could stand there beside him, and we would brave the onslaught together. But to each question he had an answer, standing up and also using a lot of hand movements. The monks were nodding at his answers. I felt relieved that he seemed to be gradually taking control of the situation, and I was very proud of him. Most of all, I was happy for him, for I could see as the testing progressed that he was proving his worth to his peers at the goemba, and to himself. I was sure they would hand the holy books over to him.

Then came the last question. Pema looked pensive, and, for a moment, I thought he wavered in his new confidence. His questioner, who was Tenpa Norbu, spoke again, in a firm voice and a challenging manner. Pema looked across the room in the direction where I sat. Our eyes met for a split second, before he averted his gaze and turned his head back toward the assembly. Then slowly, with great clarity, he spoke. Surprisingly, it wasn't a long answer. The head lama deliberated for what seemed an eternity, then rose and disappeared into an inner room, only to re-emerge shortly with the three wrapped volumes of the sutra.

Pema received the books with both hands and bowed reverently to the head lama. But it wasn't over. The lama had apparently asked him to read from the sutra, for Pema sat down again, proceeded to unwrap one of the volumes, and started chanting from its pages.

He began slowly, sounding a little unsure. Then gradually as he flipped the sheets, his voice grew stronger and louder. It resounded across the assembly hall, rhythmic with high and low notes, at times haunting in its drone, other times exciting in its urgency, until he reached a crescendo of incantations, vibrating with intensity and rapture. It was music to my ears even though I could not understand a word. I could tell the sutra must embody the high-spirited prayers of an enlightened mind. And all the while, there was a glow on Pema's face which seemed to have radiated from his inner being, an expression of ecstasy, both triumphant and humbling. He must be reliving his sublime experience in the Ajanta caves. *Standing there, in the darkness of the cave, lit only with light from the entrance, and surrounded by images of the enlightened ones I aspired to, I had an intimation of entering their realm, or at least tottering on the threshold of it, looking in.* It was as if all his life he had been working up to that climactic moment when he read from the sutra. All else seemed insignificant.

Then the head lama spoke again. This time I was sure the treasure was won. Pema looked like one who had gone into battle, uncertain of its outcome, and emerged victorious. I sat in the corner, watching his tri-umph. He was the man of the hour as the monks congratulated him. But not all the monks. Tenpa Norbu, who questioned him last, looked grudg-ingly on.

I did not tell Pema what happened next, before he and I left Thumpsing Goemba. It has remained a secret until now, Ruthie, and let it be a secret forever between us. Later that morning before we left the goemba, Pema was outside, talking to the monks and basking in his glory, while I packed our belongings hurriedly in the room he and I had shared the night before. We should be on our way, as there was no knowing if and when the Chinese soldiers might show up to search the goemba. As I was about to exit the room, a monk appeared in the doorway, blocking my way. He entered the room and immediately closed the door, locking it. It was Tenpa Norbu.

He talked to me apparently in Dzongka, all the while with a sneer on his face. I showed no reaction to what he said, from lack of understand-ing of the language rather than not being able to hear. Then suddenly he switched to Mandarin, "Let me repeat in Mandarin, in case you are lying that you are Lopen Pema's deaf and dumb Bhutanese page, Tenzing Dorji. I have watched you carefully. I noticed that your eyes followed the tingling of bells and the beating of drums in the prayer hall. Yours were not the reactions of one deprived of the sense of hearing."

I tried hard to remain calm, as though what he said had no impact on me because I could not hear. Then, coming close to me and cornering me against a wall, he brushed my cheek lightly with the back of his fingers and said in Mandarin, "I have also noticed the smoothness of the skin on your face and hands, unlike a man's, and—and is it my imagination that this bulky clothing hides the sinful shape of a woman?" Without another word, he felt my breast through the folds of my gho with one hand while he pushed back my forehead forcefully with the other, tilting my face up to meet his. He kissed me long and hard. He pushed himself on me while I fought him desperately. Then as suddenly as he grabbed me, he released his hold, stepped back, and, breathing heavily, turned and ran out of the room like a mad animal.

I was totally shaken when I joined Pema at the front entrance of the goemba. Lama Ngawang and many monks were there to see us off, but Tenpa Norbu was not there. I was in a hurry to leave, expecting Tenpa Norbu to appear any minute to expose my disguise. But he did not show up, and we soon boarded the lorry. I was extremely relieved that he did not expose me and disgrace Pema then. He was obviously in a bad shape himself when he left me, and not in a position to face his peers. As we left the goemba, he could be fighting his own demon in some dark sanctuary of the monastery. I was determined not to tell Pema what happened. It would distress him immensely. I had to put that very unpleasant incident behind me and focus on Pema's glory.

All the way to Phari, Pema told me about the test and how he answered some of the questions. Above all, he talked about the last question, how I inspired him to speak the truth, without giving us away: yes, to have served his country, and to continue on his path toward his enlightenment, no matter where he would be.

The rest of the evening, and well into the next two days on our trek back to Bhutan, Pema was rapturous, riding on a high note of triumph. I didn't think it was a question of ego, although I must say his wasn't suffering at the time. What I saw was something deeper, something to which he had blinded himself, and to which I had blinded him.

I am not sure of the exact instant of my revelation, if you could call it such. Was it at Pema's testing by the monks at the goemba, or was it when he read from the sacred sutra, that Ajanta moment? Or when the head lama finally declared him the worthy carrier of the treasure? Perhaps it was the sum of all those. By the time he brought up our future on our trek back, his plan to give up his monkhood and apply for permission to leave Bhutan, I had come to the cruel realization that, as much as I desperately loved and wanted him, Pema would find his fulfillment and happiness not by spending his life with me in Canada or anywhere else, but by living out his vocation as a monk in Bhutan. The dawning of that revelation was utter hell to me. You may think it was temporary madness that made me leave him whom I loved more than life, but what kept me determined was my strong conviction that, by leaving him, I could only love him more. I had been the wool over his eyes, preventing him from seeing himself clearly. I would not stand in his way to find his true self.

And I had to act quickly, to clear Pema's path to ultimate happiness, before it was blocked by evil. Tenpa Norbu had cast a dark shadow over me, his repulsive touch, his loathsome breath, his hateful sneer, and, above all, the fear that he could use me to expose Pema and put him to shame, the immediate shame of being stripped and whipped in front of his peers, and the lifelong shame from which he would not be able to escape, no matter where he might be. I must not let Tenpa Norbu find me.

On the third morning after we left Thumpsing Goemba, while Pema was still sleeping, I looked at him one last time in the faint glow of dawn, whispered "I love you," and slipped quietly out of the tent where we had lain all night in each other's arms. I saw him showing you a piece of paper at the dromche. It must be the verse from Corinthians that I left him. However he interpreted it, from his Buddhist point of view, he should know my love had not diminished, only entered a higher realm of understanding, that what we had was but a reflection of a greater love.

Back to the moment when I left Pema asleep in the tent. With my backpack I made my way to the junction of the paved trail to Tremo La and the main trail of the Jhumolhari trek. I was like an animal running from danger, afraid that Pema might catch up with me, but more afraid of myself, for my heart was dying for him, telling me to turn around and go back to the tent. I had to fight with all my might that inner voice, which was like a devil tempting me, gnawing at my will. As I put distance between him and me, tears were washing my face like torrential rain, so that I could not see clearly where I was going.

I had studied Pema's map the day before, and made a mental picture of the general direction I was to go, in order to return to Paro. I stayed on the main trail heading for Paro the early part of the morning, for it would be a while before Pema would realize I was gone. I would have had a good head start by then. The trail was easy, a gentle forested slope. Then I saw the river, the Paro Chhu, on my left, and knew I was on the right track. I stayed on the southern bank of the river, to avoid the army post that Dechen and I had to bypass on our way out. I went farther into the forest, away from the river. Just as I thought I had lost my orientation, I saw rice fields in the valley ahead, a farmhouse, and a chorten that Dechen and I had passed. I knew I had successfully bypassed the army checkpoint. It was early afternoon. Pema must have been wild with anxiety over my absence by then. He must have looked everywhere in the vicinity of the campsite for me, then come to the conclusion that I might have gone on ahead without him. He was probably coming after me.

I dared not rest. As I kept on walking, I ate some crackers I had brought along from Paro, not out of hunger but for energy, to keep me going. I had to find somewhere to sleep, but not along the main trail, for Pema would easily find me if I stayed on the trekker path.

I continued away from the river but was careful not to wander too far from its south bank. It was getting to be late afternoon, and I was becoming anxious. The idea of spending a night alone in the wilderness frightened me. I plowed on.

Just before dusk fell, I saw a small white, square stone structure ahead, on a gentle slope where trees had been cleared. It was an open chorten, containing a big prayer wheel once turned by a stream. The stream had dried up and the prayer wheel lay defunct. A wooden ledge about twenty inches wide encircled the prayer wheel inside the chorten. I climbed up and sat on the ledge, leaning against a corner. Wrapped in my down jacket and sleeping bag, and elevated from the dampness of the ground, under the roof of the chorten, I fell asleep as fatigue overtook me and darkness enshrouded the earth.

Next morning, I was stiff and achy from sleeping in that far-from-enviable position. I had to hurry on though. I made my way back to the Paro valley, again avoiding the marked trekking trails. The dark ruins of Drukgyel Dzong loomed in the distance, eerie and mysterious. I drew near and passed the dzong. I came close to a farmhouse. In the yard by the house was a raised cage with wooden bars, inside which was a dog. I knew why it was kept there, for Tashi and I had once passed by such a cage imprisoning a dog, and she had told me the dog was rabid, such as the one that killed her father. I soon crossed over to the north bank of the Paro Chhu on an old cantilever bridge, and came upon rice fields with some farmhouses close by.

One further blow was the loss of my rosary. I had discovered it was missing after Pema and I had left Phari on our way back. Could it have fallen out of my gho? I dared not think of the consequences if it was picked up by someone at Thumpsing Goemba. What if Tenpa Norbu got hold of it? I prayed I had dropped it somewhere on the way back to Phari, or left it at the Phari Inn after we got the treasure.

I knew that the best places to hide, until Pema gave up looking for me, would be farmhouses where no one knew who I was, and where hospitality was the norm. The farmers would also appreciate a supplement to their frugal income in the form of payment I would give them for board and lodging. I approached one of the farmhouses.

Fortunately for me, the teenage daughter of the farm couple spoke some English, having learned it at school. They were happy to provide me with a roof. I offered them three hundred ngultrums a day for my room and board, which they considered to be an exorbitant sum. I said I was a writer who wanted to experience farm life in Bhutan firsthand.

This was the first of two farmhouses I stayed at in the months after I "disappeared". For a week, I shared with the farm couple and their daughter their three meals, sitting on the floor around a bukhari stove in the kitchen, eating their curries and rice with my hands, and drinking their ara. I slept in their choesham at night, surrounded by thangkas and statues. I watched the woman weave with a backstrap loom. By the end of the week, I grew restless for news of Pema, whether he had returned to Thimphu with the treasure, how he was accepted for bringing the missing volumes home, and what his plans were for the future. Above all, I was anxious about how he was coping without me. I said good-bye to my hosts and made my way to Thimphu, hitching a ride in a car bound for the capital city. It was the seventeenth day of November. My visa had expired two days earlier.

I stayed with another farming family on the southern outskirts of Thimphu, at the opposite end of the city from Trashi Chhoe Dzong. The farmer, Dawa, and his wife, Deki, were very kind to me. Dawa spoke some English, but Deki knew very little English. I told them my name was Annie (easy for them to pronounce) and that I was a writer doing research on Bhutan. Whether they believed me or not, I had no idea, but they seemed satisfied with my story. After all, three hundred ngultrums a day was a small fortune to them. I told them not to talk to anyone about my presence in their house, giving the reason that my visa had expired. I had left the kira Tashi's mother gave me with my luggage at the Pelri Guesthouse, but Deki lent me one of hers. I helped Deki with her chores, learned to cook Bhutanese above the bukhari, and make ara from fermented wheat.

About that time, most of the monks from Trashi Chhoe Dzong were going to Punakha for the winter. I was anxious to know if Pema was going there too. I craved news of him, and yet I could not let him find me.

I also wanted badly to connect with you. On November 25th, I walked five miles into Thimphu and called you collect from a public phone across from the Pelri Guesthouse. I was desperate and worried when you told me Tenpa Norbu had called you from Bhutan and asked for me. That day, after I had called you, I tried to phone Kesang, the manager at the guesthouse, hoping to retrieve my luggage, especially since my passport and the incriminating last chapter of my memoir were in it. But believe it or not, soon after I dialed the guesthouse, I saw Tenpa Norbu outside the front entrance of the guesthouse. He had traced me there. Kesang's voice came on at the other end of the line. I spoke his name, but I was too scared that Kesang might lead Tenpa Norbu to me, so I hung up. Tenpa Norbu was a dark force with which I had to contend, from which I had to protect myself, but more so Pema. I must never let him find me.

I stayed with Dawa and Deki for over two months. I wrote you a letter filling you in on all that had happened since I left for Tibet. I asked Dawa and Deki's thirteen-year-old son to mail the letter in Thimphu for me, but I came upon the unmailed letter in his room in mid-January! He had apparently spent the postage money I gave him. I updated that letter and this time Dawa took it to town to mail, but you must have left for Bhutan by the time that letter reached Toronto.

You might question why I hadn't come home all this time. The immediate excuse was that I still needed to get my passport from the guesthouse, and I had been afraid to go near it, with Tenpa Norbu lurking by. But I could have found a way to get the passport back, such as enlisting the help of the UNV, Marvin Coe. Looking into my heart, I am reluctant to leave Bhutan, because I will not be coming back again once I leave. I love this place. I love treading the soil Pema treads, breathing the air he breathes, walking under the same clouds that glide over him, looking out to the prayer flags that are a constant sight in his eyes.

Until I came to Punakha, I had not seen Pema since I left him on the trek back from Tibet. I did not know if he was at Trashi Chhoe Dzong in Thimphu after he returned from Tibet, but the consciousness that he could not be too far from me sustained me through the unbearable ordeal of losing him. I did not intend to stay on forever in Bhutan. I would leave and go home as soon as I knew Pema was going to be fine without me.

Ruthie, I faltered at times in my conviction that Pema's ultimate happiness was in living out his religious calling as a monk. In such moments of doubt, I questioned what right I had to decide for him what was best for him. Why was I inflicting so much pain on him whom I loved more than myself? Why was I making it so difficult for us both when we both wanted to spend our lives together, loving each other the way we wanted? Was I condemning him to the life his parents had chosen for him by depriving him of myself? Then I thought of his Ajanta moment in Tibet, that sublime experience, the radiance that emitted from his inner being as he read from the sacred sutra. You had to be there to understand. I understood, and so I stood my ground.

I stayed in Dawa and Deki's house until last Thursday, when I came to Punakha. I saw a monk talking to a local by the suspension bridge to the Punakha Dzong. It was Tenpa Norbu. I was not too surprised. Luckily, he did not see me.

I saw you in the parking lot across from the Punakha Dzong the day before the dromche. How I wanted to go up to you and hug you. But for fear of Tenpa Norbu, I could not show myself to you in public. I was able to enlist the help of a Laya woman. I pointed to a shanty up the hillside behind the shops facing the river and the dzong. With hand signals and body language, I asked her to take you there, where I would meet you. I hid behind a lorry across the street to watch her going up to you. But that day her efforts were thwarted when your driver frightened her away.

On the day of the serda, I was in the crowd, watching the casting of the oranges into the river, in fact, not too far from where you and your guide were. I saw you sitting on the beach, your head leaning against his while he had his arm around you. You looked so perfect together. I was so happy for you that I started to cry. Luckily I saw the same Laya woman I had asked to help me. This time I asked her, using hand signals as I did before, to give you a seed of the Indian bean and to take you to the shanty on the hillside, across from the parking lot, where I would be waiting.

At the conclusion of the serda, I walked with the crowd back to the main part of town, on my way to the shanty. But I was becoming careless.

When I got close to the bridge, whom did I see crossing it from the dzong to the town-side but Pema. I was completely flustered by the sight of him. It was too late for me to turn away. Our eyes met in one heated moment of recognition. In that instant, all my penned-up yearning broke loose. It was as though a tidal wave of passion was hurtling me toward him. Oh Ruthie, I wanted so much to run to him, cover his face with my kisses and tears, and let the whole world condemn us if they would. He was probably thinking similar thoughts, for he broke into a run, and hurried across the bridge toward me, trying to get around the crowd in his path.

Perhaps it was his sudden swift movements that slapped me back to reason. At that critical moment of a lifetime decision, I turned and ran from him. The crowd was his biggest obstacle as he tried to catch up to me. I ran as fast as I could away from the town and the crowd. Soon I had left them behind. I came to a streamlet and crossed it on a small plank bridge. I stopped and turned around. I was crying, my heart pumping hard, my head about to explode. Then I saw Pema coming up until he reached the bridge. He stopped. He had to cross it yet. We stood on opposite banks, looking at each other, a thousand words flowing silently between us in the chasm that was keeping us apart, our eyes locked in the intensity of that eternal moment, my heart overflowing with love for him.

A voice crept into my head. *Don't deprive him of the chance to decide for himself. Let him choose.* I prayed. I hoped. And I prayed. And I hoped.

A lifetime followed.

Finally, with one last tender look at me, Pema turned and walked slowly the way he had come, without looking back.

Ruthie, I have never been more in control of myself as now. My encounter with Pema yesterday was my toughest and final test. I had hoped yesterday at the plank bridge that he would cross over to me. Life would be so much easier then. As it is, I console myself that I have not lost Pema, nor have I given him up. My love for him has only been elevated to a higher level. At last, I am free, as I believe he is too.

I am also finally ready to go home.

We should not attempt to meet in Punakha, knowing Tenpa Norbu is here. When you return to Thimphu, please book a ticket for me for Toronto; best if we can fly home together. You will probably be staying at the Hotel Druk when you get back to Thimphu. I will connect with you there in the next couple of days.

I'm ending this letter with one of my favourite verses from Corinthians:

. . . if I have a faith that can move mountains but have not love, I am nothing.

Tashi Delek!

Hugs and kisses,

Marian

47

I WAS ONE OF THE KEY PLAYERS in the drama of Marian's life, and perhaps that was why she ended her thesis of a letter to me with one of the three verses she had marked in her Bible, a wisdom for me as much as for herself, from St. Paul, a lama in his own time, a saint for eternity.

When I finally replaced Marian's letter into the envelope, I had read it three times, pondered over every sentence, mulled over every scene. I looked at my watch. It was three in the afternoon. I emerged from my room and went looking for Karma. I found him and Chimi at a game of *doegor* in the yard behind the servants' quarters, each trying to hit a stone placed at a distance with another stone, with the concentration of kids at computer games.

"I'm sorry I took so long," I began. "I needed the time."

"Is she okay? Do you know where she is?" Karma asked, leaving Chimi to his pitch.

"Yes, she's okay. She's asked me to book an air ticket for her to go home. I'm so relieved now. When can we go back to Thimphu?"

"I suggest early tomorrow morning. It may be a bit late to drive back now."

"That's fine," I said. "I really like it here." Then a thought hit me. "Karma, since we're still here, I'd like to see Lopen Pema one more time. Can we go down to Punakha Dzong and try our luck?"

"He left at the break of dawn for Bumthang. He is entering a drubda," Karma said with no uncertainty. "I found out while you were reading Marian's letter."

"This means he'll be in meditation for a long time," I said, gripped by intense disappointment, recalling what Karma said about the drubda before.

"Three years, three months and three days. Detached from the outside."

"I'll miss him. He will not be the same when he comes out."

"A holier man," said Karma, nodding.

Yes, Pema's mind would be free from the memories of people who had meant something to him if only for a short time. Silently, I wept for Marian, for the loss of her one great love, when I ought to have been rejoicing for her, and for Lopen Pema.

"I won't see him again," I murmured.

"I have something for you, Ruth, a big consolation."

"It had better be big."

Karma looked secretive but pleased with himself. "Come sit down and I'll tell you a story." He took me by the hand and led me to the patio chairs at the front of the main building.

"When you told me that the Tibetan monk who had asked about Marian at the library and the Pelri Guesthouse could be the mysterious Tenpa Norbu who telephoned you from Bhutan, I began to be careful in case he was still in Bhutan. It wouldn't be difficult for him to find out you were in Thimphu, since it's a small town and we don't get many tourists. I was afraid he might follow you to get to your sister, for whatever the reason. My instinct had never been more correct." Karma was apparently enjoying his own tale. "I saw a monk loitering just outside the entrance of the Hotel Druk when I left the hotel the evening after we took Marian's suitcases from the guesthouse back to the hotel. I saw the same monk again the next day outside the hotel when I came by to take you to meet Tashi Campbell at the Swiss Bakery."

"You know, it could still have been my imagination, but the first night I was in Thimphu, when I was walking back to the hotel after a stroll through the town, I saw someone standing below the clock tower, someone who

212

could be watching me. It was a bulky form. It could have been a monk in a robe, though at the time that idea did not occur to me."

Karma nodded and continued, "When I came by the Swiss Bakery after your lunch with Tashi, I saw the monk again pacing near the southern traffic circle. When you said you would walk to the library by yourself to find Sonam, I decided I would stick around, as you might say, to make sure you were safe. Sure enough, the monk followed you to the library. He was stalking you the whole time you were in Thimphu. I didn't think he would harm you, though—he had no reason to—but I believed he was hoping you would lead him to your sister."

"That was why you and Chimi were so secretive when we left the hotel for Phuentsholing the next morning, trying to shake him off my scent."

Karma nodded. "And same with going to Bumthang. Well, he was at the Punakha dromche."

"I know. I believe he was the creepy monk I sighted at Chimi Lhakhang and possibly at the Black Hat Dance at the dromche. Marian in this letter I just read said she saw him in Punakha. That was why she couldn't get close to me. You see, Marian knew Tenpa Norbu, and she had good reason not to let him find her." I could not tell Karma more, and he did not ask.

"This morning, while you were reading Marian's letter, I went into Punakha. I saw our man just outside the Punakha Dzong. I confronted him, to put an end to this nonsense."

"You did?"

"I asked if his name was Tenpa Norbu. Was he taken by surprise! He was stunned by my sudden question, but admitted he was. I asked him why he was stalking my client, Ruth Souza. He was tongue-tied, as you would say. Then he invited me to sit down under a tree. He told me he was from Thumpsing Goemba in Tibet, and about Lopen Pema's journey there to bring back the three books of the sutra, which raised several questions about Lopen Pema and his deaf-mute page and guide Tenzing Dorji. He looked severe, like a policeman relentlessly carrying out his duty. I was able to address all his questions by telling him the story of Tenzing Dorji. Now do you want to hear it, Ruth?"

"Yes, I want to hear the story of Tenzing Dorji," I said, bewildered.

"Tenzing Dorji was a deaf-and-dumb fellow whom Marian Souza befriended while she was working in Thimphu. He would wait outside the library for her to finish work and walk her home sometimes. They had formed a close friendship. Before Marian left Thimphu to go on her travels following the end of her work contract, she gave Tenzing Dorji a backpack which had belonged to her. It would be something useful to him, and also remind him of her.

"Now Tenzing Dorji had crossed Tremo La before to bring horses back from Tibet for a horse contractor. Lopen Pema Tshering had heard about him. He asked Tenzing Dorji to go with him to Tibet across Tremo La, as his guide and page. Tenzing Dorji was happy to oblige, since it was for a good cause, would help him accrue good karma, and, besides, he had not much else to do. However, on their return from Tibet, Tenzing Dorji did not go back to Thimphu with Lopen Pema. He got on a bus bound for Eastern Bhutan where he had some relatives. Lopen Pema has not heard from him since."

"Good story," I said, seeing a new side to my guide. "But how did you know all this about Tenzing Dorji?"

"You were the one who told me all about him, Ruth."

"I was?"

"Yes. You see, Marian had written to you about him while she was in Thimphu. Then when you were interviewing Lopen Pema during the dromche, for the book you are writing, the lopen told you about his trek to Tibet to bring the missing volumes of the sutra back, and about his page Tenzing Dorji. You realized what a coincidence it was that both Marian and Lopen Pema knew the same young deaf-mute fellow, Tenzing Dorji."

"Yes, I told you all that, didn't I," I echoed, following his drift. "Tenpa Norbu found something at Thumpsing Goemba after Lopen Pema and

Tenzing Dorji left, something that would be harmful to Lopen Pema's reputation. Did he say anything to you about it?"

"You mean the rosary beads? Yes, Marian must have left her rosary beads inside the backpack when she gave it to Tenzing Dorji, without either one's knowledge. It must have fallen out of Tenzing Dorji's backpack at Thumpsing Goemba."

"Oh?"

From out of the front pouch of his gho, Karma produced the red beads of a rosary, Marian's rosary.

"How did—?" I was dumbfounded, and, yes, utterly relieved for Marian and Pema.

"Tenpa Norbu gave this to me. He said, 'Take this to Ruth Souza. I don't think her sister intended it for Tenzing Dorji when she gave him her backpack.'"

"Wonder what he thought of your story," I murmured. I could not reason why Tenpa Norbu played along with Karma's concocted tale, in spite of his certainty, unknown to Karma, that Tenzing Dorji was a woman, and in all likelihood Marian. What made him return the rosary?

"Is it important what he thought? A smart gambler knows when to quit, even if he guesses his opponent is just bluffing." Karma looked pleased with himself. "After he heard Tenzing Dorji's story this morning, he said to me, 'You have just given me the answers that I need, to account for Tenzing Dorji to my superiors in Tibet. I thank you.'"

"One thing still puzzles me. How did Tenpa Norbu know to go to the Thimphu Public Library in the first place?"

"Tenpa Norbu said he found a plastic label in the room shared by Lopen Pema and his page at Thumpsing Goemba and, not knowing English, took it with him to Thimphu. He showed it to people on the street. Someone told him it said "Marian Souza, Thimphu Public Library," and directed him there."

Marian and her carelessness!

"Does Tenpa Norbu know Lopen Pema is entering a drubda?"

"It was he who told me about it. He saw Lopen Pema leaving Punakha Dzong at the break of dawn today. After Lopen Pema was gone, he asked at the dzong for Lopen Pema, in order to find out where he was going, and was told Lopen Pema had left for Bumthang to enter a drubda for a strict retreat. Tenpa Norbu also told me it was time for him to return to Tibet. He said he crossed Gori La from the Tibetan side to Haa on the twelfth of November, barely missing the snow. Yak herders at the border showed him the way. He came that way because he would not have survived Tremo La without a guide, he said, even though Gori La meant a much longer distance for him to travel on both the Tibetan and Bhutanese sides. He had permission from the head lama at Thumpsing Goemba to stay in Bhutan until spring, when he could cross the pass again. Even as I speak, he is heading out to Haa, to await crossing Gori La back to Tibet at the first chance."

"Oh, Karma, I'm so happy he's going back to Tibet," I said, nursing Marian's rosary in my hand, happy beyond measure that Tenpa Norbu would be carrying the secret of Tenzing Dorji's true identity to his grave. "I still wonder what caused his change of heart. There had to be more to it than your story of Tenzing Dorji."

"He said he witnessed an unusual drama yesterday that began at the cantilever bridge to Punakha Dzong and ended at the small plank bridge further upstream. That, together with Lopen Pema going into three years of meditation, was a sign for him to leave Bhutan."

"What drama?"

"He didn't say. One thing he said was 'I cannot stand in anyone's way to nirvana.'"

48

WITH MY MISSION TO FIND MARIAN ACCOMPLISHED, I was more relaxed than I had been in a long time. That night, my last night in Punakha, I requested that Karma have dinner with me in the dining room of the Meri Puentsum Resort. He was pleased to oblige. We picked a small corner table. Most of the guests who had come for the dromche had left that morning. I ordered a French red wine for the two of us. I was able to truly enjoy my dinner that evening. Not that the food was any different from the usual fare, but my heart was light, and for the first time, I felt I was dining not in the company of my guide or travel companion, but of someone I wanted to be with, to whom I could not express fully my gratitude.

After dinner, Karma and I made our way to the guest sitting room of the main building, to have coffee. Chimi soon found us, and reported some problem with the car. Karma left with him, promising he would return.

Feeling alone and idle, I looked around the room. It was furnished with redwood chairs padded with cushions covered in woven fabrics of traditional designs, much like the piece of yak weaving I had bought at the Yatra Factory in Bumthang. A wet bar stood in the corner, decked with bottles of hard liquor. The walls were scattered with beautiful painted stencils of auspicious designs, the lotus flower, the wheel, and the endless knot.

A young woman came into the sitting room, a baby in her arms. She looked Asian. I recognized her as a guest at the resort. We nodded at each other. Soon after the woman had settled in the sofa across from me, the baby started to cry. The woman unbuttoned her blouse and held the baby to her breast. The baby stopped his cries as his small mouth found its target quickly. Soon, her husband entered the room, and sat down beside her. He put his arm around her while the baby sucked at his source of sustenance. She turned her face toward his, and they kissed. Feeling heat in my face, I looked away.

Karma returned. He looked relieved that they finally got the car started. A battery problem, he said. Chimi would start it early the next morning, with a boost if necessary, and keep it running for a while before we set out for Thimphu.

"Karma, let's go," I whispered, anxious to return to the privacy of my room. "I'm tired."

Karma probably noticed the flush on my cheeks. He must think it was the wine, or else the sitting room was too warm for comfort. Once outside, I took in deep gulps of the cool fresh air. Karma took my hand and guided me down the steps leading from the front yard of the main building to the lower building where my room was. It was dark on the path lit only with lanterns. We reached the bottom of the steps and stopped outside my door.

"Thanks for your company tonight. I really enjoyed the dinner," I murmured, as I fumbled for my room key in my purse.

I felt him close behind me. My hands shook. I could not find the key. I turned to him, and my face almost touched his. This time, I did not shy away. I closed my eyes, and before I knew what was happening, we were smothering each other with kisses, while he held me in a tight breathless embrace. His hands firmly groped the small of my back. Finally extricating myself, I fished for my key again. This time, I found it. With a trembling hand I gave it to Karma, who unlocked the door and opened it. I went inside, pulling him in after me.

49

WE LEFT FOR THIMPHU on the morning of February 26th. What I had failed to appreciate on my way to Punakha, the flora, the light green terraced rice fields, the wild red rhododendrons and occasional white ones, the spruces and hemlocks, even the migrant road workers along the highway, I was appreciating this time. Somewhere on the side of the road, where a herd of cattle were grazing in the field, a cow was licking the face of another cow, perhaps a bull. The sight was a first for me. Such harmony among animals.

We crossed Dochu La. I joined Karma and Chimi in shouting out "*Lha Gyel Lu!*" I was still dazed, yes, stunned, by all that had happened in the last twenty-four hours. It was as if I had taken a panacea that was therapeutic and liberating. The euphoria would die down, but for the moment, I was indeed on top of the world.

We stopped at a small café beyond Dochu La, called Karma Café.

"Named after me," said Karma, smiling. "In Bhutan, you can't go very far without meeting a Karma."

"I like the name. It's—"

"Buddhist?"

"Yes, and it's non-fatalistic. It's saying you've got free will, to choose how your life is going to turn out. I like that."

"Not only do we get to choose how this life is going to turn out, we determine what our next life will be by what we do in this life. Everything we do in this life is for our karma, good or bad."

"I don't believe in reincarnation, but I agree with your Buddhist view of cause and effect. You reap what you sow. That's Christian too," I said.

"You see, we're not that different," Karma said. There was deep tenderness in his eyes.

We reached Thimphu at three in the afternoon. Karma checked me in at the Hotel Druk. The receptionist gave me a note. It was from Marvin Coe.

February 25, 1999

Dear Ruth,

I just heard from Marian. She sounded well. If you are back in Thimphu, call me at the Pelri Guesthouse in the evening at 413490, or at the Department of Public Works during the week between nine and four at 454872.

Sincerely,
Marvin Coe

I called Marvin immediately. Yes, Marian phoned him the day before, he said, and she sounded okay. No, he did not know where exactly she was.

"She said she'd been in touch with you. I understand she's planning to leave Bhutan with you. She sounded very regretful, though, that she would be leaving this country. I told her I could look into work for her here through the UN or other organizations. The fact that she's already here puts her at an advantage, since there'll be no traveling expenses for the hiring organization to pick up."

"What did she say?"

"Much as she wanted to stay, she said she had to leave. After she called, I thought about the Montessori School here in town. I know the director and they are in need of English teachers. Marian may be a good candidate."

Karma reserved an air ticket for Marian on Druk Air to leave Bhutan for Bangkok the same day as I, March 2nd. I then called Air Canada and booked a ticket for her to be on the same flight as mine from Bangkok to Toronto. I was living up to Dad's expectation that I would bring Marian safely home.

That night, Chimi went home to his wife and children. Karma walked me back to the Hotel Druk after dinner in town. Below the clock tower by the hotel, we embraced. He would stay with me at the hotel if I let him, but I was firm with him, and with myself, and I asked him to return to his home in Thimphu for the night.

"Karma, what we had was spontaneous and memorable," I said, "but let's not make it harder for us to part."

Next morning, Karma was waiting at the hotel when I went down for breakfast. I wanted to say good-bye to Tashi Campbell, but Karma said she might have left for Sherubtse College in Kanglung in Eastern Bhutan. Early March was the time the new term started. Still, we walked up Norzin Lam in the direction of the Memorial Chorten, and past the chorten to the house where Tashi lived with her mother.

Karma was right. I had just missed Tashi by a couple of days. Choedon welcomed us into the house. She led us upstairs to her kitchen and served us butter tea and sep. By the warmth of her hospitality, I gathered she didn't know about Tashi's desire to go to Canada after she graduated from Sherubtse College.

"Have you found your sister?" Choedon asked with concern as soon as we sat down on a mat on the floor. Tashi must have told her that I was in Bhutan looking for Marian.

"Yes, I've heard from her. She loves Bhutan so much she has stayed longer than she should, but she's going home to Canada with me."

"I am glad she is safe. I don't blame her for liking this country. This is a paradise, no war, no crime, no begging on the street, no drugs. Our poppies grow wild in the fields and nobody picks them for bad drugs. We may not have much, but we are happy," said Choedon, looking contented and proud. "Oh, I almost forgot, Tashi left you her address at Sherubtse. She had a feeling you would stop by." So saying, Choedon retrieved a small, unsealed envelope from her room and handed it to me. My name was scribbled on it. I took out the note which simply bore Tashi's address in Kanglung. Below the address, she wrote: "Write me if you have news of Marian. Good luck, Tashi."

"I have one other place to visit," I said to Karma over lunch at the Swiss Bakery. "The public library. I have a book to return."

Karma and I found Sonam at the library. He asked about Marian as soon as he saw me. I gave the same answer I gave Choedon.

"I just want to drop in to say good-bye." Taking *The Jesuit and the Dragon* out of the wool bag that Karma got me, I handed the book to Sonam. "You may not know it, but you have done me a great favour, Sonam, in lending me the book. It has helped me understand my sister better."

That evening, Karma and I attended a performance of folk singing and dancing in the high school playground. A few men in uniformed ghos and wearing white headbands played various musical instruments, the dramyen, the yangchen, the flute, drums and bells. The combination of their sounds was like the continuous gurgling of a clear mountain stream, with not many variations of notes, but nonetheless pleasing and soothing. Then the dance troupe emerged from the school building, teenage girls from the village in uniformed black kiras with white blouses and peach jackets. They sang and danced to the music, keeping a moderately slow rhythm, tapping their heels, swaying their bodies, and gesticulating with their hands.

Karma gave me a translation of their songs. *With joy we welcome our honored guests. We wish the rays of heaven which glitter with the spiritual power of the gods to shine on this beautiful world.* Various numbers described the joy of the people meeting on happy occasions, like the warmth emitted from a clear sky, and expressing their hope to meet again under similar circumstances. Friendly ambience radiated from the dance and song, happiness and goodwill reflected on the faces of the audience, and harmony pervaded among all sentient beings. The concluding song and dance was the *Tashi Laybey*, intended to wish those present good fortune and success. The dancers formed a circle and invited the audience to join them in the dance. Karma went in with me. *May the blue heavens and the radiant sun shine on us, and bless us with all that is good.*

"Going round and round in a circle signifies that the dancers will meet again and again in future times," whispered Karma behind me.

I was crying.

50

MARIAN FINALLY CALLED ME at the Hotel Druk on February 28th, two days before we were scheduled to fly out of Paro. She had returned to Dawa and Deki's farm outside Thimphu, in case Tenpa Norbu was back in Thimphu.

"Marian, forget Tenpa Norbu. He is history. No, I didn't kill him off. He is now in Haa, waiting to cross back to Tibet when spring comes. He's not looking for you anymore, and he's not after Pema anymore," I blurted in one breath.

"And Pema?"

"He has entered a drubda in Bumthang to meditate. Will be there for three years, three months and three days. He'll be holier than thou when he comes out." I regretted immediately sounding flippant.

That afternoon, Marian and I met at the Hotel Druk. We cried into each other's shoulders for a long while. When our talking began to make sense, Marian asked, "When is our flight out of Paro?"

I did not answer her immediately. When I did, it was with the gravest decision.

"Marian, Marvin Coe told me the other day he could probably get you something here, so you can extend your work visa, if you wish."

Marian looked at me for a long moment, studied my face carefully, then slowly a faint smile formed on her lips, which grew broader as she continued to look me in the eye.

"What about you? I mean, what will you think if I stay?"

"I'm happy if you are."

Marian was a picture of bliss. "I love you so much, Ruthie!"

Then, from my purse, I took out her rosary. "This is for you from Tenpa Norbu."

"What?!"

I proceeded to tell her the story of Tenzing Dorji as Karma told it to Tenpa Norbu.

"By the way, did you have a label with your name and the library's on your backpack?"

"Why, yes, I made different labels with the new label maker I got for the library. I made one for my backpack, a red one. I remember peeling it off the first night I went into Phari with Dechen, to avoid suspicion, and I put it inside my backpack."

"It probably fell out when you were packing at Thumpsing Goemba, in your hurry to leave after Pema got the books. Tenpa Norbu found it and it led him to the library."

"Good thing I didn't even miss it! Imagine having one more thing to worry about." Marian was laughing.

I told Marian all that had happened between Karma and me.

"I'm very happy for you, Ruthie. You're finally listening to your heart. Remember I once said I wanted to hook up a wire from your heart to your head?" Marian looked more excited than I ever was about my relationship with Karma.

"And I had often asked you not to just go with your feelings."

"I got mad with you so many times for acting big sister. I once said I was sorry I was in the womb with you for nine months, remember?"

"Don't I remember!" We laughed, reminiscing. Then I said more soberly, "When you wrote that you were in love with Pema, I was mad that you were giving your feelings full rein again, and, in so doing, also messing with the emotions and life of a monk. But what I have learned about you, and what you are capable of, since I came to Bhutan, has only filled me with awe and respect. I cannot ever live up to you. And I'm so proud you're my sister." My voice broke as I ended in tears.

"Hey, why so serious? Be happy!" Marian gave me a bear hug, and I hugged back. Then she said, "Remember we were dreaming of a title for the memoir I was going to write before I came to Bhutan? I have a title for it now."

"What is it?"

With the jubilant look of one about to make a grand announcement, Marian articulated slowly and clearly, "The Heart of the Buddha."

Marian hoped I would stay on in Bhutan but did not attempt to persuade me. Karma and I planned to leave for Paro that night, so that we could have the next day, which would be my last day in Bhutan, to hike up to the Taktshang Monastery. Marian would go with us to Paro to see me off. But she would wait for me at the Paro Druk Hotel, so I could have some time alone with Karma.

51

FROM A VANTAGE POINT across a deep ravine I looked over to the steep granite cliff on which was perched Taktshang Monastery, nicknamed Tiger's Nest, comprised of several lhakhangs, or whatever was left of them after a fire destroyed a great part of the monastery the year before. Even in its damaged state, there was a poetic and mysterious aura about it, an inspiring piece of the kingdom's cultural and religious heritage.

"Once a year Bhutanese people can go in and see the cave. I have been there many times. It was most inspiring," said Karma, referring to the cave in the cliff where Guru Rimpoche had meditated, flown there on the back of a flaming tigress.

"I can understand how you must feel when you are there, for Christians also have saints and miraculous apparitions, holy relics, and sacred grottos." Scanning the monastery on the cliff, I said, "I can visualize how magical it must have looked before the fire, and how wonderful it will be again when it's eventually restored. I'm glad you've brought me here."

"A grand finale to your trip?" There was a bitter edge to his question.

I looked up at him. The moment we had both tried to put off had come.

"I don't want this to end." I was crying, as Karma held me and covered my wet face with kisses.

"Don't go, Ruth," he finally whispered in my ear.

"I have to. You and I have known all along that we belong to two different worlds. Just take Taktshang Monastery. I can't even enter it that one day a year when you are allowed to see the cave. You'll be up there while I am here, separated by this wide abyss, unable to reach you. I have to return home, to the life I'm accustomed to, while you belong here, with your chortens, dzongs and prayer flags, among your people and your saints."

Karma was quiet. Deep down, he must have realized the truth in my words. We clung to each other, trying to savor our final moments together. After a while, he said, "Your sister is staying in Bhutan, Ruth. If she can stay, why can't you?"

I touched Karma's sad boyish face.

"She's a saint, and I'm not."

Karma gave me an intent and knowing look. Gently, he brushed a strand of hair from my cheek. He touched his lips to my forehead.

"You are not so different," he whispered.

Epilogue
June 2002

M ARIAN AND I NO LONGER WRITE LETTERS to each other. We have been e-mailing ever since Bhutan launched its first Internet provider in June, 1999.

Soon after I left Bhutan in March of that year, Marvin Coe got Marian a job teaching English in the Montessori School in Thimphu. She was forgiven for her overstaying the term of her first visa and was issued another work visa, which would be valid as long as she was employed in Bhutan. She e-mailed to say that she found teaching Bhutanese children exhilarating and gratifying. In her words, "They are angels from heaven, the most innocent of God's little creatures."

However, she did not consider teaching in the Montessori School her ultimate calling in the little Himalayan kingdom. The children attending the school came from parents who could afford to send them there, not that they were rich by any standard, for there was simply no affluence in Bhutan, and every ngultrum spent on a child's education entailed some sacrifice on the parents' part. Marian really wanted to go where she would be needed most, which meant where the inhabitants were most deprived, which also meant where her own basic comforts would be greatly compromised. Life was never simple and easy for her. Her dream was realized last year, when Tashi Campbell turned twenty-one.

Tashi's Canadian grandmother, Virginia Campbell, had left a part of her husband's estate to Tashi. When she told me over three years ago in Bhutan that her grandmother had left her some money, I had no idea of the size of her inheritance, so was I in shock when she wrote me last year to say she had inherited a million dollars. She decided to keep a third of the money for herself, for her future education and use in Canada. She has just graduated from Sherubtse College. I had given her a listing of Canadian universities, and she is waiting to hear from the ones to which she has applied. She has set up a trust account for her mother, with a fixed annual allowance to be paid out to her for the rest of her life. And the remaining money, in the area of three hundred thousand dollars, she signed over to Marian, to be used for the interest of the people of Bhutan in whichever way Marian saw best.

Marian wasted no time in buying a few new computers for the Thimphu Public Library, which she said would always have a place in her heart. She then went to Haa Dzongkhag in Western Bhutan, south of Paro, one of the most remote districts in the kingdom. The inhabitants of Haa are mostly wheat, barley, and potato farmers, yak herders, and traders of yak products the like of butter and cheese. The timing was good for Marian, for she had just received the money from Tashi when the government opened up the district to foreigners.

She rented a double-sized storefront in the town of Haa where she set up a library. Marian felt the residents of the dzongkhag should have their own public library, specially catered to their needs. That English was used in schools and understood by many in the kingdom made it possible for her to carry out her plans. She ordered books and periodicals from Bangkok and India, and furniture from Phuentsholing. She had a couple of computers delivered from Thimphu and taught local residents on their basic use. She gave lessons to local students on research skills and opened up for them the limitless avenues of knowledge, beyond the confines of the library and the boundaries of their kingdom. She read to local children, to foster a love for books from a young age. And she taught interested high school students the basics of librarianship. "They will not be full-fledged librarians, but they will know enough to run a small library after college," she e-mailed. With a large portion of the money from Tashi still earning interest in a Canadian bank, Marian plans in time to set up more libraries in other remote parts of Bhutan, based on the Haa model.

"Don't you see I'd be helping an underprivileged nation, and at the same time doing what I do best where it counts most?" Those were her words before she left for Bhutan to reorganize the public library in Thimphu over four years ago. She is finally living her dream.

Nowadays Marian is able to write about Lopen Pema dispassionately. It has been over three years since he went into meditation. She has heard that he has come out of the drubda, and is living in Paro Dzong, as a teacher in dialectics and dance. She has not seen him again.

"I can now think of him without longing or regret," she e-mailed recently. "He is happy, and so I am happy. I love my work here, ministering to his people. What more can I wish for?"

As for myself, in the first year after I came home from Bhutan, Karma and I kept in close communication, first by letters, then by e-mail when it became available.

"Last night, I dreamed of you coming back to me, riding on the back of a flying tiger," he wrote soon after I left. He begged me to return to Bhutan in every letter and e-mail message he sent.

But all the while, I knew I could never belong to Karma, or to Bhutan. Like the little cloud in the song Yee Ying taught Marian and me so long ago on Lantau, after wandering across the heavens, riding on the wind, and touching the wings of birds, I had to return to where I started out, where I felt I belonged: back to my job at Precious Blood Hospital, attending weekend services and monthly social functions at St. Luke's Parish in my Toronto neighbourhood, meeting friends on weekends for movies and dinners, and taking vacations once or twice a year to less exotic places than Bhutan. To me, Bhutan will always be that *untravell'd world, whose margin fades for ever and for ever when I move*, mysterious, beautiful, elusive.

Three years and four months have elapsed since Karma and I loved and parted. I have not heard from him in the last six months. I don't know if I'll see him again when I return to Bhutan this September with my father, to visit Marian.

Glossary

ara	home-distilled alcoholic drink made from fermented wheat or rice
bodhisattva	in Buddhism, saintly one who delays enlightenment and chooses to reincarnate to help others to enter enlightened state
buddha	one who has broken out of the cycle of rebirth, and entered the enlightened state
bukhari	kind of stove introduced by the Swiss to Bhutan
bumpa	flask for holy water
cham	dance
chhu	river
Choekey	classical language used in Tibetan and Bhutanese Buddhist text
choesham	altar room
chorten	Buddhist monument containing relic
dahl	kind of lentil paste or soup popular in India and Bhutan
dharma	Buddhist teachings
doegor	game of throwing stones at another stone
dorji	in Buddhism, instrument signifying the thunderbolt, to control demons
dotsho	outdoor hot rock bath
dramyen	kind of lute
dromche	festival in Bhutan in honor of local protector deity, held annually in some cities
drubda	meditation center
dzong	fortress-like structure, used in the old days for defense, and which now houses temples, monks' quarters, and administrative offices

Dzongkha	language spoken in Bhutan
dzongkhag	district
emadatsi	chili in cheese sauce
gelong	ordained Buddhist monk
gho	national dress worn by Bhutanese men
goemba	Buddhist monastery
gomchen	lay practitioner of Buddhist rites
Je Khenpo	Chief Abbot, spiritual head of Bhutan
kabney	long scarf worn by men to enter temple
kadrinche	thank you
Kagyu	official sect of Tantric Buddhism in Bhutan
kangdu	human thigh bone used as horn
karma	in Buddhism, condition in one's next existence generated by one's actions in the present life
kira	national dress worn by Bhutanese women
la	mountain pass
lam	street
lama	Buddhist teacher
legzhembe zhug	good-bye
lhakhang	temple
lopen	teacher-monk, respectful form of address for monk
Lopen Dorji	director of chanting, one of four high lamas just below the Je Khenpo
Mahayana	one main school of Buddhism
mandala	in Buddhism, cosmic diagram
mani wall	prayer wall
momo	dumpling stuffed with meat, vegetable and cheese

Namo Amitabha	prayer formula to Buddha Amitabha
Lam Neten	title given to head of central district monastic body in Bhutan; representative of the Chief Abbot
ngultrum	Bhutanese currency unit
nirvana	in Buddhism, state of enlightenment, being free from cycle of rebirth
Nyingma	sect of Tantric Buddhism, originating in Tibet
okhang	lowest floor in farmhouse, for animals
rachu	shoulder cloth worn by women at festivals
rimpoche	reincarnate lama
roti	kind of bread, resembling pita bread
Sakyamuni	the historical Buddha, Siddartha Gautama
sep	corn snack
serda	procession ceremony on last day of Punakha dromche
sutra	Buddhist text
Tantras	treatises of Tantric Buddhism, branch of Mahayana school of Buddhism
Tashi Delek	Good Luck, a popular form of greeting
thangka	scroll painting or embroidery of Buddhist saint
torma	ritual cake made from flour and butter, placed at altar
tsechu	festival in Bhutan, celebrated annually in different cities in honor of Guru Rimpoche who brought Buddhism to Bhutan
utse	top of central tower in dzong
yangchen	kind of dulcimer
yin-yang	two opposing forces in Chinese philosophy
yuan	Chinese currency unit

ABOUT THE AUTHOR

Elsie Sze grew up in Hong Kong and currently lives in Toronto with her husband Michael. They have three sons, Benjamin, Samuel and Timothy. A former teacher and librarian, she is an avid traveller, often to remote places which form the settings for her stories. Her first novel, *HUI GUI: a Chinese story*, was nominated for Foreword Magazine's Book of the Year Award in Fiction, 2006.